'A REFRESHING TAKE ON THE FANTASY GENRE BY A BRITISH MUSLIM AUTHOR.'
Manda Benson, *Pilgrennon's Beacon*

'NOOR PLUNGES READERS INTO AN ACTION-PACKED SETTING INVOLVING AN UNFORGETTABLE HOST OF CHARACTERS. THE CHANGELING KING GUARANTEES TO TRANSPORT READERS INTO A WORLD FILLED WITH MAGIC.'
Nerine Dorman, *What Sweet Music They Make*

'THIS IS EPIC FANTASY AT ITS BEST.'
Barbara G Tarn, *Books of the Immortals Series*

NOOR A JAHANGIR

About the Author

Noor A Jahangir was born and raised in Lancashire, England. He grew up in a town very much like Affrington and knew at the age of seven that he wanted to be a writer. Most of his teen years were spent in an Islamic boarding school for boys, set in the Pennine Moors and overlooked by Peel Tower. He is a qualified Muslim scholar, holds an honours degree in English Studies with Media Studies and Creative Writing, a post-graduate Diploma in Management Studies, and is currently studying for his Masters. He is an associate lecturer at the University of Central Lancashire and also works as a chief officer for a non-profit organisation. The Changeling King is his first novel.

THE CHANGELING KING

NOOR A JAHANGIR

NOOR A JAHANGIR

This is a work of fiction. Names, characters, places and incidents are either the product of the author's imagination, or if real, are used fictitiously. All statement, activities, stunts, descriptions, information and material of any other kind contained herein are included for entertainment purposes only and should not be relied on for accuracy or replicates as they may result in injury.

First Print Edition 2012

Copyright 2012 © Noor A Jahangir

The right of Noor A Jahangir to be identified as the author of this work has been asserted by him in accordance with the Copyright, Designs and Patents Act 1988

All rights reserved. No part of this book may be reproduced, transmitted or stored in an information retrieval system in any form or by any means, graphic, electronic or mechanical, including photocopying, taping and recording without prior written consent from the author.

The Changeling King
Noor A Jahangir
ISBN: 978-1-4717-4504-1

www.trollking.co.uk

THE CHANGELING KING

Dedications

To my family

NOOR A JAHANGIR

THE CHANGELING KING

CHAPTER 1: THE TRAVELLERS

ENGLAND (NOW)

A lone tower stood on a forgotten hill, its crumbling walls choked with creeping ivy and lichen. A mouse scratched away at the mortar at the base of the tower to widen the portal into its home. It paused momentarily as a solitary barn owl winged by on a late night hunt.

The hill began to quiver as wild energy rose from deep beneath the ground and swirled up through the tower's foundations. Ancient wards, long worn from the passing of ages, snapped and fizzled out of existence. Power snaked through stone, making the edifice thrum to the luminescent tattoo of white fire. Fearing the approach of a predator, the mouse bolted down its hole to a fiery death.

A beam of blue energy surged out from the battlements into the night, rupturing the sky with a halo of clouds and lightning, pursued by the wailing howl of disturbed winds. A blackness tore a gash in the starry night. The beam subsided but the tower continued to smoulder like a dying ember.

The darkness rippled as a host of meteorites shot forth from the rift, burning yellow-green as they separated, spearing towards the ground, trailing stardust. The sky boomed angrily as the meteorites screamed over the tower and ploughed into the hillside, throwing up sheets of earth.

A thick forearm, covered with tufts of white fur, reached out from one of the newly formed craters. A three digit hand, ending in thick, cracked nails, dug into the singed grass. A second arm followed as the traveller struggled to escape the steaming embrace of its cocoon.

The traveller lay panting, his close-set eyes and wide snout weeping uncontrollably. His lungs burned with the effort to separate oxygen from the toxic air. His arms, proportionately longer and thicker than his legs, felt as if they were being forcibly held down. Even his tough hide seemed to be galvanised by this planet's atmosphere. Spasms gripped his limbs and chest like the jaws of a nicor, the land-bound dragons of his home-world.

The alien sounds of the new planet laid siege to his protesting ears. Layers of noise compounded together into a constant roar. He reached for his axe as something large flew by above him; fire flashing under its wings and its wail resonated for miles around. Far below him smaller armoured creatures moved in a train across an inky river, their eyes projecting a wash of amber luminance.

Beyond the hill a deep valley cupped a number of small settlements with firelights webbing back and forth across them. On the horizon, the first ray of daylight warmed the sky. The traveller shielded his eyes from the glare and cast about the hillside looking for members of his warband. Shakily, he raised himself onto his feet. Some of them had managed to extract themselves and now lay on the grass, like beached sea-mammals. He needed to get them together and move them into the tower.

By the time he had located all of his warriors, the sun had crested the distant moors. This world had an older sun, but despite its pitiful size, its yellow rays were burning his exposed flesh. The traveller swathed himself with his oil-cloth. Ten of his warband were strong enough to walk. The other four survivors were too feeble to make the short trek to the tower.

Normally, he would have cut their throats to end their misery. He had no room in his unit for weaklings. But the traveller could ill afford to squander his resources. Already six of his command lay splattered about the hillside.

'Get those grunts into the tower,' he called to the more able-bodied warriors.

'Vasch, what of our dead?' asked one of his comrades as they entered the tower, his nostrils flaring and his green eyes glimmering at the prospect of meat.

'You want to go out again, Grenld?'

The one called Grenld shook his head sullenly, his face already covered in sores from exposure.

THE CHANGELING KING

'We'll eat whatever keeps until after sundown; otherwise we'll bury our dead like the alvor do.'

'That's disgusting,' said Agilerd, the oldest member of his crew. 'They were warriors. They've earned the right to be eaten by other warriors; not by maggots and worms.'

'I don't like it either, but we have our orders. We cover our tracks and stay out of sight. Grenld, you get first watch. Rest of you, get some sleep.'

Vasch strode to the back of the circular room. Udulf, a big bruiser who had recently joined his unit, stared at him with unfriendly eyes. Vasch would have to watch for him. Vasch dropped his gear onto the floor and settled down under the sweep of the stairs, out of Udulf's line of sight. From inside his leather hauberk, he drew out a glass bauble. It was the size of a rook's egg, inscribed with frosted symbols just beneath the surface. He held it gingerly before his face. It began to softly pulse red, almost making him drop the damn thing. Something invisible reached out from within the orb to examine his face with a fluttering caress.

Vasch's lip curled back over his tusk in revulsion. Magic was for goblins. If the Trollking hadn't been so specific about keeping the bauble safe, he would have smashed it with his axe. Despite his revulsion, Vasch peered closely at the orb as an image began to form within the pearlescent shell; a human child with straw coloured hair and blue eyes. The child would soon die by Vasch's hands.

CHAPTER 2: THE LAKE

ENGLAND (NOW)

Nathan Celic stood before a mirror looking dejectedly at the slight bulge of his stomach against his top. He pulled his jeans a little higher up his midriff, choosing to ignore the fact that his wide belt and buckle were cutting into his skin.

'Logan! Bro, we're running out of time. Get her to hurry up, will you?' he called.

His brother grunted from behind a stack of old books on a counter. They were in an antique shop, picking up Logan's girlfriend, Katrina. The place smelt of musty books and old things. Her granddad, a scrawny World War II veteran with a white, walrus moustache and thick prescription glasses, stood behind the till. Nathan could feel the old guy's eyes follow him around the room.

Nathan pushed his black hair behind his ear and scowled. Logan had been going steady with Katrina for nearly a year now. The brothers had been in this shop at least a hundred times, but still the codger watched them as if they were convicted criminals. Had this been any other shop, Nathan would have seriously contemplated throwing a brick through the window.

Hoodlum and vagrant they had labelled him, ever since he'd turned eight. Adults questioned his right to stand on a street corner or to hang out in a playground. The way he walked and dressed were reasons to condemn him. Their stares nettled him to want to do what they already accused him of.

'What's taking her so long?' he groused to Logan.

'I have to look good for my boy,' said Katrina as she parted the beaded curtain that divided the shop front from the house. She twirled on the spot for Logan's benefit, wearing a low-cut crop top

THE CHANGELING KING

and trousers. Her large green eyes, diminutive nose and raven bob made her look like a manga character.

'Granddad, I've left a slice of pie in the oven for your lunch. The timer is already set. You just need to hit the "start" button when you want to eat it. I should be back by teatime,' called Katrina as Logan led her to the door.

Katrina's granddad nodded absentmindedly while keeping his eyes on Nathan. Nathan stuck up a finger at the old coot behind Katrina's back. The old man responded with an equally rude gesture of his own. Nathan grinned despite himself.

The three walked several blocks to the more affluent part of town. Georgian terrace houses and corner pubs gave way to large semi-detached Victorians and green areas. They were supposed to meet up with Salina, Nathan's girlfriend, at the bus-shelter around the corner from her mum's place. Salina's mother didn't approve of her daughter's association with Nathan.

Nathan caught sight of her when they were still half a block away. She had wavy, golden hair, with eyes bluer than the sky and a smile that did funny things to his stomach. But then he noticed her geeky brother, Adam, beside her. Salina spotted them and waved.

'What's he doing here?' asked Nathan as they drew close enough not to have to shout.

'He's my brother. Where else would he be?'

'Home, perhaps? Go on, bugger off home, Adam. You're not old enough to come with us,' said Nathan, shoving Adam back in the direction of his street.

'Leave him alone. If he doesn't go, neither can I,' said Salina testily.

Nathan draped a conciliatory arm over her shoulders but she pulled away from him. He glared at Adam, who caught the look and stepped closer to his sister.

Adam stared out of the greasy window of the 313 bus. Suburbia rolled on by, giving way to the verdant rolling landscape of the Pennine countryside. Adam imagined wolves and bears roaming around in the thickly wooded hills, though he knew that badgers were the largest predator in these parts.

NOOR A JAHANGIR

The bus deposited them at a lonely stop on a winding road. Adam strained to hear the comforting sound of passing traffic as they climbed over a stile. They cut through a farmer's field to a public footpath, which led them into the wood. They hiked for about an hour along a trail that ran parallel to a wide stream. Occasionally, the alders thinned enough for them to see a picturesque town that had escaped industrialisation, nestled in the valley below. The arches of a railway viaduct cut across the valley like a brick leviathan. Adam was finding it difficult to keep up with the others.

'Can you guys slow down a little? I've got a stitch,' said Adam, already out of breath.

'I told you it was a mistake bringing him along,' grumbled Nathan.

'Lay off him, Nathan,' said Logan as he slowed his pace to allow Adam to catch up.

Adam sighed as Nathan threw him yet another evil look over his shoulder.

Eventually, they encountered the source of the stream, a lake that meandered for a mile along the moors. To Adam's embarrassment, the girls began to undress. The Celic brothers disappeared behind a bush to change into their trunks. Adam turned away as the girls pulled off their tops and concentrated really hard on the lake itself.

The far shore was heavily bearded with beech, birch and holly trees. The mountain ash and sessile oaks on their side grew further apart, allowing the golden rays of sunlight to touch the bluebells and the bracken that braved the woodland floor. An ancient oak, with craggy bark and thick boughs, grew close enough to the shoreline for it to reach out over the lake with its twisted limbs. A faded blue rope hung suspended from a branch two thirds of the way up the tree.

Adam watched in awe as Katrina, dressed in a one-piece swimsuit, climbed up the tree, making it look easy. She clambered up until she could grab the rope and then swung out into space, letting go as she hit the apex. Katrina dropped into the water with a squeal of joy. Adam sighed in wonder.

Nathan went next, then Logan and finally, even Salina scaled the tree, ululating like Tarzan as she sailed through the air. Finally, Adam found himself in the predicament of being the only one still standing on the shore.

THE CHANGELING KING

The sun grew warmer on Adam's back as he planned his route up the oak. Behind him, Salina splashed water on Nathan; shrieking with laughter as he splashed back. The other two shouted out encouragements at the combatants.

'Come on Adam, the water is nice and cool,' called his sister, 'forget about the tree, it's not safe.'

'Yeah, Adam, it's much too dangerous for a little tyke like you. Just slip into the water now,' added Nathan.

'Leave him alone, Nathan,' said Salina. 'You know he doesn't like it when you talk about his height.'

'Nathan, stop acting like a prat,' said Logan.

Adam looked back over his shoulder, squinting through the sun's glare. They were watching to see what he would do next, except Katrina who floated placidly on her back. Adam suddenly felt unbearably warm and flustered.

'I knew he wouldn't climb,' said Nathan with a smirk.

Adam felt like running into the water and knocking the sneer off Nathan's face. Nathan was big, like his brother, with wide shoulders and big arms. He wasn't as athletic as Logan, unless you counted throwing eleven year olds into wheelie-bins as a sport. Adam didn't know what his sister saw in him. Nathan had greasy hair and his 'goatee' barely passed for fuzz. Why couldn't she have gone out with Logan instead? He was slimmer than Nathan, good looking and popular at school.

Adam rested his hands on the tree, feeling the texture of its cracked bark, trying to draw strength from its sturdy trunk. He pulled himself up onto the first branch. The others fell silent as he laboured his way up. At one point, he developed a cramp in his foot and had to wait in agony as it worked its way out. Finally, he pulled himself onto the last bough and inched out until he was directly beneath the rope. Only then did he realise that the rope was out of his reach.

Why mum had to send him with Salina was beyond him, thought Adam, recalling the big row they had over breakfast. He would have been happier in front of his games-console, playing through campaign mode on Horizon Commando 2. Even Salina hadn't wanted him to come. Who the hell climbed trees nowadays anyway? This was definitely Salina's fault. She should have buggered off before mum woke up.

Adam looked down at the four treading water below him, psyching himself up for the ridicule that would surely follow. Luckily, they seemed more concerned with something happening further out in the lake. He sighed in relief and began to make his way back down.

'What is that?' he heard Katrina ask.

He paused to gape at the phenomenon that had captivated the others. Lights shimmered under the lake's surface, forming a queasy pattern that left Adam cross-eyed. The water above the lights bubbled as large pockets of air exploded into white froth. Salina edged towards the shore. Adam wasn't that far off the ground now but he found his eyes drawn to a depression at the centre of the light-show, increasing in size and momentum.

'Salina, get out of the water,' he said urgently.

She seemed transfixed.

'Salina?'

The water began to funnel inwards.

'SALINA, GET OUT OF THE WATER NOW!'

Salina's gaze snapped away from the lake and turned to Adam. Her eyes were large and round with terror. She raised a hand towards him. Adam leapt to the ground but landed badly. The shock rode up to his groin, making him wince. The water drew away from the banks and into the gaping maw of the vortex.

Adam reached out desperately for his sister's hand, scared to enter the water. Her fingers strained towards his.

The whirlpool ripped her away from him.

Adam cried out again.

Salina and Nathan were swimming hard against the current as the vortex continued to reel them in to its maw. Adam continued to watch in horror as Katrina disappeared below the surface. Nathan shouted something at him as the whirlpool swung him past Adam.

'Call . . . for . . . help.'

Adam ran to his sister's handbag and pulled out her mobile phone. He fumbled with the lockscreen as Logan went under too. Adam

THE CHANGELING KING

dialled the emergency services number and then looked back at the lake. Nathan went next. A voice spoke urgently into his ear. Only Salina remained visible. He couldn't remember speaking, but the voice reassured him that help was on the way. The brushed aluminium casing slipped through his nerveless fingers and the phone fell onto his sister's neatly folded jeans.

Salina screamed. Adam waded out into the shallows but hesitated when he felt the pull of the undertow.

'Oh, God, please don't make me do this. Let them be okay now, please, let them be okay,' he pleaded through his tears.

The funnel had begun to collapse in on itself. Adam splashed forwards again, only to lose his footing as the lake-bed suddenly dropped away beneath him.

Water closed in over his head and filled his mouth and nose. Panicking, he flapped his arms wildly, trying to claw his way back to the surface.

A snarl of energy snaked out and snagged his leg, pulling him relentlessly towards the core of the vortex. A frisson of pure fear coiled around his stomach. Prayers tumbled unbidden from his lips. The surface lifted away from him. He couldn't breathe.

Something awoke deep inside him. Darkness wriggled up his chest, like a parasite that had grown within his gut and now sought a way to escape his body. Adam braced himself as the sinister force lashed out.

Suddenly he was free. He broke the surface, spluttering hard, his body wracked with spasms as his lungs sought to clear themselves.

Strong hands grabbed him from behind and pulled him back to shore. His saviour deposited him in the shallows and forced his eyes open.

'Are you okay, kid?' asked the voice of a stranger.

'I'm fine. My sister is still in there. So are my friends. Please, help them,' said Adam, coughing out more water.

The man nodded and ran back into the lake.

Adam continued his vigil with his knees drawn up to his chest for warmth. Steam rose from him as the sun dried his clothes, but Adam continued to shiver. The cold emanated from inside him.

NOOR A JAHANGIR

Minutes went by but the man did not resurface. Eventually, he heard the thumping of helicopter blades drawing closer. Salina's phone rang but Adam ignored it. He watched as the funnel finally disappeared in a wash of bubbles as the helicopter descended from above.

CHAPTER 3: SULTAN

INDIA (1586 AD)

Prince Sultan rode around a sandy paddock on the back of his father's latest purchase, an Arabian thoroughbred. He held a short Indian lance, aiming it at a wood and leather mannequin.

His father, Shah Suleiman of Azamabad, stood at the paddock gates carefully observing his performance. A small retinue of guests, advisors and guards stood behind the Shah. Amongst them was a gangly, square-jawed Englishman, recently come to Hindustan with the East India Company. He had arrived in Suleiman's court just a few days ago with a letter from the Mughal Emperor, Akbar. The letter strongly requested that the Englishman be accommodated in his endeavour to study the flora and fauna of Northern India.

Sultan's father had so far avoided giving an audience to the Englishman. He knew this because his father insisted on discussing the kingdom's business with Sultan.

'Karram Singh. That will do. The foal is a good purchase, don't you agree?' asked Suleiman of the horse master.

'Yes, Your Majesty, it is an excellent purchase. And I think young highness is quite taken with him too,' replied the horse master.

'It appears so, Karram Singh. Sultan, come join me here. You rode well. I am proud of you, my son.'

Sultan sighed in exasperation as the huge man from the Punjab province strode across the sand. Sultan considered charging at him with the padded lance. Karram Singh smiled as if he knew exactly what the prince was thinking.

'Father, I'm not tired yet. Can't I ride for a little while longer?'

'You must study as well as learn to ride, Sultan,' said Suleiman.

NOOR A JAHANGIR

'Why, father? I can fight with a shamshir better than any of the other boys.'

'That is true, but a land is not maintained with a sword and people are not fed by princes riding on horses,' said his father with a laugh.

'Englishman,' said Suleiman, without looking back, 'I have just thought of a use for you. Which of the European languages do you speak? Do you speak Portuguese, French, German?'

The Englishman marched forward with a vigorous stride. He didn't much look like a man given to study.

'I am proficient in all of those languages, your Majesty.'

'What is your name?'

'Hubert Giles Williams, your Majesty.'

'You look like a soldier, Williams. Are you sure all you want to study is plants and animals? Or are you really here to gauge my defences and to learn the lay of my land?'

'It is true that I did a term of service in the Royal Navy, but my true calling is science, Your Majesty.'

'Honesty. That is a good sign, Williams. It means we may get along yet.

'The French and the Germans are making great leaps in their musket designs. I hear that the Germans have muskets with the flint loaded on a sprung arm and that the French are trying to improve the mechanism of the striking surface and flash pan. I foresee that conflict in the future will not be decided by how skilful one's swordsmen are, but by how advanced one's firearms are.

'My son must be able to speak the language of the people that will influence the future of this land. Do this and you have my permission to study the plants and animals of Azamabad.'

'That is a most generous offer, Your Majesty, but might I suggest . . .' began Williams.

'No, you may not suggest, Williams. And one more thing: everything you learn about the plants and animals of Azamabad, you will share with my scholars. Sultan will be your understudy.'

'You are too kind, Majesty.'

THE CHANGELING KING

As of that day, Hubert Williams gained a protégé and assistant. When Sultan wasn't practising horse riding, archery, swordplay or shooting, he wandered amongst the woods and parks in and around Azamabad. He carried cages and jars for Williams, made notes on scraps of parchment and repeated sentences in several languages. Always, wherever they went, a retinue of armed guards followed.

Once Williams had Sultan draw a sketch of a weed growing at the base of the city walls, while he himself sketched a creeping vine. Shah Suleiman appeared on the parapets above.

'Mr Williams, there are plenty of weeds to sketch away from the city's defences. The Emperor would be very interested in sketches of these walls, but it would cost you your head.'

Williams remained in the court of Azamabad for a full year before he was given leave to return to Delhi. Sultan's father had been greatly displeased with this arrangement but did not hinder the Englishman's journey. Akbar had personally requested his presence. By this time Sultan had developed a good command of the Western languages and had acquired a deep appreciation of the province's flora and fauna. His father, however, fell into a dark mood and began to spend long hours with his advisors and generals.

Unused to being excluded from important meetings, Sultan spent his newfound freedom by looking for ways to sneak into his father's study and eavesdrop. His father, however, had an uncanny knack for knowing exactly where to find Sultan, at which point he would be dispatched to the family wing. There he was subjected to the art of personal hygiene. A long bath, a change of clothes, hair oiled and brushed and then forced to partake in a meal.

Sultan took to loitering around the training grounds to watch the soldiers drilling and practising armed and unarmed combat. Sultan tried to convince the soldiers to spar with him too. In the past, two soldiers had been discharged from active duty for having accidentally struck the prince. Another had ended up in the hospital wing with his head bandaged when the enthusiastic prince had gotten the better of him. The guards had learnt their lesson.

***

NOOR A JAHANGIR

Three weeks after the departure of Williams, an old man dressed in a long white tunic and turban, leaning on a knotted staff, arrived at the palace gates. He did not speak a word, but stood waiting patiently. Eventually, news of this stranger's presence reached the Shah. Suleiman descended to the gates, followed by his first wife, Princess Gulbadan, Sultan and the usual cadre of aides, advisors and guards. The watchmen at the gates saluted smartly as the royal family approached. The old man watched from under his bushy eyebrows, stroking his long white beard.

When they drew closer, the Princess Gulbadan exclaimed softly and stepped close to the Shah to whisper in his ear. He nodded and whispered something back before turning to address the old man.

'Peace, mercy and blessings upon you, Sheikh Inayatullah. It would bring great honour to my humble home if you would kindly permit me to be your host and offer you food, water and shelter,' said Suleiman.

'Peace, mercy and blessings also upon you and your family, Shah Suleiman. Your offer is most generous and the honour would be mine to accept.'

Suleiman gestured with his hand for the Sheikh to enter. The old man moved forward slowly as if the very act of walking caused him agony, though no sign of pain showed on his face. Suleiman fell in step with the Sheikh and the rest of the procession followed in their wake.

'Who is that man?' asked Sultan.

'Sheikh Inayatullah is a very pious saint. I went to speak to him after your sister Gulzarin was born and he told me about you,' replied Gulbadan.

'How old was I then?'

'You were minus eight at the time.'

'Oh,' said Sultan, perplexed.

The Sultan threw a feast for all the poor of Azamabad that evening, though the poor of Azamabad were considerably wealthier than many merchants in other provinces. The city's finest poets sang couplets and religious ghazls. They were followed by acrobats and jesters for the entertainment of the common-folk. All the while, Suleiman spoke quietly to the Sheikh, seated on a series of cushions

THE CHANGELING KING

arranged at the foot of the throne. Sultan couldn't make out what they were saying, so instead he watched the acrobats form a human pyramid.

Later that night, as Sultan was being chased around his bedchamber by servants trying to get him ready for bed, his father strode into the marble-clad room. Immediately, Sultan slid to halt with a sheepish grin. Suleiman smiled indulgently. The servants used the opportunity to pounce, dressing him quickly as he stood checked by his father's gaze.

'I see you have been behaving as befits your station,' remarked Suleiman.

Sultan nodded his head vigorously even as one of the servants tried to brush the knots out of his tangled hair.

'Sheikh Inayatullah has kindly agreed to take up your religious education. I want you to report to him every day after the mid-afternoon prayer. Treat him with great respect, Sultan; he is a man of God and a possessor of great mystical powers. If you can exercise patience and discipline in equal measures, you may find his teachings enlightening. He may even share with you something of the mysteries.'

After delivering this revelation, his father spent an hour with him, relating to him stories of djinns, sorcerers and flying carpets. But when Sultan finally slept, he didn't dream of magic carpets and princesses. He dreamt instead of a faraway land, of a jewelled city and blue-grey mountains.

CHAPTER 4: FIRST CONTACT
ENGLAND

Adam waited until his mother had locked the front door before announcing that he was going to his room.

'Do you want me to make you a sandwich or something?' she asked, sounding drained.

Adam shook his head then silently made his way upstairs. He paused on the landing outside Salina's room. The door stood wide open and he could smell a lingering hint of Salina's favourite perfume, candy floss mixed with bubble-gum. The room was tidy, shoes organised by colour on their rack, teddy bears and dolls crowding shelves in orderly regiments. Only the duvet appeared slightly rumpled. His mother had lain there last night, clutching Salina's most recently worn pyjama top. A lump formed in Adam's throat, sticking like a hard-to-swallow tablet.

Adam closed his own bedroom door, letting the familiar chaotic sight sooth him. He sank onto his bed and stared sightlessly at his Winterman comic book poster. The last twenty-four hours had been the worst in his life. He had stood by the lakeside for three hours, watching the emergency services run through their procedures. Various uniformed officers had questioned him before his mother had been allowed to take him home. Then he witnessed her rant and rave for half an hour, going by stages through grief, anger and finally guilt. Eventually, she shut herself in Salina's room.

Adam spent the night crying soundlessly into his pillow and waking from disturbing dreams of his sister floating through an endless void, calling to him for help.

Then, this morning, they had to go to the local police station to give his 'official' statement. A pair of detectives, a Pakistani man with

THE CHANGELING KING

a gentle voice and a stern blonde woman, had cross-examined him for an hour. No one believed Adam when he told them about the lights, the whirlpool – and the thing that had tried to take him too. They spoke of his sister as if she was dead. Was she? Adam couldn't bring himself to think it.

The tears came again, trickling into his hair. If only dad were here, he would have known what to do. He would have believed Adam.

Detective Karen Rainbow rubbed her eyes wearily and glanced at her watch. Karen's partner, Hussein, sat slumped in the passenger seat of her Ford. Neither of them had been home since the incident at the lake. Supper and breakfast had been lukewarm coffees from a vending machine.

The interview with the boy, Adam Phelps, had been unproductive. His story had started off believable, but quickly turned fanciful, fairy lights and sea-monsters, traumatised hallucinations. Mrs Phelps hadn't helped either, sobbing inconsolably throughout the interview.

A soldier by the name of Ryan Scott, recently returned from active duty in Iraq, had drowned trying to save the kids. The lake was on army land and the soldier had been out jogging in the area. His body now lay in the district morgue.

Hopefully, the pathologist in charge of the soldier's autopsy would have some kind of lead for them.

'Hussein, why do you think the soldier drowned? His commanding officer said he was a strong swimmer.'

Hussein sat up and rubbed his tired eyes.

'Helicopter, probably. The down-force generated by the helicopter's propellers must have pushed him under,' said Hussein, illustrating the effect with his hands.

'Plausible, but the Phelps' boy claimed that the soldier had already been under for five minutes before the chopper arrived. So why did he drown?'

The morgue was situated in Rushdown, a small town ten minutes away from Affrington, separated by a short stretch of country-road. Karen let the speedometer climb to fifty before easing off the accelerator. Green fields, dotted with woolly tufts of sheep, slid by.

NOOR A JAHANGIR

A specialist CSI unit had been sent down from Manchester, equipped with sonar. The lake had been combed several times. No bodies had been recovered.

Karen slowed the car as they entered Rushdown. The road narrowed considerably, congested with cars parked, end-to-end, on either side of the road. The morgue was by far the largest and ugliest building in town. It sat next to a row of regal Victorian houses, a product of bureaucratic design and efficiency. Karen parked up and, together, the detectives walked to the entrance.

The automatic door had been smashed in. Fragments of glass littered the reception area beyond. A commotion from within warned that the arsonists were still inside.

Karen ran back to her car and began to whisper urgently into her car's radio-mike.

'Dispatch, this is Detective Rainbow. I'm calling from the morgue. My partner and I are on the site of a break-in. We need armed back up.'

It took Vasch's warband two nights to cross the gently undulating moors, segmented and divided by wooden gates and stonewalls.

They were crossing one of the many glistening black pathways when a huge, armoured creature lumbered out of the night. Berherd had been bringing up the rear. Its single rectangular eye reflected his terror, fiery beams shooting out from its widely spaced nostrils. The beast screeched and slammed headfirst into the warrior. It churned him under its broad discus-shaped legs and then spat out his mangled body.

Vasch stood frozen long after the beast disappeared. Berherd's pack-brother, Durke, was first to stir as a second beast lumbered by and bumped over the corpse. By the time they had retrieved Berherd, there wasn't much left of him that remained edible. They buried the body in a shallow ditch by the side of the road. Berherd had been with Vasch for three years.

In the early hours of the morning, the warband skirted through the cobbled backstreets of a small settlement and dashed across an island of greenery. The orb, clutched possessively in Vasch's hand, led them straight to their destination.

THE CHANGELING KING

Curly flowing runes, punctuated with occasional straight lines, decorated the temple's entrance. Vasch ordered Udulf to smash through the transparent doorway. A mournful wail sounded from somewhere within.

The warband hunkered down and waited to see if Udulf would die a horrible death. When nothing happened, they made their way inside and destroyed the source of the noise, a small cabinet filled with flashing lights. It gave off a few sparks and then fell silent.

The building smelt like a goblin-shaman's hut, of chicken guts and the sharp tang of sulphuric potions. It was lit harshly by elongated tubes containing white fire, suspended from a panelled ceiling. Vasch could smell something else, something that made his stomach rumble with hunger; dead flesh. Vasch consulted the orb again. This was the place. They would wait here for the prey to arrive. Until then, they would feast.

Karen and Hussein had strapped on protective vests and armed themselves with X26 taser-guns from the Ford's boot. In the distance they could hear a siren fast approaching. The intruders inside the morgue were arguing in a foreign language that neither of them had heard before. Every now and then the burglars would take out their frustrations on the furniture.

A dark-blue van screeched to halt by her Ford with the siren still blasting. Four Armed Response Team officers dressed in navy-blue boiler suits jumped out and ran over to join them. They were armed with Heckler and Koch sub-machine guns and Glock side-arms.

'Detectives,' said the young officer in an overly dramatic whisper, pale eyes twinkling in anticipation. 'I'm Scholes. These lads are Johnson, Bragg and Barnes. What's the situation?'

'Great entrance. What's the plan? Are we going to try taking them by surprise?' asked Karen.

'What?'

'Never mind. We've counted four perps so far, but there could be more. They're all big fellows and seem to be armed with clubs and axes. The coroner may be in there too.'

'Okay detectives, ART will take it from here. I suggest you wait in your car until we've got them boxed off. Johnson and Bragg, I want

NOOR A JAHANGIR

you two to go around the back and block off their exit. Barnes you're primary through the front. Flash-bang and clear. Check your targets and fire only if provoked.'

Karen sighed in exasperation and considered pulling rank on the young constable. Hussein patted her on the shoulder and shook his head. No point in arguing.

'Go, go, go,' yelled Scholes.

Barnes raised his gun and charged in through the door, followed closely by Scholes. A moment later there came two loud bangs followed by the muffled cough of gunfire.

CHAPTER 5: HEAVEN'S WRATH

KRYLLON (NOW)

Beneath the wings of carrion birds and the shadows cast by feathered arrows, a battle raged between two great hosts. Closer to the ground, the air became thick with meat flies and the stench of maimed bodies. The broken cries of the wounded and the dying were mercifully drowned out by the clash of weapons.

Goblins jeered at the alvor and waved their clan totems, staves mounted with animal skulls, hide and feathers.

Gillieron, Lord General of the alvorn army, fought fiercely against the first wave. He slammed his leaf-shaped shield into an enemy's face. The goblin's eyes glazed over momentarily. Gillieron rammed the goblin a second time and knocked it to the ground to be trampled by its comrades. More goblins pushed forward, their large bulbous eyes, better suited to the twilight of tunnels and caves, narrowed to filter out dust and the sunlight.

The goblins were generally a head shorter than the alvor, but their bony frames were ripped with lean muscle and protected by patchwork leather armour. They grinned fiercely as they fought, bearing needle-like teeth from lipless mouths. Their triangular blades and chisel-headed picks rose and fell, tearing flesh and spraying blood. The goblins forced a wedge into the alvorn line, seeking to isolate the general.

Gillieron's shield took a hammering as he held it before him, rallying out from behind its bronze rim with his tapered short sword, which ran dark with goblin-blood.

A hand-blade crashed into his shield, splintering the wooden base and twisting its bronze banding. Gillieron countered by ramming his sword up through the goblin's jaw. He gagged as russet blood spurted on his face, filling his nose with its metallic stench. The goblin fell, twisting away from him, wrenching the sword from his hand.

Gillieron threw the broken shield at his enemies and ripped out his sabre, three feet of curved bronze, from its scabbard. He began to lay about him, lopping limbs and shredding armour until his arms grew weary. The goblins fell back.

The ground beneath his feet began to rumble with the muted precursor to a cavalry charge. Gillieron could see Captain Quinlan roaring to his pike company to form up ranks at the centre. The goblins cheered as iron-armoured trolls mounted on nicors, wingless dragons native to Kryllon's wetlands, smashed into the alvorn front line.

Gillieron shouted desperately at the archers to provide cover for the infantry to fall back as the pike units were swept aside. The nicors were barded to protect them from the alvorn pikes. Champrons covered their horned heads, with segmented plates protecting their snaking necks and peytral armour for their muscular chests.

Sheets of sequoia shafts rained down, but the arrows clattered harmlessly off raised shields and armour.

Captain Nenmacil sallied forth at the head of the alvorn cavalry with sabre and lance, hoping to staunch the charge. The alvorn riders managed to unseat a few trolls from their terrible steeds, but many more of their own number fell to the snapping jaws of the reptiles.

Nenmacil led the cavalry clear then turned about to attack one more time, smashing into the enemy cavalry's flank. Blood roared in Gillieron's ears as wounded troops scurried pass him.

The sky suddenly darkened as behemoth clouds rushed together from across the horizon. Lightning crackled, followed by peal after peal of thunder. The battle ground to a halt as combatants turned to look up at the heavens. The animals were first to bolt, as horses shrieked and nicors scrambled on clawed feet for the safety of the forest.

Powerful winds beat down. Screams of terror rang out from both sides of the field as the sky tore open.

The air howled like a hungry wolf as it rushed up to fill the vacuum. A halo of clouds exploded outwards from the rift in waves,

THE CHANGELING KING

causing the atmosphere to crackle as static energy formed a bolt of pure light and heat.

It slammed into the ground.

The earth reverberated from the impact, throwing all who stood to the ground.

The tear in the sky began to close.

Rain lashed down on the colourless strips of grass and the stunted tree trunks that protruded like skeletal fingers from the wasteland. The downpour added to the confusion as the recently firm ground turned to slippery mud.

Gillieron got to his feet and stumbled towards the newly formed crater. It was shaped like a sunburst, eight feet across at its widest point. His curiosity overcame his fear and he leaned forward to look. The bodies of four human children lay sprawled at the bottom of the pit.

CHAPTER 6: SHADOW OF THE EMPIRE
INDIA (1591 AD)

Sheikh Inayatullah remained in Azamabad for five years. Sultan increased in wisdom and diligence under his tutelage. Even his other studies and training benefited from his new discipline. Sultan grew in body as well as in mind.

At the age of thirteen, Sultan was a tall, handsome boy. His silky black hair curled at his shoulders. He favoured his father's brow and nose, lending him gravity, but had his mother's hazel eyes and high cheekbones.

At the beginning of the sixth year, as new blossoms crowned green shoots, the Sheikh bid farewell to the royal family. He left as he had come, on foot, dressed in the same clothes he had arrived in.

The East India Company had been growing in influence over the years and the other Europeans seemed to be growing nervous. In the meantime, Akbar had sent countless invitations to Suleiman to visit the capital. Suleiman had turned them down as diplomatically as possible.

Sultan had never seen his father this agitated before. The only thing he could do to help was to work even harder at his lessons. His determination did not go unnoticed.

One Friday, a few weeks after the Sheikh's departure, his father sent for him. Sultan entered quietly and waited for his father to acknowledge him. Suleiman sat upon a divan with two administrators standing in attendance. The Shah pressed his signet ring into a freshly poured wax seal.

Sultan's eyes were drawn to the bookshelves that lined the walls. Texts on statesmanship, war, economics and religious commentaries, sat side by side with books on farming. Sultan's eyes hungrily

THE CHANGELING KING

devoured the names written in gold leaf along the leather spines. Some titles were illuminated with Arabic calligraphy, in fanciful shapes such as boats, flowers and even buildings, linking together volumes in collections.

'Sultan, come join me,' called his father.

The administrators packed their missives into leather satchels and hurried out of the study. Sultan strode over to his father and with his permission sank gratefully down on the cushioned seat. Sultan found himself being appraised by his father.

'Sultan, I am aware that we have not spent much time with each other these past months,' said Suleiman.

'Father, I understand that you are very busy with state matters and assure you that you need not justify your actions.'

'Nevertheless, I am failing to attend to my family's rights.' The Shah fell silent, looking reflective. 'We should go on a picnic. There is a tiger rampaging in the jungles close to the Bengal Mountains. We can go hunting while the women-folk enjoy the amusements of a safari.'

'That would be wonderful, father. We haven't gone hunting together in years.'

Suleiman nodded in pleasure and patted Sultan's back. Sultan kissed his father on both cheeks and then excused himself.

By Sunday morning, the entire royal family, as well as a troupe of thirty servants, ten Russian amazons and seventy men-at-arms were packed and ready to leave for the safari. The royal ladies were mounted on brightly-coloured palanquins atop elephants and guarded by the platinum haired amazons, who were armed with matchlock rifles and stiletto knives. Sultan, his father and a large number of retainers rode escort on horseback. Suleiman was about to give the order to ride when they heard a horse galloping towards the palace gates.

The men-at-arms quickly moved to form a protective crescent around the royal family. The amazons readied their rifles. A rider burst into view and skidded to a halt, caught off-guard by the ensemble of weapons ranged against him. He was dressed in the Emperor's livery. The man passed a scroll to one of the halberdiers manning the gate. The guard brought the scroll to the chief-of-staff, who then proffered it up to Suleiman. The Shah unfurled the parchment and scanned through its contents.

'The young prince Murad, second son of Akbar, wishes to pay our humble kingdom a visit,' said Suleiman. 'He is a day's ride away from Azamabad and is being chaperoned by Chancellor Abdul Fadl.'

'I guess that means the picnic is not going ahead then,' called down Gulbadan.

Suleiman shrugged his shoulders in apology. He turned to his chief-of-staff.

'Make everything ready for the prince's arrival and double the security in the palace. Inform our spies that I want to know exactly what that snake Abdul Fadl is planning.'

Prince Murad and his entourage arrived the next day at dusk. There were no women with the party, which in itself wasn't unheard of, but the prince had an additional escort of a hundred Imperial lancers with the customary hundred men-at-arms.

Murad rode in on an open-sided palanquin, carried by burly servants. He wore a knee-length, red silk tunic, belted at the waist with an orange sash. Beneath the tunic he wore tight, orange pantaloons. On his head rested a large silk turban, pinned with a ruby brooch.

A second person rode in the palanquin with him; Chancellor Abdul Fadl, rumoured to be the highest in the Emperor's confidence and, perhaps, the second most powerful man in the Mughal Empire. The reception was subdued.

Murad started drinking shortly after arriving. He had brought his own liquor, despite the laws proscribing alcohol in Azamabad. For the best part of an hour, the Shah listened politely to Abdul Fadl's small talk and gossip from the imperial capital. Meanwhile, Sultan fidgeted with a knife and a bowl of mango, papaya and watermelon.

Eventually, Prince Murad drank himself into a stupor. As the sound of his snores grew louder, the tone of the conversation turned to more serious matters.

'Your position is most precarious, Highness. An independent kingdom within the borders of the Empire is unheard of. I am in awe

THE CHANGELING KING

of His Imperial Majesty's tolerance of your continued autonomy,' said the viper-faced seneschal.

'Akbar's tolerance is famous throughout Hindustan. The taxes he levies on kingdoms such as mine are ample enough to give even a hardened miser a turn towards forbearance,' responded Suleiman.

Sultan looked quickly to Abdul Fadl's face to see how he would react to his father's sarcasm. The seneschal, a veteran courtier however, evinced a thin smile that didn't reach his cold reptilian eyes.

'My prince is tired from the journey, Shah Suleiman, and, for his sake, I beg leave to retire to our chambers,' said Abdul Fadl.

'But of course, my people will show you the way.'

'Oh, one last thing, Shah Suleiman. Our courier informed me that when he arrived with the prince's message, you were preparing to leave for safari. It is not His Highness's wish that you forestall your programme on his behalf. In fact, the prince and I are both avid hunters and would be honoured to join you on this trip.'

Suleiman inclined his head in mock respect as the besotted prince was carried out by his men. Abdal Fadl raised a hand in salutation and followed them out.

The Shah immediately signalled his advisors to abandon their positions behind various curtains to attend him. Sultan remained seated, though he fully expected his father to dismiss him.

'Akbar has finally revealed his hand. I have no doubt that Abdul Fadl plans to use the hunting trip to assassinate me,' said Suleiman.

'Your Majesty, you must refuse to go on this trip,' implored one of the advisors.

'The prince will not take no for an answer. He will insist that insult is implied by my refusal and, come nightfall, the Imperial army will be sitting on our doorstep.'

'His Majesty is right,' said the Wazir of Interior Defence, 'we've already received intelligence that a sizable Imperial force is camped three leagues west of Azamabad, at the village of Unakshavar. We will have to be subtle in our planning.'

'I agree. We cannot refuse to mount a hunt, but we can set the pace and the terms. We will hunt on foot after the fashion of my forefathers; without dogs and beaters. No rifles. Only spears and

NOOR A JAHANGIR

bows. Abdul Fadl will insist that we take the prince's men along, so I want five of your best trappers, Shere Singh, to accompany us. The land will be our only other defence.'

Sultan's heart raced as his mind conjured images of his father and himself cleverly evading the Imperials in the dark hollows of the jungle.

'Abdul Ghani, you and your household guard will ensure that once the hunt is underway, my family is removed immediately to Kashmir, to my brother-in-law's fort in the mountains. Sultan will remain with me on the hunt, otherwise Abdul Fadl will see through our plans. Once my family is clear of Azamabad, I want every available fighting man on the city walls. Azaad Baksh, you were my father's greatest general. You will command the defence of the city. Victory or defeat, word must be sent to my brother-in-law. If God wills it, Sultan and I will live through this to receive your message there. Now go and begin the preparations.'

When the advisors had filed out of the audience chamber, Suleiman turned to Sultan and placed his hands on his shoulders.

'Sultan, our lives will be in imminent danger. Attack may come at any time. Though my heart desires to spare you this ordeal, the safety of our loved ones will not allow it. But I will not have you walking into this without fully understanding the risks.'

'Father, I understand completely. I won't let you down.'

'One more thing, Sultan. If I fall, you must not come back for me. If the worst comes to pass, you must press on to Kashmir. You know the way. Follow the river up to the Bengal Mountains and then through the mountains to where the river splits in two. There, amongst the heights, you will find your uncle's fort. If you lose your way, stay alive. Even if Azamabad falls, our family's legacy will live on through you.'

Sultan nodded, not trusting his voice, but his eyes turned traitor as large tears ran down his cheeks. His father smiled and wiped Sultan's face with his sleeve before drawing Sultan into a fierce embrace.

THE CHANGELING KING

CHAPTER 7: DEAD MEN TELL NO TALES

ENGLAND

Vasch's eyes and ears were in agony.

The warband had been feasting on a human sacrifice they had found laid out on a steel altar, its chest stitched closed, possibly after having its heart ripped out. Then something clattered into the sacrificial chamber and in the next instant a brilliant explosion of light and sound assaulted their senses.

Something struck Vasch hard enough to stagger him. Winded, he dropped to the ground. They were under attack, but where from? Vasch crawled forward until his head struck the altar. He grasped the rim and peeked over the reflective surface, blinking rapidly to clear his vision. Two warriors in dark breastplates and rounded helmets stood framed by the open doors. The warriors held aloft bulky crossbow-like weapons that spat fire at his comrades. Vasch felt his chest where he had been struck. A crumpled piece of metal had lodged itself in his hauberk. The missile had barely broken his skin.

'Everyone stay low. Try and flank them,' he called out to the others.

Chas charged out from cover and ran straight at the enemy warriors. The humans' weapons flashed rapidly as they yelled at each other in their own tongue. Chas staggered and threw himself behind a metal cupboard. Vasch wrinkled his snout in disgust. One of these days, he would have a serious word with young Chas about following orders.

Haig rose up behind the humans and grabbed one of them in a bear-hug. Hot metal sprayed across the room. Grenld roared in pain and clutched at his left eye. Vasch placed one hand on the altar and vaulted over. The second human aimed his weapon at him. Vasch yanked it from the human's hand then dropped it as red hot pain seared his palm. The human stood frozen, staring in horror at his contorted face. Vasch knocked the man unconscious with a punch.

Tangred and Udulf charged into the chamber. They were supposed to be watching the front. Another two humans followed them through in close pursuit. Vasch drew his dagger and threw it to Haig, who snatched it deftly out of the air to hold it to the human's throat. The newcomers froze.

'Get out the back way. Haig, if these meat-sacks so much as flinch, cut the human's throat,' said Vasch backing slowly towards the open doors.

The warband exited the building with their hostage and the humans followed. Vasch and Haig were the last to stumble down the embankment.

Without warning, the two humans opened fire. Haig yelped as a projectile ripped into his hand, making him drop the knife and release the prisoner. Vasch grabbed Haig by the arm and dragged him through a shrub and into the woods beyond.

Karen and Hussein entered the reception area cautiously. They held their tasers at the ready as broken glass crunched beneath their boots. There was no sign of the ART guys or the arsonists. Hussein moved past her to a set of double doors and peeped through the safety glass. He signalled with his chin for Karen to join him. The doors opened onto a short corridor with only one office leading off from it. The office was empty but for broken furniture. A second set of doors at the end of the corridor led into the examination room.

One of the ART guys lay on the floor, looking dazed. It was either Bragg or Johnson, Karen couldn't remember.

'Are you okay?' asked Hussein.

'Yeah, that thing caught me by surprise that's all,' said the officer gruffly.

Some of the freezer drawers were open in the examination room, but thankfully empty. A mangled body lay on a gurney. Karen averted her eyes. The fire exit doors stood ajar.

Outside, a steep embankment led down to a tall hedge wall. Scholes and his other team mates stood at the bottom. Beyond the hedge rose a dense wood. Long, thin trunks crowded close together, their thick foliage conspiring to blot out all traces of sunlight.

'What the hell were those things?' asked one of the shaken ART guys.

'Just big lads in Halloween costumes, mate,' replied Scholes, as he turned to look at Karen.

'What happened?' asked Hussein.

'We were well outnumbered, at least four to one. They took Bragg hostage and were going to haul him off into the woods. I shot one in the hand.'

'Why didn't you give pursuit?' asked Karen.

'Like I said, we were outnumbered.'

'Your friend back there looks like he might be concussed. You'd better call for the paramedics,' said Karen.

'I'm going to go check out the examination room again, see if I can find out what they were up to,' said Hussein and then followed the ART guys back inside.

Karen waited until they were gone, then bent down to peer at something large caught beneath the hedge. She pulled an evidence bag over her hand like a glove and used it to retrieve the item. It was a knife. The grip was sheathed in reptile skin and the blade itself was a serrated nightmare. With her prize in her hand, Karen trudged back up the embankment to the morgue.

CHAPTER 8: ALVORN REACH

KRYLLON

The forest was cool and an occasional burst of sunlight dappled the green realm they travelled. Nathan Celic sat quietly with his brother and friends, having only just regained consciousness. He was terrified.

Where were they? How had they got here? The last thing he remembered was water closing in over his head and then everything had gone blank.

Nathan studied their captors from between the vine-mesh on the back of the cart. At first he had thought he was hallucinating. The gaolers were human in shape but skinnier than supermodels. They had protruding arum-shaped ears that twitched like a dog's. Their skin was covered in some sort of body glitter, in varying shades of gold and copper.

'Am I dreaming?' he asked aloud.

'If you are, then can you please wake up, because we seem to be stuck here too,' said Katrina.

Nathan looked back at her and then yelped as Logan pinched him hard on the thigh.

'No, bro, you're definitely not dreaming. Keep your voice down though. We don't know if these things are friendly or not,' said Logan.

'They've shoved us in a cage and they're holding us prisoner. What part of that sounds friendly?' asked Katrina.

Salina hugged her knees unhappily, seeming close to tears. Nathan crawled over to her and held her hand. One of the aliens walked right up to the cart and pushed something through the mesh. It was a water-skin of some sort made from thick leaves, held together by a

THE CHANGELING KING

white rubbery substance. Logan picked the seal clear and sniffed at the contents before taking a small sip.

'It's water,' said Logan, before taking a deeper swig.

The alien watched them as they passed the skin around. Its round eyes were dominated by large pupils that reminded Nathan of a bird of prey. Nathan shuddered involuntarily and hoped that the alien wasn't thinking about dinner.

'What do you think they are?' said Nathan.

'For some reason I keep thinking of fairies,' said Salina.

Katrina snorted in derision, 'You're such a girl, Sal. They look more like umpa-lumpas to me.'

The cart rolled on. With no idea of the time or destination, the four began to feel restless. Nathan wondered whether the umpa-lumpas were planning to stop for a break soon. He could really do with going to the toilet. Then the aliens began to sing.

'It's beautiful,' whispered Salina.

The four gathered at the end of the cart and pushed their faces against the mesh to get a better look. They could hear cheering now coming from all around them. Globes filled with a luminescent liquid lit up a broad causeway as they passed into a city. Huge sequoias that made Dawn Redwoods look like Bonsai lined the streets. Hollows spotted the trunks as if some huge woodpecker had excavated them. Translucent amber filled various openings, probably windows and doors, observed Nathan. Thick boughs were being used as catwalks and bridges as the inhabitants of the city thronged the heights to welcome their warriors home. Soon the tired fighters were being mobbed by well-wishers. The cart came to a halt as the celebrating crowd swept around them. Children stormed their parents, and husbands and wives cried with joy.

Nathan felt very uncomfortable watching the homecoming. He knew now that he was the alien here and not his captors.

The guard shooed them back. The four complied immediately, scared of antagonising him. It was definitely a 'him', thought Nathan. He had seen some females amongst the warriors and the crowds. Though whippet thin, the females still had curves in all the right places. Their facial features were also less pronounced, except for the large predatory eyes.

NOOR A JAHANGIR

The guard removed the mesh hatch from the wagon. Two warriors appeared behind him, including one wearing a heavy cloak and a helmet with a tapered cranial ridge. Nathan and the others clumsily clambered down from the cart, their legs stiff from being cooped up.

'Welcome to Alvorn Reach. I am Gillieron. Nod if you understand me,' said the umpa-lumpa with the helmet on.

Nathan looked at the others. They shouldn't have been able to understand them. He couldn't have been speaking English. The pronunciation of the words sounded too foreign. Logan nodded his head to show that they did.

'Please accept my apologies for keeping you locked up for so long. I hope you have had time to recover from your ordeal of crossing the ether. You are now guests of the alvor of Kryllon.

'There will be much celebrating tonight, said Gillieron. 'It was the first major skirmish against the Trollking in a long time, and though many of our brothers and sisters have fallen, the victory proved less costly than we had dared hope. But first, we must go and see the Archmagus.'

The alvor led them to a platform constructed of woven branches and lacquered leaves. One of the guards drew a bit of vine-mesh across the front of the platform. The platform ascended smoothly as a counterweight, adjacent to the lift, descended slowly.

The lift stopped far above the ground and the passengers alighted onto a series of steps made up of over-lapping fungi circling the girth of the tree. They climbed until they reached a landing. Gillieron knocked on an amber portal and requested permission to enter. The door swung open to admit them.

Inside, the tree was cramped and smelt of must. Shelves and tables were cluttered with book and jars, with scrolls wedged into every other nook and cranny. A fire burned within a large amber egg, heating the room without damaging the living structure. Light-brown mushrooms formed a modest-sized table and eight stools in the middle of the room. An alcove by the fire formed a ninth chair, occupied by a hunched figure in blue robes. His long, silvery hair fell over his shoulders. A wispy beard trailed down his chest.

'Ankh, fetch some drinks for our guests. Please, be seated,' said the old alvor.

THE CHANGELING KING

A gnome, whom they had not noticed before, hastened to do the mage's bidding on short stubby legs. He returned almost immediately with six goblets of wine on a tray. The mushroom stools were surprisingly spongy to sit upon.

'I am Archmagus Amras, the Guardian of Kryllon. Tell me everything and leave nothing out. Begin with your names and then continue with how you got here.'

Nathan suddenly felt a strong compulsion to tell this strange man everything. His tongue began tripping over the strange syllables before his mind had even begun to form a coherent thought.

'I'm Nathan, erm, from Affrington, which is in . . . ah, England. This is my big brother Logan and our friends, Salina and Katrina.'

'What is the name of your world?' asked the Archmagus.

'Our world? It's called Earth.'

'That's not a name, it's a description. This world is known as Eridani. What is your world called?'

'Earth, that's what we call it. It doesn't have any other name.'

One by one, the Archmagus made each of them retell the story. He continued to question them at great length, often cross-examining all four of them for details, as if trying to catch them in a lie.

'I think that is enough talk now,' announced the Archmagus, finally. 'The children are tired and need rest. They must sleep, yes. Sleep is the best thing for them. It will heal the hurts of their bodies and minds and help them forget the horrors they may have witnessed.'

Nathan found his eyelids growing heavy and his mind growing dull. He fought to keep them open, but his eyes refused to focus and he slipped into a soft, fuzzy darkness.

The water closed over his head. He was drowning. His lungs fought against his will, begging him to open his mouth. Something had his leg. It was pulling him down. Salina was right above him, her pale hair fanning around her face like a golden halo. She turned around slowly, her eyes wide and empty, her mouth open in a silent scream.

NOOR A JAHANGIR

Nathan jerked awake, gasping for air, his body drenched with perspiration. He looked about himself in panic. This wasn't his bedroom. The walls were bleached white and merged seamlessly with the ceiling and ground. Where was he?

A translucent yellow door stood opposite his bunk, a green pod filled with flower petals. Nathan rose unsteadily to his feet. The floor felt warm under his soles. He stumbled towards the door. It swung open at the touch of his hand.

Logan, Salina and Katrina sat at a table drinking and talking quietly with the alvor, Gillieron. A child played by Gillieron's feet. Nathan's heart pounded with fear as he recalled the events of yesterday. It hadn't been a dream. He, Salina and the others had drowned in that lake. Somehow, they had been transported to this strange place.

Nathan walked unsteadily over to the table and sat down between Salina and his brother. Salina handed him something to drink. It tasted and smelt of flowers. He looked around the table and took strength from the familiarity of their faces. Finally he looked at Gillieron and found that he couldn't read his expression.

'Are we prisoners?' asked Nathan.

'You are guests,' replied the alvor.

'Then we could just walk out of here, anytime we want to?'

'I witnessed your arrival through a tear in the sky amidst a terrible storm,' said Gillieron. 'You survived an impact that would have crushed a dragon. Does any of this describe your normal circumstances?'

Nathan answered the query with pursed lips.

'The truth is that we do not know why you are here, or whether you pose a threat to our people. Sadly, it is therefore necessary for us to err on the side of caution. It is for our safety and yours that you remain within your quarters until we ascertain the purpose of your coming.'

'Then we're prisoners, in everything but name,' said Nathan.

'The Archmagus is the wisest and most knowledgeable person I know. If anyone can help you, it is he. Now please, eat. The Archmagus is expecting you after breakfast.'

THE CHANGELING KING

Nathan felt a knot of unease curl in his belly at the mention of the Archmagus. Nathan was pretty sure that the old alvor had done something to them last night, making them blab out everything he wanted to hear. Nathan would have to try and keep his wits about him. Normal rules obviously didn't apply in this world.

They ate the crispy petals, dried fruit and nuts placed before them and washed them down with a hot drink that tasted similar to heavily honeyed camomile tea.

'This isn't breakfast,' said Logan miserably as he munched on a leaf stuffed with diced nuts. 'Haven't these people heard of eggs and bacon?'

'What is bacon?' asked Gillieron, his eyes wide with interest.

'Meat,' said Logan as he drained his fourth mug of tisane.

'That is disgusting. I didn't think humans would ever fall as low as the trolls and goblins and feast on flesh.'

'Don't knock it until you've tried it,' replied Logan.

Gillieron looked as if he was about to throw up. Logan smiled and continued to clear the plates of every last crumb. When they had finished, Gillieron gave them a brown cloak each to wear over their new, black tunics and leggings. The alvor led them outside and, for the first time, they were able to see the alvorn city properly. Lights stretched out in all directions, hanging amongst the branches and boughs like droplets of dew on a giant protracted web. Thick boughs supported whole boulevards thronged with alvor socialising and going about their business. The humans gazed around wide-eyed with wonder.

'It's like a squirrel's version of Disneyland,' stated Katrina.

Gillieron led them higher up amongst the trees, until they could see the enormous orange sun blazing through the canopy. Alvor stopped what they were doing to stare at them as they went by. They crossed a narrow catwalk that swayed gently as they passed over it. Gillieron took them down the spiral, fungi staircase that ended on the landing outside the Guardian's home.

Ankh, the gnome, waited for them with drinks and waved them to their seats. The Guardian was still ensconced in his easy chair, smoking something in a fluted pipe while studying an ancient manuscript.

NOOR A JAHANGIR

'Isn't it rude to stare in your world, boy?' asked the wizened alvor without looking up from his reading, 'I trust you are rested enough now for us to discuss the matter at hand? I know you must have many questions to ask of me and I will try and answer as many as I can.'

The Guardian's voice was much more kindly this time around, almost grandfatherly. Nathan, however, remembered how the alvor had manipulated them last time. He wasn't going to let his guard down.

'There is a place between worlds that exists beyond the normal perception of mortals. The Void is a transitory place that acts as a passage between realities for those who know how to access it and work its secrets. Most enter it not knowing what it is and spend the remainder of eternity lost in its madness. Others more fortunate find themselves in new worlds. To enter the Void one requires a portal or a gateway. In more primitive cultures this is often a ring of stones, a crude and unreliable means of entry. The most effective gateways are viscous, but require great skill to locate and activate.' The Guardian rolled up the scroll and placed it carefully on the shelf behind him, before continuing.

'The portal you passed through is a stone gateway, reinforced by water. Your planet was once the site of many a great battle between good and evil, but the magic weakened and the war moved on to other arenas. According to my texts, the gateways to your world were sealed. It would take a very powerful individual to have channelled enough energy to reopen them. For what purpose you were transported here, or how you have come to know our language, I cannot say. Your memories have been tampered with, of this I am certain. Parts of your minds have been blockaded with powerful wards, which I cannot overcome.'

'Who could be so powerful?' asked Gillieron.

'Shadel'ron,' said the Archmagus, his lip curling in agitation. 'He is a renegade Guardian and cannot be trusted. He shunned our powerful fellowship near five hundred years ago. Gladly, this plain is beyond his reach.'

'How do we get back?' said Nathan.

For an instant the alvor gazed at Nathan with a watery smile on his face. Nathan fought the urge to fidget.

THE CHANGELING KING

'Nothing would give me more pleasure than to send you home. While you have slept the day away, I have studied every tome and scroll in my possession. Gateways are complex constructs, built by a higher power than the Guardians. When activated correctly they can take you directly to a fixed destination with little danger. To my best knowledge there are only two gateways in Kryllon that may take you back to your world and time. The first is the way you came, but that can only be reached by flight. Unfortunately, no living wivere remain in Kryllon to fly you there.

'The other gateway is many miles north of here, a cauldron pool at the heart of a fortified city. Your only way home is in the very throne room of the Trollking.'

'Who is this Trollking?' asked Katrina.

'It is enough for you at present to know that he is very powerful and very evil. He has brought great suffering to Kryllon. It is he who forced the alvor to abandon their ancestral homes. He will not rest until all the people of this land are either enslaved or wiped out.'

'If this Trollking is as powerful as you say he is, then what chance do we have of defeating him? I don't suppose he's just going to let us walk right into his castle and use this gateway thing, is he?' asked Logan.

'We are not soulless creatures like our enemies. Of course we will not send you on your way as you are. We will teach you the ways of this land, train you to fight and provide you with weapons, equipment and provisions. We will teach you all the skills necessary for you to infiltrate Ranush and pass undetected through the gateway itself.'

'But you will not come with us, right?' asked Nathan slyly, seeing through the alvor's grand words.

'Nathan's right. Even trained and equipped, the four of us still don't stand a chance in hell,' added Katrina, 'we're only kids you know.'

The Guardian drew himself up, his eyes flashing with power.

'By the time you reach Ranush, the Trollking will have a war waiting on his doorstep.'

CHAPTER 9: MAN-EATER
INDIA

Sultan smiled as pleasantly as he could at Prince Murad, who looked to be suffering from a terrible hangover. The prince's silk garments had the dishevelled appearance of having been slept in.

It had been three days since the arrival of the prince's retinue and Sultan had spent the time saying farewell to his family and friends. On the day of the hunt, he had risen early to devote himself to the spiritual exercises the Sheikh had taught him, to be carried out at false-dawn.

Sultan turned to look at Abdul Fadl, who even now fumed over the rushed arrangements. He had only just learned that the hunt would be on foot, without even the benefit of the basic amenities.

Sultan listened with relish as his father explained to the befuddled prince and his chaperone the Azamabad style of hunting. No servants, no mounts, no muskets and no beaters. They would eat what they hunted and carry no additional supplies.

Abdul Fadl had insisted on bringing along twenty of his best lancers. The lancers were not happy about their new assignment either. The lack of horses made their elite status redundant.

Suleiman raised a lacquered hunting horn to his lips and signalled the start of the hunt. With a last lingering look at his home, knowing full well that this may be the last time he saw it, Sultan turned about and fell in with the hunting party.

The trappers set a steady pace so that even the overweight prince could keep up. But within minutes, Murad began to pant like a man bereft of oxygen. The trappers fanned out into the bush, checking spoors to make sure that the party didn't accidentally run into trouble. It was python mating season and there was risk of chancing upon snakes wrestling over a female. They would also be passing through the territory of a two tonne rhinoceros that had a penchant for charging at poachers with its two foot horn.

It was clear that Murad was in no fit condition to be out hunting. Sultan wondered if it were possible for a man to die of over-exertion. Perhaps, if they picked up the pace a little, he would find out. To his disappointment, his father called a halt after just fifteen minutes of easy running. Murad flopped to the ground like a beached whale. His damp silks clung to his quivering flesh.

'No more,' he gasped between ragged breaths, 'please, no more.'

'Your trappers are pushing us too hard. I still do not understand why we couldn't at least bring horses,' said Abdul Fadl, also breathing hard.

'Horses are useless over this terrain. Besides, the smell of horses will warn our tiger of our approach. Then he becomes the hunter and we the prey. The pace the trappers are setting for your prince has already put us several leagues short of today's target. If you can't keep up, you should turn back now. The going only gets harder from here on in. I can spare a trapper to guide you back.'

'No, that will not be necessary,' said Abdul Fadl, shocked by the sudden steel in Suleiman's voice.

'We will rest for half-an-hour and then we must press on,' said Suleiman.

Abdul Fadl pulled off his boots and threw them carelessly aside. Sultan looked at his father with a mischievous smile, who purposefully turned away.

Sultan wandered into the brush to circle behind the party. It didn't take him long to locate some stinging nettles. Noiselessly, he emerged behind Abdul Fadl and slipped his find into the balding man's boots. Undetected, he withdrew to share intelligence of his prank with the trappers.

By nightfall, Abdul Fadl limped from blisters caused by more than just hard travel. The lancers set down the litter they had made for Murad, to ease their backs. The trappers shot some wild rabbits and roasted them over an open fire. Once everyone had eaten, the trappers set watch duties. The lancers didn't volunteer to share the responsibility. Sultan was pleased with this arrangement, preferring not to sleep with an enemy standing guard over him.

At some point on the following day, the tiger had picked up their scent. It took one of the trappers so stealthily that the party didn't miss him until they stopped for lunch. They back-tracked but only found his bow and a large blood splatter.

Sultan stayed close to his father, just behind their lead scout, hunting spear in hand. Eventually the racket of the royal lancers faded to the background. As the silence grew around them, his father froze and signalled silence. A scream sounded from somewhere behind them.

Two lancers lay dead on the jungle floor, their throats torn open. The tracks on the ground suggested that a few of the lancers had run off in terror. The others had fallen back to defend their prince and the royal advisor.

'What happened here? Surely one tiger didn't do all this?' asked Suleiman.

'That isn't a tiger,' said Abdul Fadl, 'it's a demon in the form of a beast.'

'A manticore? I thought only the Europeans see such fantastic creatures in our jungles. Did it then have the body of lion, the tail of a scorpion and the head of a man on its shoulders?' asked Suleiman.

'Don't mock me,' said Abdul Fadl, as solemnly as he could muster while still quivering with fright.

Suleiman signalled for the party to follow the fresh trail left by the predator. A guttural roar came from a hundred feet to their left. Suleiman charged forward, while Sultan brought up the rest of the party. Of the trappers there was no sign. Sultan ordered the lancers to form a half circle and to start beating through the underbrush, to frighten the tiger away.

The sound of excited shouting and the angry sounds of a cornered tiger drew Sultan forward, keen not to miss the endgame. He slipped on something viscous and landed hard on his rear. Winded, he was forced to sit still and regain his breath. The body of a trapper lay concealed beneath a bush beside him.

THE CHANGELING KING

The trapper's throat had been cut open. The wound was too clean to have been made by claws or teeth. Sultan's heart began to pound, constricting his throat. Treachery was afoot.

Sultan scrambled to his feet and launched into a mad dash. Low hanging branches whipped his face and exposed roots tried their best to trip him. He wanted to scream a warning ahead to his father, but he knew that stealth and surprise were his only allies.

Sultan burst into a clearing just as the tiger leapt at his father. The Shah braced his spear against the ground. The tiger bore down on the spearhead, steel shredding through hide and muscle. Suleiman let go of the spear and jumped aside. The tiger, mortally wounded, kept its feet. It batted at the shaft until the spear snapped. Unarmed except for the hunting dagger that remained sheathed at his hip, Suleiman called to the lancers to put the beast out of its misery.

Sultan charged forward sword in hand as his father turned to see why his order had not been followed. He roared a warning, even as a lance struck low in his father's side. The Shah roared in outrage and twisted the lance from his assailant's hands. Sultan hamstrung the first lancer he ran past and met the second head on with a reverse cut that severed the man's arm at the elbow.

Suleiman drew his knife and lunged at his assailant. The lancer deflected the blow as another man impaled the Shah. Suleiman threw his knife at his attacker, catching him in the throat.

Sultan came up behind the first attacker and buried his own dagger between the man's shoulders, before turning to finish the two he had wounded. The lancers worked together to force Sultan back. Behind him, his father staggered forward to aid him. Weakened from blood loss, the Shah fell to his knees, humbled, as the tiger had been just moments before.

Fuelled by rage, Sultan pushed past his enemies' guard and pelted them with a barrage of strikes. The one-armed lancer went down first from a riposte that nearly decapitated him. Sultan pounced on the hamstrung soldier and slid his blade through the man's ribs.

Sultan dropped his bloodied sword and moved to his father's side. Suleiman held the lance in his abdomen steady, his face contorted with pain. Sultan raised his father's head to his lap and examined the wounds. The task proved difficult, his vision distorted by tears.

NOOR A JAHANGIR

'My son, leave me be. I can feel my life ebb away with each breath I take. I am already dead. You must see to your own safety.'

Sultan gently worked the lance free. Dark blood gushed out over his hands as he pushed down on the wound.

His father smiled wearily.

'Run for the mountains and follow the river up into Kashmir. Rejoin your mothers and sisters when you can. Give them my love.'

'Hush father, you can tell them yourself, these are just flesh . . .' Sultan could not continue. His father smiled courage to him and squeezed strength into his hands with his own.

'There is no God but God, and Muhammad is His Messenger,' said Suleiman with his last breath.

Sultan clutched his father tight to his chest. His heart told him to stay this way forever, but his father's final command compelled him to let go. Dazed, Sultan found himself standing over his father's body. His assassins lay dead around him. Of the tiger there remained only a broken spear and yet another trail of blood.

'To God we belong and to Him we return,' intoned Sultan, as he had been taught.

He ran then and this time not even the jungle could slow him down. Though it flayed him and tore at his skin; it could not stop him. Terrible emotions ripped through his core, threatening madness, as loyalty to his father's command conflicted with thoughts of revenge.

THE CHANGELING KING

CHAPTER 10: OFFICER DOWN

ENGLAND

Adam awoke with a start. His console's control-pad slid off his bed to crash to the floor. His mouth was dry but his pyjamas were drenched with perspiration. A thread of light filtered in from under his bedroom door. The television still showed the Horizon Commando 2 pause menu. He remembered switching it on but losing interest because he was too distracted.

He had been dreaming about Salina again. This time she had been behind a glass wall, screaming and smacking her palms against the partition. Strangely, she had seemed older, but so weak and pale. But that wasn't what had woken him. He concentrated; trying to remember what had scared him so much to make his pulse race even now.

The image came to him suddenly. He lay, twisted amongst the roots of a large tree. A huge monster stood over him, its face a mask of horror, clutching a cruel looking knife in its hand. It had been the bite of that serrated blade sawing through his scalp that had awoken him.

Adam listened to see if he had disturbed his mother. He could hear the television on downstairs, but otherwise the house was quiet. Adam slid out of bed and switched off his own set and console. He checked his bedside clock. It was only ten o'clock. He lay back down and closed his eyes. He prayed quietly, hoping without conviction that he wouldn't dream again.

The ambush at the temple of death had caught Vasch off guard. His orders had been to avoid engaging the native forces. It was clear that the local militia possessed advance projectile weapons. They had been lucky to have escaped with only flesh wounds. Morale was low amongst the troops. If he wasn't careful, he would have a mutiny on his hands.

Vasch took his bearing from the orb, its core turning from blue to red to mark their heading. He signalled for the warband to regroup on him. They made good ground across open fields, pausing only to wonder at the tall skeletal towers, linked together with thick cables, which dotted the countryside. Soon they arrived at a place where several roads met, centred on a round island of grass. Many metal beasts herded together around the island before breaking off to follow their own paths. Vasch looked beyond the island to the rolling hills that formed a natural enclave for a sprawling metropolis. Overlooking the city, on one of the hills, a multi-towered structure cut into the horizon. The orb vibrated, indicating that this was their destination.

Vasch waited for a lull in the passage of the metal beasts before leading the warband across the grassy island. They passed into a valley of squat buildings constructed of ribbed metal, red stone and wood. Sounds of industry and strange smells emitted from windowless buildings. There was little activity in the forecourts, but Vasch didn't want to risk another encounter with the local militia. The warband headed into the wilderness beyond the eerie valley.

This world seemed to have an abundance of resources and the humans flaunted their mastery over metal. They seemed oblivious to the metal beasts crawling along the ground and the metal dragons that left huge gouts of smoke in the skies above. Vasch wondered whether he and his crew had bitten off more marsh-viper than they could chew. He had not survived war, strife and famine to forfeit death on this inhospitable, alien world.

They arrived at their destination just as night began to bleed in from the east. The warband were anxious for action, sharpening their weapons with whetstones and warming aching muscles with light exercise. Vasch ignored their fidgeting and instead gazed at the city that nestled in the valley below. Hundreds of golden globes, strung grid like through the city, lit up almost as one. It was the most beautiful thing he'd ever seen. Vasch sucked in a lungful of thick, greasy air. It was time.

The warband sneaked into a yard full of slumbering metal beasts, heading for an unguarded entrance. The door was locked. A few strikes from his axe broke the lock. Inside, it smelt of alchemic compounds and human flesh. Vasch drew out the orb, and moved his arm until the orb flashed red to indicate their direction.

The warband came upon a few humans. They were unarmed, hardly worth the effort. The humans screamed and tried to run. The trolls dropped them with thrown axes or chased them down before cutting their throats. Grenld wanted to take scalps, but Vasch pushed him away. These were not warriors. Their scalps were worthless.

Suddenly, a cacophony of sounds erupted as a voice shouted urgently from somewhere above them. Screams of panic could be heard in the corridors. The warband was soon confronted by a number of guards in matching livery. They were led by a dark skinned human, wielding a small black weapon in his hands. The orb vibrated angrily between Vasch's fingers. The dark human was their target.

The human barked a command at them. It was a strange language, abrupt in places and sibilant in others. The man repeated the command again, raising his weapon to emphasise his words.

Udulf advanced on the human, his club cocked over his shoulder. The human raised his arms and fired. Udulf's body convulsed hard. Two bits of string led from his body to the weapon, transmitting a strange clicking sound. Udulf yanked the barbed ends from his abdomen and threw them aside. He swung his club from his shoulder. The spiked shaft struck the dark skinned human across his ribs. The human hit the wall and crumpled to the floor. Then the warband fell upon his companions.

Several police vehicles were at the hospital already. They had set up a police line and were keeping the regional press at bay. The local television news crew had arrived too. One of the constables recognised Karen and waved her through. Karen parked near the entrance and, a minute later, found Assistant Chief Superintendent Ryan Sullivan waiting for her at reception.

'Karen, you shouldn't have come,' said Ryan.

'You know I have to be here, sir. How is he?'

'He's in a bad way. His arm and ribs on the left side are shattered and there was a lot of internal bleeding. He also suffered massive concussion to the right side of his head. He slipped into a coma on the operating table.'

NOOR A JAHANGIR

'I have to see him.'

'Karen, wait. Bodies are turning up all over the hospital. I've got a bad feeling that this isn't over.'

Karen stopped in her tracks for an instant and looked back at Ryan as his words sank in. She nodded tersely and continued towards the lifts.

'Karen,' said Ryan once more.

'Yes, sir?' she called back over her shoulder.

'He's in D29.'

Karen found herself fighting to keep back her tears. She kept telling herself to be strong. The bland hospital corridors were all too familiar. She had to stay in control. Her throat felt swollen. The lift stopped and the doors opened.

Hussein had been given a room to himself. His head was swathed with bandages and a breathing apparatus covered the lower half of his face. A set of monitors and an IV drip surrounded his bed. It was happening again. She was losing someone else important to her. Karen exhaled sharply to ease the tightness in her chest. Karen looked at Hussein's face. Someone would pay for this.

CHAPTER 11: TRAINING DAZE
KRYLLON

Arazan, Captain of the Alvorn Guard, looked like he was just a few years older than Logan, thought Nathan. He wore a military uniform over his compact body, a bronze mail shirt over black trousers tucked into knee-length cavalry boots. He waited for them in a clearing within sight of the only stone structure in Alvorn Reach, the Alvorn Guard barracks.

'You know who I am and Lord Gillieron has told me what he knows about you; so we'll dispense with the introductions. I have been asked by the Guardian to prepare you for your journey. Weapons, hand-to-hand, survival techniques, geography and strategy are what I will be teaching you. Pay attention and work hard, otherwise I have better things to do with my time. We will start with unarmed combat. Logan, step up.'

Logan looked a little amused as he moved out into the sanded area. Next to him, the alvor looked like children. He rolled his shoulders and then fell into a fighting stance, left foot forward and right foot behind and slightly to the side. He raised his fists – one out front, parallel with his chest, and the other guarding his face.

'Ah, the classic fighting stance,' said Arazan, standing easy with his hands at his side, 'very practical but it has some shortcomings. You must remember, while all stances are very good to start from, they all have weaknesses. For instance, Logan's leg is open to a sweep. Raising it and shifting your weight to the back foot may work in some cases, but . . . I think it will be better if you saw it for yourselves. Are you ready Logan?'

Logan nodded and raised his fists a little higher. Arazan feigned a sweep at Logan's leg but Logan deftly raised his leg clear. Arazan brought his leg back in and snapped out a push-kick, sending Logan to the ground. Logan grinned and rubbed his stomach.

'What happened?' asked Arazan.

'My balance was messed up, because I was on one foot.'

'Correct. There are two ways of resolving this. Logan, you come at me this time.'

Logan got up and fell back into his stance. When he was ready, he kicked out, aiming for Arazan's legs. Arazan slid to one side and threw a punch, stopping a whisper shy of Logan's throat.

'That is the first method. Don't be where your attacker wants you to be. Again,' said Arazan.

Logan repeated his move, this time feigning first before flashing a kick to Arazan's stomach. Logan buckled over as Arazan's foot jabbed him under his arm.

'That is the second method. Don't wait for your opponent to strike again; your best defence is to attack first.'

Salina raised her hand.

'You have a question?'

'Do I have to do that?' she asked querulously.

'What, learn to fight? Yes. You all do, if you are to stand even a modicum of a chance of surviving in our world.'

'I don't like getting sweaty,' said Salina.

'I'm afraid that is going to be unavoidable.'

'There is no way I'm doing this. There's no safety mats or anything.'

Arazan stared at her without expression.

'Um, Salina, I think we better just do as we're told,' said Katrina in a low voice.

'Well then, I want to speak to the manager or whoever's in charge . . .' Salina broke off as Arazan's face became even sterner.

'You are next, Salina,' said Arazan.

Salina's face flushed red and she crossed her arms in front of her chest. Arazan moved quicker than Nathan's eyes could follow. Like an illusionist he popped up behind Salina and forcefully propelled her out on the packed earth of the practice ground. Nathan moved to protest, but was silenced by Arazan's scowl. For the next few minutes Salina desperately back-pedalled, side-stepped and rolled to avoid being struck, before Arazan signalled Katrina to take her place.

The morning wore away as Arazan put them through various techniques. By the time the sun reached its zenith, they were completely exhausted.

'Good, you are all fast learners. If you keep this up diligently we will have no problems. You have several hours to rest and eat. By the time the shadows double, I will meet you in your quarters for your lessons on strategy and tactical use of geography. Knowledge of the terrain and how to use it to your advantage is a necessary skill. I will see you then.'

The alvor turned about and walked away. The four watched as he disappeared into the foliage. Their faces were glowing and their clothes were torn, dirty and damp with sweat.

'This Arazan's a strange one. I wouldn't want to cross him,' panted Nathan.

'Let's go find something to eat and somewhere to wash. My stomach hurts from hunger,' moaned Katrina theatrically.

They all got up in agreement and limped away, nursing the various bruises that Arazan had inflicted upon them.

Afterwards, while Logan took a nap and Katrina nursed her aching muscles, Nathan and Salina went out together to explore the forest. They came across a wide stream that bubbled out from under a stone ledge and meandered away beneath the trees. Salina sat down by the ledge and pulled Nathan down beside her. They enjoyed the warmth of the Kryllon sun, in silence for a while, and the strange, but pleasant, smells of the forest.

'What's on your mind, Sal?' Nathan asked eventually.

'Nothing; I just thought of the stream back home, up in the woods near the park. Do you remember? We used to go there all the time to get away from everyone?'

'It's a little difficult to forget; we've been going to the same stream since we were seven. You used to call me a bully, as I recall,' said Nathan, his eyes twinkling mischievously.

NOOR A JAHANGIR

'Only because you used to call me names when your friends were around, so they wouldn't think you were a big softy for playing with a girl.'

Salina laughed as Nathan pulled a face.

'What did we talk about by that stream?'

Nathan straightened up and gazed into Salina's eyes. She remembered well enough, but he realised she wanted to hear it from him.

'You used to talk about what kind of house we would live in, how many kids we would have, you know? Mostly girly stuff like that. I swear if Gavin and the boys had found out, they would have beaten the crap out of me.'

Salina smiled and gave his arm a quick hug.

'Nathan, what's going to happen to us? Do you think we'll ever see home again?'

'Of course we will. As long as we stay together, we'll be fine. Everything is going to work out,' said Nathan.

He hoped he sounded reassuring because, secretly, he was terrified that they wouldn't. Somehow, he had to get his friends back home.

Nathan and Salina jumped as a couple of alvorn sentries bled out of the foliage in front of them. Nathan stood up and offered a hand to Salina.

'What are you doing out here alone? The forest isn't safe for saplings. Please return to the barracks immediately.'

Nathan and Salina looked at one another and giggled, feeling like a pair of naughty school children.

'When you are engaged in combat, you must not think of the opposition as anything but the enemy. Don't see them as someone's parent, sibling or child. It will weaken your resolve to fight for the kill. A war has no place for niceties. As long as you follow the warrior's code, you are committing no crime,' lectured Arazan, pacing the breadth of the barrack's mess-hall.

Nathan and the others sat on chairs, at a long stone table, spanning the length of the hall. Smoky, amber doors led off from the hall to the sleeping chambers. The ceiling was vaulted and set with skylights that spotted the stone floor with yellow pools of light.

'The warrior's code is to protect the weak from the strong, fight evil wherever you find it, never burn a holy place or defile a food source. Never kill unarmed men and women, and never harm a child or an elderly person. It is a simple and righteous code to live by.'

Arazan stopped pacing the room and turned to face the four. He looked each one of them in the eyes, perhaps to see if they understood.

'The code for a leader is not as easy to follow. A leader must look out for their troops. A leader must see to it that they are fed and have a regime to follow. You must make sure that they are prepared mentally for each skirmish. The leader must have no scruples in making tactical decisions. A leader must know when to surrender and when to run. Most of all, a leader must know his limitations and those of his troops.'

'A weapon is an extension of the hand. Most people forget that they have other parts of their body that can be used in a fight when they have a weapon. Give a person a poniard and he will try to stab you with it, continuously over-stretching to get at you. A goblin with an axe will try to swing it at you, becoming inefficient in close quarters. Turn your opponent's advantage against them. These weapons are only effective when there is a distance between you and your opponent. When you're in close, it becomes a liability.'

Arazan slashed sizable shavings out of Nathan's training armour as he spoke, slats of bark held together with a durable vine. Nathan hadn't landed a single strike yet.

'You mustn't think about scoring points. This is not a sport and I don't intend to let you get used to tapping with your weapons. In battle you must always aim to dispatch you opponent as quickly as possible, maim if you can't get in a killing blow. When faced with multiple opponents take the fight to the side which attacks first and carry it until you defeat them. Remember, even a crippled enemy can crawl and throw a knife. Deal with your most immediate threat, finish the wounded afterwards.'

NOOR A JAHANGIR

The barracks smelt of warm wood, amber and teenagers. Nathan and the others were back in the mess-hall again, listening to Arazan droning on about the geography and people of Kryllon.

'To the west of Alvorn Reach, across the River Caprice, lies dvargar country. What the dvargar lack in height, they make up for in muscle, girth, superior armour and ingenuity. Their land is uneven, full of rolling hills, with miles of catacombs running right through them. The dvargarn fortress, Amundborg, is hidden somewhere deep within the hills and marshes.'

Nathan glanced over at Logan who snoozed contently, his head propped up on his hands, elbows resting on the table. Salina chewed on her chipped and broken fingernails, while Katrina scratched her initials on the table with a dagger. Nathan sighed and continued to take notes. Absorb, absorb, absorb, he chanted his mantra under his breath. Outside, the sun finally began to set on their first day of training.

CHAPTER 12: YMIR ISLAND
KRYLLON

Over the weeks of training, their bodies grew accustomed to the gruelling training and, somehow, they still found enough energy to slip away from the barracks to join the younger alvor revelling at Islmir's Knoll, overlooking the sea. On other nights they would go skinny-dipping, or pilfer food from the kitchens to roast over an open fire and tell the greener recruits stories about Earth.

About a month after their arrival in Kryllon, one early morning, they found themselves riding through the forest in the company of Arazan and four cadets. Nathan exchanged glances with the others, wondering what form of training they were going to be subjected to next. Perhaps Arazan would have them swinging from tree to tree, or base-jumping from the cliffs. The stoic alvor seemed even more distant than usual. His face was haggard, his ears drooping and his bronze eyes somewhat dimmed, as if he had been awake the entire night.

By midday, the trees began to thin and finally gave out completely. The sea lay before them, framed by the brightening sky and black sand. Several Alvorn Guard troopers stood waiting by an alvorn long-boat drawn up on the beach. The boat was beautiful, seemingly crafted from a single, hollowed-out, white tree. Nathan and the others helped push the vessel into the surf before clambering aboard and grabbing an oar each.

The sea was choppy and the four were unused to the rhythm of the vessel. They found themselves struggling to keep time with the alvor. Luckily, after an hour, Nathan spotted landmass on the horizon; an island.

They landed in a small, natural cove. Arazan ordered them and the other cadets out of the boat and onto the seaweed-choked beach.

NOOR A JAHANGIR

Nathan grabbed his gear and leapt into the shallows besides his friends.

Without a word, the Alvorn Guard turned in their seats and began to row back out to sea. Nathan and the others watched until the longboat became too small to discern.

'Right, this is obviously another test. We all need to work together,' said Nathan.

'We don't work with humans,' sneered a cadet named Amroth. He signalled to the other three alvor to follow him and set off down the beach.

'What's got him all hot and bothered?' asked Katrina.

'Whatever it is, it's going to have to wait. We've only got a few hours of good light left to us,' said Nathan, 'I suggest we make camp right here on the beach for today. Salina, I want you to inventory the gear we've been given. Katrina, gather some wood and get a fire going. Logan and I will build a lean-to to give us some shelter from the wind.'

There was no discussion amongst the four as they moved swiftly to carry out their individual assignments, thankful for something to do to keep their minds occupied for the moment. As the first stars appeared in the sky, a modest fire pushed back the oncoming darkness, creating a comfortable circle of light. The four gathered around the fire and began to munch on cakes and cheese made from deer's milk.

'Okay, Salina, what have we got?' asked Nathan.

'We have a day's worth of fresh food. All of it is perishable. Dry rations, we can stretch out for two days. Four sleeping rolls, four daggers, a hatchet, a pot, four cups, our heavy travelling cloaks, string, two hooks and a compass.'

'It all depends on how long Arazan is planning on leaving us here. We can do this. Tomorrow we will scour this island for a good campsite and alternative food sources. On approach, the island looked fairly large. I'm guessing there might be a spring or even a small freshwater lake somewhere. Salina, hand out some more food; we may as well eat good while we still can.'

THE CHANGELING KING

'This reminds me of that film, Cast Away. You know, the one with Tom Hanks in it,' said Katrina, looking out dreamily at the surf caressing the beach.

'I prefer the version with Oliver Reed,' said Logan.

'It's so romantic, isn't it?' said Salina.

They all sat by the fire late into the night, talking about movies and their friends at school. Nathan finally got up and grabbed a sleeping roll. He unrolled it with a flip of his hand and lay down with his back to the fire. The others eventually bedded down too.

Nathan lay awake long after everyone else had gone to sleep. He'd always wanted people to like him and look up to him the way they did Logan. Strangely, it felt like things were beginning to go his way here, so far from home. Perhaps being stuck on this island would give them time and space to work out what had happened to them. He lay awake for a while longer; listening to the unfamiliar sounds of the island's nocturnal habitants.

By sunset on the third day, the four had managed to establish a functional camp in a large clearing. They had set up a perimeter of traps for small animals and alarms in case of bigger game. Of the team of alvor, there hadn't been sight or sound.

The clearing was located near a natural spring that emptied into a small pool. They had also discovered a large variety of berries and other edible fruits and nuts to supplement their diet. The four, trim from their training, grew even leaner and their spirits began to dip into a reflective melancholy.

They spent their time foraging, training and discussing all that had happened to them – the lake, the mystery of how they had been transported to Kryllon, the journey that they would inevitably have to make, and what they would eat when they got back to Earth. It wasn't until the fourth day that trouble came looking for them.

They had just finished skinning and spitting a couple of rabbits when one of their perimeter alarms clattered off to the west. Startled, the four leapt to their feet and hid in the bushes.

They watched as a huge beast lumbered out on all fours. Its rear legs were short in comparison to its thick arms, much like an ape's. Shaggy grey fur covered its shoulders and back. The rest of its body was protected by large grey plates covered with cracked skin. It paused near the camp, its small beady eyes glaring from under a heavy brow, flanked by curved horns. The ogre sniffed around the fire, its pink snout furrowing in concentration. It pawed at the rabbits, yelping as it singed its paws. A few repeat efforts ceded the same result. The ogre roared in frustration before ambling away.

The four remained hidden for several minutes, listening to the fading sounds of the beast. Eventually they came out to stand around the fire. Ever practical in the matter of food, Logan removed the spitted rabbit before it burned beyond edibility. Salina wrinkled her nose and pressed her sleeve over her mouth.

'What was that, and more importantly, what the hell is that smell?' asked Katrina.

'An ogre,' said Nathan quietly.

'Are you sure? It looks nothing like Shrek,' noted Katrina.

'I'm pretty sure. Arazan described them in our geography lessons,' added Nathan, 'but that's not important. What is important is that we prepare for its return. It knows we're here now.'

The ogre returned two nights later, setting off the alarms on the western side of the camp, its stench preceding it as it approached upwind of them. Nathan lay hidden in the underbrush. The ogre appeared at the edge of the clearing, its hide glowing from the reflected light of the fire. It looked carefully at the four sleeping mats, hopefully not realising that the lumpy shapes beneath the blankets were just rock.

The ogre sniffed at the air, then moved towards the fire. It dragged a large club behind it. Nathan wondered how many times it had crept into the campsites of unsuspecting alvor, smashed their heads in and then dragged them away to its lair. Nathan vowed that today would be its last foray.

A net dropped from the darkness over the ogre. The beast roared in anger as it struggled to free itself. Logan charged out from cover and jabbed a sharpened stave into the ogre's side. The beast roared again and swept Logan off his feet with a backhanded blow.

Nathan leapt up, shouting at the top of his voice as he sprinted towards the creature from the opposite direction. He rammed his own spear into the beast. It yowled in pain, then tore free of the net and ran for the safety of the trees.

The girls dropped down from their perch and came over to join Nathan as he helped Logan up. They were all breathing heavily, the adrenaline still coursing through their veins.

'We have to hunt it down,' said Nathan.

The others nodded.

They followed the ogre's trail of blood through the wood to a cave on the far side of the island. The ogre was wounded, but this was his territory. Cautiously, they edged into the mouth of the cave, moving slowly, letting their eyes adjust to the darkness within. Nathan's heart beat so hard against his ribs that he feared it would give them away. His mouth was dry and his stomach knotted with fear and further aggravated by the stench of carrion.

The entrance went back about twelve feet before the cave opened up into a larger chamber. Light poured in through a natural chimney. The cave's walls had been smoothed down by constant tenancy and were covered with primitive drawings that had a childish look to them. They found the ogre cowering in the furthest nook, clutching its sides.

The four spread out and held their lances at ready.

'Man-things come to death Gwyrt?' spoke the ogre in a low guttural voice.

'Oh my God, Nathan, it can talk!' cried out Salina.

'I guess Arazan forgot to mention that in his geography lessons, huh, Nathan?' asked Katrina, 'What now? We're still going to stick him, right?'

Nathan found four pairs of eyes looking to him for a decision. He toyed with the idea of killing the beast; God knew how many alvor the ogre had consumed. There were a fair amount of bones littered throughout the cave, some of them uncomfortably familiar in shape and size. He would save a lot of trouble for anyone else that came by this island.

'Nathan, take my lance,' said Logan.

Nathan and the girls looked at Logan as if he were crazy.

NOOR A JAHANGIR

'We can't kill it in cold blood, it isn't right. Not even a thing as foul as an ogre deserves that,' said Logan.

'No deathing Gwyrt?' asked the ogre.

'No, no deathing Gwyrt. We're going to help you,' said Logan as slowly as he could.

The ogre snorted incredulously before passing out.

Logan and the girls patched the ogre up and, to Nathan's disgust, spoon-fed the monstrosity rabbit broth. The thing ate a whole potfull. Salina tried to convince Gwyrt to bathe, but conceded defeat when the ogre came back from the beach smelling even worse.

Nathan still fumed about what had happened in the cave. Logan had no right to step in and take over at the last minute. The ogre could have easily ripped him to pieces. He would bet a hundred pounds that no one in Amroth's team would have done something that stupid. The others could fuss over that monster all they liked; Nathan wasn't about to make a fool of himself.

The ogre stayed with them even after it had recovered from its wounds. Logan spent a considerable amount of time fishing in the shallows with the ogre. Most of the catch went to keeping the beast's hunger at bay.

Nathan took to ranging along the beach, hoping to come upon signs of the other team. The alvor, however, seemed more than adept at covering their tracks. Then on the sixth night, he caught sight of a ghostly face peering out of the wood.

Nathan barely stopped himself from calling out in fear before the face disappeared. His heart raced with fright, though his mind reassured him that it had been an alvor.

Nathan thought about telling the others what he'd seen, but then decided against it. What were the alvor planning? Tomorrow, he would redouble his efforts to locate their camp. When he knew something worth sharing, he would tell the others.

Nathan found the alvorn camp almost by accident. He had decided to scale the mountain above Gwyrt's cave to get a better vantage of the island. The mountain was an old volcano that had vented its fury in ages past. Nathan skirted around the peak and marked the most likely spots for a camp. Then, as he made his way to the first location, he caught sight of one of the alvor lugging a couple of skins of water.

Nathan dropped to the ground as the alvor passed by, just several meters below him, and muttering curses at his fellows. Nathan followed cautiously, trying his best not to give himself away by stepping on a twig or something stupid like that. The alvor led him on for another half-mile into a dead-end gully.

The alvor was confronted almost immediately by Amroth, who cast a wary eye along the alvor's route, before relieving him of a couple of skins. Nathan hunkered down behind a bush to watch. The other two alvor were busy fashioning a sturdy looking cage at the back of the gully. Amroth passed a skin of water to the others before settling down by a small fire.

Nathan watched them for a short while until he felt certain he knew what the alvor were planning. He studied the area around the gully, memorising landmarks, choke points and defensive features, before slipping away as stealthily as humanly possible.

It took Nathan the rest of the afternoon to find his way back to his own camp.

Logan lay snoozing in the shade of the lean-to. Gwyrt, sitting watch over Logan, smiled at Nathan; it looked more like a grimace of pain. Nathan ignored the ogre and continued down to the beach. He saw the girls swimming a little way out and waved to them. They waved back but didn't look as if they were coming back in yet.

Nathan could smell his own sweat. He stripped down to the waist and waded into the shallows for a quick bath. The water was warm on top but felt colder beneath the surface. He waved to the girls again, signalling for them to come to shore. The girls nodded and Katrina held up her hand, her fingers splayed; five minutes. Nathan headed back to camp and sat down to wait.

Nathan sat up and looked around, disorientated. The sky had darkened to a deep violet. He must have dozed off. The girls were talking quietly by the fire, cooking mussels and clams. Logan was awake too, but lazed on his bedroll.

'Guys, why didn't you wake me?' asked Nathan.

'We tried, but you were really bushed,' replied Salina.

'Listen, I've got something important to tell you,' said Nathan rubbing the crust from his eyes with his fingers. 'The alvor are planning something.'

'The alvor? When did you see the alvor?' asked Logan, sitting up.

'I saw one spying on us last night, so today I went and found their camp. It's on the other side of the old volcano, in a little ravine with only one way in.'

'Dude, when were you going to tell us about this?' asked Logan in an annoyed voice.

'I wanted to tell you all earlier, but you guys were busy. That's beside the point now. I think they're going to raid our camp tonight.'

'Why would they want to raid our camp?' asked Salina.

'They were building a large cage or pen or something at the back of the gully. Wait, where's the ogre?' asked Nathan.

'He's around. What's this got to do with him?' countered Logan.

'Everything, you idiot. We have to find him. The whole point of this exercise is to capture the stinking ogre,' said Nathan, clambering to his feet. 'Now, where exactly is he?'

An angry roar from the direction of the beach answered his question. The four grabbed their staves and sprinted through the trees. It took them just under a minute but, by the time they reached the beach, the ogre was gone.

'Damn!' shouted Logan.

The alvor had hardly left a footprint to give them away. But there were still signs of a scuffle impressed on the sand. Nathan tracked the markings, picturing in his mind how the alvor had snuck up on the ogre. He guessed they must have swum around the island and come out of the surf around Gwyrt; otherwise, the ogre would have caught their scent. Here and there were marks of where the alvor had cast their net over Gwyrt; the stone weights had left their own indents in the ground. Spoors of blood, blotted by sand, showed that the alvor had battered Gwyrt senseless before dragging the ogre back into the sea with them. Nathan was impressed by how quickly they had managed the task.

THE CHANGELING KING

'What do we do now?' asked Salina, her hair blowing around her face.

'We have to find Gwyrt before the alvor kill him,' said Logan.

'It's alright guys. I've got a plan,' said Nathan, smiling. This was going to be fun.

The alvor were in high spirits, their laughter carrying far over the night air. Amroth sat smiling amongst them, basking in the praise of his comrades. They were regaling each other with their contributions in the capture of the ogre. Gwyrt sat quietly in the cage at the back of the gully.

Nathan and the others watched from the ridge above the alvor. Together, the boys slid back from the edge and began to circle their way down. Salina and Katrina had already gathered a small arsenal of pebbles from the spring. The girls would wait until Nathan gave the signal for them to start bombarding the alvor from above. With the alvor distracted, Nathan and Logan would charge out of the darkness and take them out. At least that was the plan.

Nathan and Logan had barely reached their position at the mouth of the gully when something large dropped into the alvor camp-fire, sending up a dazzling spray of embers.

'What the hell was that?' asked Nathan.

'I guess Katrina got tired of waiting,' replied Logan.

The alvor were already on their feet. Amroth shouted angrily for his comrades to arm themselves as the girls began to pelt them. Nathan wondered if they had misjudged the size of the missiles. The girls were drawing blood and even managed to drop an alvor to the ground.

'Have some!' roared Logan and leapt out of cover, holding his stave in a double-handed grip. Nathan cursed and ran after him.

Off-guard, the alvor turned to face the new threat. Amongst the people of Eridani, the alvor were known for having the fastest reflexes. But in training they had discovered that they were more than a match for them in strength and their equal in speed. Arazan thought it had something to do with them being from another world. But right now, the 'how' didn't matter.

NOOR A JAHANGIR

Logan went straight for Amroth, pounding down on the alvor's stave with mighty overhead slashes. Nathan found himself defending against a tandem attack from the other two. Gripping his stave around its middle, he spun the shaft left and right to keep them back.

The sound of wood clacking against wood reverberated through the ravine. Gwyrt began to roar and shake the bars of his cage. An alvor turned to see if the ogre was about to break free. Nathan whacked him across the back of his head, knocking him unconscious. The other slid his staff along Nathan's, rapping him hard on the fingers.

Nathan dropped the staff, shaking his hand in pain.

The alvor swung at his head. Nathan swayed under and then came back with an uppercut that staggered his opponent. Before Nathan could follow through, Logan stepped behind the alvor and clobbered him over the head.

Two days later, the alvorn long boat arrived on the morning tide.

Arazan leapt from the bow-spirit into the surf and strode up the beach to where Nathan and the others stood waiting. Amroth's team sat at their feet, scowling unhappily. They had endured a day's indignity in the cage they had designed for the ogre and looked the worse for wear.

'I see you've all spent your time constructively,' said Arazan. 'Where is the ogre?'

'In his cave, I suspect,' said Nathan.

'We've already said our goodbyes,' added Salina.

'Indeed. You can tell me all about it on the way home,' said Arazan as he headed back to the boat.

CHAPTER 13: ASSAULT

ENGLAND

Karen was on her way to the Phelps' place. She wove through some light traffic, made up of mothers doing the school round, white vans and public transport. Karen sighed as the fourth set of traffic lights turned red before she could slip through.

The empty passenger seat played on her mind. A loner by nature, she had come to rely heavily on Hussein for social contact.

Earlier that day she had been called in to see Ryan Sullivan at Divisional Command. Ryan had informed her that two CID detectives from Scotland Yard were going to take over her case. She had been reassigned. She was furious, but understood why it had to be done; though it still stung her professional pride.

Once free of the traffic, it only Karen another six minutes to get to the Phelps' place, a large detached house with white-washed walls and a red-tiled gabled roof that broke over the two attic windows.

Karen parked up behind a silver Mercedes-Benz. From her handbag, she removed the Glock pistol she had been issued for her new assignment. The weapon felt heavy but familiar, its bevelled grip cleaving snugly into her hand. The distinctive smell of gun-oil brought back memories of the fear and guilty excitement that preceded jobs that had required the hardware. She slid a fresh box-magazine into the base of the grip, and checked the safety. Hopefully, she wouldn't need it. She slid the gun back into her handbag and stepped out of the car.

The front door opened to reveal Mrs Phelps, dressed in a pair of jeans and a black top.

'Hello, Mrs Phelps, I'm Detective Sergeant Rainbow,' said Karen.

NOOR A JAHANGIR

'I remember. Have you found out anything else about my daughter?' asked Mrs Phelps.

'I'm deeply sorry about your daughter, Mrs Phelps, but I'm no longer handling that case. I think it would be best if we went inside and discussed why I'm here,' said Karen.

Mrs Phelps opened the door wider to admit Karen. She led Karen through a generous hallway into a spacious kitchen.

'Please sit down. Would you like some tea?' said Mrs Phelps.

'Yes, thank you. Is Adam at home?'

'He's upstairs playing videogames. Is something the matter?' said Mrs Phelps as she went about her kitchen, wiping down the pristine granite worktops.

'Actually, I'm afraid what I'm about to say concerns his safety. You'd better sit down,' said Karen. 'Your daughter's case has been given over to CID, due to some complications.'

'Is it about the attack at the hospital? It's all over the news,' said Mrs Phelps.

'My partner, Detective Hussein, was severely injured. He's in a coma,' said Karen, a large lump forming in her throat.

'Oh my God, I'm so sorry. The news mentioned that some people had been badly wounded, but didn't say who.'

'My commanding officer feels that there could be a link between the attack and your daughter's disappearance, although there's no evidence yet to support that theory. But we don't want to take any chances. I've been assigned to place you and Adam in protective custody.'

Mrs Phelps swayed in her chair and for a moment Karen thought that she would faint. She watched as several emotions passed across the woman's face. Karen fetched a glass of water for her and placed a comforting arm around her shoulders. Eventually Mrs Phelps wiped her damp cheeks with a tissue and looked straight at Karen.

'What do we have to do?' asked Mrs Phelps.

'Well, first of all, you and Adam should pack some clothes and anything else you think you may need. You may be in protective custody for a while. Is your husband at home or at work?'

THE CHANGELING KING

'My husband is an army officer. He went M.I.A over a year ago in Iraq,' replied Mrs Phelps.

This lady had already been through so much, thought Karen. And yet she carried her grief with such grace.

'I'm sorry, I didn't know. If there is anyone else you want to contact, you'll be able to do that from Division. That's where we'll be headed first. After that, we'll go straight to the safe house. Time is not something we have a lot of. You best get started with your packing. Do you want to speak to Adam yourself, or would you like me to explain to him what's going on?'

'No, I think he doesn't need to know yet. There's no point in scaring him,' said Mrs Phelps, 'I'll tell him when I think it's the right time. Just give me a few moments to get ready.'

Mrs Phelps stood up and straightened her shoulders, wiped her tears away again and forced a smile. Karen found herself admiring Mrs Phelps' courage.

'Is she going with us too?' asked Adam, staring at the lady detective, recalling her stern face and disbelieving eyes.

'Yes, she is, Adam,' replied his mother.

'Why?'

'Adam, you're being rude to our guest. No more questions.'

Adam scowled at Karen. He didn't trust her. She made him feel guilty, even though he hadn't done anything.

'Shall we go then, Detective?' asked his mother.

'Yes, and please call me Karen. You can call me Karen too, Adam.'

'Sure, Detective Rainbow,' replied Adam, hating the way his own voice sounded high pitched, like a girls.

The detective sighed under her breath. His mother hadn't noticed, but he had. He could tell that Detective Rainbow wasn't used to being around kids. He wondered whether she was the type that would try and treat him like an adult. Grownups did that when they didn't know how to handle you. Adam hated it.

Outside, Detective Rainbow began to put their luggage in her car's boot. Adam waited outside the front door as his mother set the alarm.

'Mum, why can't we take our own car?'

'It's better that we all stay together,' said Detective Rainbow. Adam ignored her and continued to look at his mother.

'Adam, please, just do as Karen tells you to.'

His mum climbed into the back of the Ford and fixed Adam with a hard stare. Adam walked around the car and climbed into the front passenger seat. Immediately he flipped open the glove compartment and began to sort through the stack of CDs. He didn't recognise any of the names on them.

'Who are Bach and Schubert? I don't think I've heard of them? Are they like some kind of Euro-pop types?' he asked.

'Why don't you put one on and see?'

'Nah, I don't think so.'

By the time they reached the station, Karen was ready to strangle the kid. Everything he said and did seemed to have been calculated to cause her the maximum amount of irritation. She could see Mrs Phelps in her rear view mirror smiling bemusedly at Adam. Karen took a deep breath, counted from ten to one and told herself to be calm.

It was with great relief that she finally turned into Divisional Command's car park.

The reception ladies waved at Karen as she led the Phelps in. Karen nodded to them and then took the Phelps up to her office.

'I'm just going to go and see the Assistant Chief-Superintendent and find out where we're headed. Adam, don't touch anything. In fact, don't even move or I'll lock you up for the night.'

Mrs Phelps smiled, mistaking Karen's aggravation for humour. Karen sighed again. She wondered at Mrs Phelps' calmness and speculated whether she was in shock.

Karen knocked on Ryan's door and entered. He smoked his pipe at his desk as he read through a report. He looked up as she entered and waved her to a seat.

'You know, it's against the law to be smoking in here now,' chided Karen.

THE CHANGELING KING

Ryan smiled and nodded absent-mindedly. Karen sat down and glanced at the array of certificates and photographs that hung on the wall behind him. There was a picture of Karen and Ryan at her graduation, alongside images of his wife and sons.

'Do you miss the Met, Karen?' asked Ryan.

'Sometimes. How about you? Do you miss the buzz?' asked Karen.

'At first I did,' said Ryan, as he tapped out the ashes from the pipe into a steel bin. 'But I am content here now. I have time aplenty to enjoy quiet evenings with my wife, play football with my sons and drink coffee with you and Hussein. Ah, poor Mrs Hussein, what must she be going through now? I think I'll go and pay her a visit before I go home. I spoke to his doctor today. She says the danger has passed and that there's a good chance he'll wake from the coma.'

'Well, that's something, I suppose. I'd be happier if he was on the case with me, though. Hopefully, God-willing, he'll make a full recovery,' said Karen, feeling her heart lighten a little under its cloak of grief.

'You know, I don't think I've ever heard you mention "God" before,' said Ryan, raising an eyebrow as he refilled his pipe with fresh tobacco from a small packet.

'It's something Hussein used to say. I guess it's rubbed off on me,' replied Karen.

'Well, maybe there is hope for your soul yet. Anyway, back to the job. There is a small farmhouse in the Pennine Moors, a few miles from Ewes End. It's a safe house that falls under the Met's jurisdiction, but I've had a word with the chief there. You'll have to drive into Ewes End first to pick up the keys. The house is stocked with everything you and the Phelps will need. The food should last you a month or two. Off the record, the chief also told me that there is a shotgun and rifle in a cabinet in the study, in case of an emergency.'

Ryan was about to add something else when the clarion call of the station's alarm cut him off.

NOOR A JAHANGIR

CHAPTER 14: TIGER'S LAIR
INDIA

Sultan awoke face down in a puddle. He rolled to one side and came up against some exposed roots of a tree. Slowly he sat up and felt his limbs for breaks. Steep embankments rose to either side of the little brook he lay in.

He must have fallen down.

His mind flashed on snippets of his flight and why he had been running, until he was beleaguered by waves of grief. Hot tears cut wide trails through the grime on his face. His body shuddered as he fought for mastery over his emotions. Remember, he told himself, remember what the Sheikh would say. This life is but a brief sojourn, a passing shadow. The true and eternal life only begins after we pass beneath death's cloak.

Far away, in the distance, a dog bayed. The hunt was on again, but now he was the quarry.

The Imperials were using hounds to track him. Somehow, he would have to throw them off his scent. The jungle was his only ally now. Sultan forced himself to his feet and staggered along the brook. He had been this way before, on a hunt with his father. The brook deepened and grew wider further along, until it emptied into a river. Sultan waded into the ice-cold water. It tasted of mountain snow. Sultan took a few hungry gulps before striking out against the current. The dogs would get the hunters to the river eventually, but it would gain him time. His muscles stiff from his reckless flight from the night before, Sultan clambered up the opposite bank.

Sultan's fire burned itself out. He had run out of kindling but didn't have the strength to gather more. The night had passed and he had not slept at all. His clothes were still damp, making his flesh pucker from the cold. The sun had yet to show itself. He erased signs of his camp before setting off once again.

The jungle canopy thinned as he drew closer to the mountains. The river would have been the easier route to follow, though it added some extra miles with all its twists and bends. But the hunters would expect him to do that. The high ground was the most direct route but the terrain ahead would be very unforgiving. To make matters worse, Sultan was starting to feel feverish. Every inch of him ached. His head hurt so much that he feared he would pass out.

By noon, Sultan suffered from fatigue and altitude sickness. He stopped to rest every twenty yards as he climbed higher and his body grew weaker. Progress was slow but there hadn't been any sign of the hunters today. Perhaps his strategy had worked.

When his muscles began to cramp, Sultan realised that he needed to find shelter and rest. It would not do for him to die of exposure on the mountainside.

Eventually, he lucked upon a cave. It was well concealed with brambles. Too exhausted to check for signs of occupancy, he clambered straight into its cool darkness.

The cave stank of bat droppings. Fruit bats he could handle, but there was also another, more familiar smell. It reminded him of something comforting from his childhood, but his fevered mind was unable to decode its secret. Satisfied that there were no snakes, scorpions or poisonous insects, he curled up on the cave floor and closed his eyes.

The sound of snapping bones and tearing flesh sawed through Sultan's dreamless slumber. He reached for his sword but his hands closed on air. He had dropped it in the clearing where his father had died. Sultan opened his eyes and waited for them to adjust to the darkness. He rolled his head towards the grisly sounds. The metallic stench of carrion and blood attacked his nostrils. A dust-charged shaft of light filtered into the gloom of the cave, revealing something large feeding.

Sultan's blood turned to ice as he recognised the fell shape, a head easily as wide as his own torso, with flared whiskers and triangular ears, flanked by tall, powerful haunches. Sultan drew in an involuntarily breath. The beast raised its head from its feasting. Eyes that had inspired tales of a mythical monster glinted in the half-light.

Sultan slowly rolled onto all fours, his left hand seeking the hilt of his dagger. The tiger continued to watch him, statue-like over its dead prey. The moment hung frozen between them.

Deliberately, the tiger looked away and went back to snapping the limbs of its catch. For now it was content to leave him alone, but straddled the only way out of the cave. Judging from the size of the catch, the feline was not likely to move for a while.

The beast rose from its feast and stretched its large frame. The splintered end of a broken shaft protruded from its underbelly. His skin crawled with a fresh thrill of fear. This was the man-eater that his father had injured at the climax of the hunt. Wounded, this tiger was a bigger threat than when it had been healthy. He had to get a better view of the carcass to establish how it had died.

The kill's legs were quite long and dainty for a creature of its size; probably a wild goat or a small deer. If the animal was carrion then he would become the next meal. If the tiger had taken the animal down itself, it meant that the wound wasn't as fatal as it seemed.

The tiger glanced at him again, licking the blood off its chops. Untroubled by his presence, it stretched itself across the opening and closed its eyes. A few minutes later, the deep rumble of its breathing filled the cave. If he had been a gambler or a foolish man, Sultan would have ventured sneaking over the tiger. Sultan was neither. Something rustled outside the cave. The tiger's head snapped up, eyes wide and alert. The sound passed out of hearing and the tiger lowered its head and went back to sleep.

Sultan crossed his legs beneath him. He drew his hunting knife as quietly as he could and laid it before him. The tiger's ears twitched slightly. Sultan closed his eyes, no less aware of his surroundings than the tiger, and began to meditate on the path that God had laid before him.

The tiger stood suddenly, facing the exit. Every line in its body illustrated alarm. The yipping barks of a team of dogs carried over the

THE CHANGELING KING

distance to Sultan. The tiger threw an accusatory look at him. He had led the hunters to its lair. The beast dropped to its haunches.

The hunters thrashed about for several hours. The hunting dogs had gone mad the minute they had picked up the tiger's scent. The beast stayed low but remained alert. Sultan knew it was just a matter of time before they came upon the cave.

When a hunter finally exclaimed over his discovery, the tiger churned out of the cave and attacked. Sultan pressed himself further back into the shadows. The hunter screamed in terror, but was abruptly silenced. Shouts of alarm were followed by the clatter of arrows against rock. Sultan listened quietly, picturing in his head the beast's struggle for survival. The big cat snarled and snapped bones. Men cursed and cried out in pain. 'Muskets,' someone shouted, 'shoot the damn creature!' They opened fire. The tiger roared.

Silence.

Something primal rose up in Sultan's stomach, urging him to charge out like the tiger and face his enemies. Sense soon prevailed, and he remained hidden where he was. Above him, the hunters debated who should take the tiger's head and hide as a trophy.

'What about the cave?' asked a man with a gravelly voice, interrupting the debate.

'What about it?'

'Shouldn't we check it?'

'Why? Do you really think you'll find anything alive in the lair of a man-eating tiger? The prince is a seasoned hunter and would have steered well clear of a tiger's hunting ground.'

'Maybe he's counting on us thinking that, but really he's hiding nearby.'

'That is possible. Fine, set up a patrol in this area, in fact you can lead it yourself. Take three days provision and see if anyone will volunteer to join you. If the prince doesn't show up by then, return to Azamabad and report to His Excellency, Abdul Fadl. The rest of us will press on and see if we can pick up his trail on the way to Kashmir.'

Sultan silently cursed the man for his obstinacy. He would have to skulk in this cave for a while longer. Eventually, the main body of the hunting party moved on up the mountain. Gravel Throat, as Sultan decided to call him, had remained behind with three other footsore lancers. To his disgust, the four lancers set up camp a few meters above the cave mouth and began exchanging crude jokes while they ate. Sultan returned to his meditation.

As time wore on, he began to realise the full extent of his troubles. Gravel Throat and his select group of slackers had no intention of commencing a patrol. They seemed fully intent on lazing on the mountainside for the three days they had been given.

Sultan's stomach cramped from hunger, but he was resolute not to touch the now maggot infested leavings of the tiger. The Sheikh had taught him that a Salik, a true seeker of enlightenment, with practice, could sustain himself on the remembrance of God alone. When Sultan questioned how this was possible, the Sheikh had responded with a riddle.

'The sustenance of every man, woman and child is a responsibility that God has taken upon Himself. So, whether one believes that he is providing for himself, or is being provided through another, it is God who really is the Provider.'

'I do not understand. How is one sustained without provision?'

'My child, sustenance, as with many other things, does not have to be seen, smelt or indeed tasted for one to receive it.'

Even then Sultan had not understood, but chose not to press the Sheikh any further on the matter. Over time, he had begun to understand that there was much more to the world than could be perceived by the five senses. The Sheikh had opened his eyes to this hidden world.

Sultan settled into a cross-legged position, back straight and hands resting, palms up, on his thighs. Slowly his body temperature fell to match that of the cave. His heartbeat slowed until it was in-step with his breathing, as he silently chanted the Lord's Names of Power.

The alternation of day and night soon lost meaning for Sultan. His ears no longer registered sounds, and the stench of engorged maggots was inconsequential. Sultan travelled ever deeper inward; cocooned from the hurts and aches of the world around him. Emptiness filled his mind as his spirit soared high above the mountain, the clouds and the cosmos beyond.

THE CHANGELING KING

After two and half days of sleeping and eating, Gravel Throat's curiosity overcame his laziness. As Gravel Throat lowered himself through the cave opening, Sultan crossed space and time, until he entered the atmosphere of a distant world.

Gravel Throat ducked into the cave and toed through the bones of the tiger's last meal.

Sultan's spirit rushed to the surface, towards an island that lay west of a large continent.

Gravel Throat peered into the gloom of the cave, wishing he had brought a torch with him or had waited until morning.

Sultan hit water and went under. His mouth filled with foul liquid and mud. He lurched awake, coughing to clear his lungs.

Gravel Throat crouched at the back of the cave. There was nothing here. Disappointed, he made his way out and told his fellows that they would leave for Azamabad in the morning.

Sultan looked about. He sat hip deep in a bog, far removed from any mountain. A large dollop of rain splashed hard on the crown of his head. He looked up as an alien night sky crackled with the energy of an oncoming lightning storm.

The reeds that grew on the edge of the bog parted. The massive head of a horned reptile snaked towards him. Sultan yelled in terror and scrambled backwards. Lightning flashed as the lizard stalked forward, revealing a demon mounted upon its back. Sultan shrieked once again.

CHAPTER 15: LAST SUPPER
KRYLLON

After a breakfast of fruit and yoghurt, Nathan and the others grabbed their cloaks and made their way to the Guardian's place. It was the morning after their return to Alvorn Reach and they had been summoned to attend a meeting with the Archmagus.

Ankh waited for them just inside the doorway. The gnome was dressed in a brown felt suit with a matching wide-brimmed hat. He led them into the Guardian's study and motioned for them to sit. Lord Gillieron nodded to them in greeting. Captain's Arazan and Tinuvil were also present, as well as a youthful alvorn lady they had not met before. Ankh brought them all goblets of fruit juice.

Nathan surreptitiously checked the woman out. She was remarkably beautiful, her complexion silver instead of the variations of gold and bronze seen in Alvorn Reach. Her hollow cheeks, sharp nose and hoary mane gave her a predatory look. She was dressed in chocolate coloured leggings and a thigh-length belted tunic. The alvor woman looked up from her goblet and smiled inquisitively at Nathan. He blushed and dropped his gaze.

The Archmagus cleared his throat and, suddenly, Nathan realised that the ancient alvor had been sitting in his chair all along.

'Captain Arazan tells me that you have exceeded his expectations and that your training is now complete. I believe congratulations are in order,' said the Archmagus. The other alvor in the room smiled politely at the four.

'I had hoped that you could have stayed a while longer, but to delay now would be dangerous. The Trollking has despatched a second company to try and cross through the Belt. You must leave before they get through. Tomorrow you will set off on your journey. Lord Gillieron will make sure you have everything you need.'

The Archmagus pulled out a rolled scroll from his sleeves and passed it to Katrina, who sat closest to him. She smoothed it out on a little table and held it in place for the gnome to weigh down the corners with large acorns.

'This is the most detailed and accurate map of Kryllon in my possession. I have marked the best course for you to follow.'

Amras pulled out another map and passed it to Katrina. She spread it open over the first map.

'This is an original street map of Ranush, supplied to us by Lady Merenwen. The safest route to the Trollking's fortress has been marked on it. Once inside, you must find your way to the throne room.'

'What about the Trollking's horde? The four of us can hardly fight them all,' said Nathan, intimidated by the scale of the task ahead of them.

'The alvorn army will leave Alvorn Reach in three weeks under the command of Captain Tinuvil. They will travel by longboat up and around the northern coastline. At the same time, Lord Gillieron and Lady Merenwen will be travelling to Amundborg on a diplomatic mission. Hopefully, they will be able to charm the dvargar out of their burrows to join the war effort.'

He said the word dvargar as if it soiled his mouth to say it.

'It would be better if you avoid direct confrontation with the Trollking, but that seems unlikely. The combined forces of the alvor and dvargar will deal with his armies. Does that set your mind at ease, child?'

Nathan would rather have preferred to go in with the might of the alvor behind him.

'I will leave the rest of the details to Lord Gillieron to brief you. You are strangers to this world but, despite that, we have prepared you as best as we can. I pray that you are successful in your mission, but now I bid you farewell. Kige watch over you.'

Nathan and the others, human and alvor, filed out of the Guardian's home. Arazan broke silence first.

NOOR A JAHANGIR

'I've got duties to see to. I'll see you four back at the barracks. Please excuse me, Lord Gillieron, Lady Merenwen.'

Arazan's gaze met the lady's and lingered for a moment, before he bowed and continued on his way.

As the sun disappeared beyond the treetops, the four said their goodnights and began the long walk back to the barracks. The petals of the pink and baby-blue nightbrights, strung amongst the higher branches, began to glow gently with the captured sunlight and the phosphorus-filled globes lit up the walkways. It was a pleasantly warm evening, scented lightly by queen-of-the-nights and other wildflowers that grew on the forest floor.

Back at the barracks, the four retreated to their beds. Nathan, however, found it impossible to sleep, his mind plagued with apprehension of the uncertainties morning would soon bring.

THE CHANGELING KING

CHAPTER 16: MUD, BLOOD AND RAIN
KRYLLON

Nathan was a little disappointed. Only a handful of their alvorn friends had turned up to say goodbye to them.

Lord Gillieron and Lady Merenwen were leaving on their mission to Amundborg at the same time. Gillieron's family were there to see them all off, as was Arazan. The girls hugged everyone and Arazan offered them a few words of advice on riding. His concern for them was obvious, but he seemed somehow distracted. Nathan was sure that it had something to do with the way Lady Merenwen kept slipping the alvorn captain doleful glances. Finally, the four mounted their horses and waved goodbye to the alvor and Alvorn Reach.

The first two days of their journey proved uneventful and pleasant. They stopped at each of the three alvorn watchtowers as planned. They ate hot food and slept on moderately comfortable pallets every night. On the third day they arrived at the final tower.

They walked out to the crater that the alvor called Heaven's Wrath, the place they had touched down. Small blue flowers and green shoots bravely patterned the crater's nadir – a minor miracle or, perhaps, a sign of greater changes to come.

Nathan looked up to see if the heavens bore a similar scar, perhaps a tear in the atmosphere or a shimmer of colours. Lilac skies stretched as far as he could see.

They awoke to the catcalls and war-cries of a hundred goblins and trolls who had surrounded the tower.

The enemy clearly had the advantage of numbers, the tower only having a compliment of six alvor. But the tower was well-fortified and stocked and the alvor had lit the signal fire that would bring a contingent of the Alvorn Guard by late afternoon on the following day.

Nathan and Logan sat hunched together beneath the battlements of the watchtower. Black feathered arrows overshot the ramparts and shattered against stone. When the goblins stopped to reload; Nathan, Logan and a handful of alvor stood up and returned fire, then quickly ducked back down again.

The captain of the tower, Truvalor, came and hunched down beside them.

'You will have to leave tonight, Nathan. The Trollking's mongrels cannot keep this up for more than another day, but the river will be swollen by mountain rain, making it dangerous for you to negotiate it,' said the alvor.

'How, Captain? They have us surrounded,' said Nathan, as he stood up with the others to fire off another volley.

'There is an old bolt-hole leading from the base of the tower to the river. We used it in the past to sneak our scouts out. You will get wet, but there is no other alternative. I've already dispatched one of my warriors to prepare your boat,' said Truvalor, as they dropped once more behind the crenulations.

'Will you be able to hold them off until Captain Arazan gets here?'

'They've already lost a good number of their troops. I wager they'll have advance scouts keeping an eye out for the Alvorn Guard. They'll retreat at the first sign of dust on the horizon. Now go and prepare yourselves.'

Nathan nodded and signalled to Logan. His brother returned the nod before sending a last volley into the goblins. The brothers slid down a ladder into the tower. They found the girls waiting for them on the first floor. They were covered with dust from the bolts that they had been loading onto the ballistae emplacements.

'What's happening out there? We can't see much from in here,' asked Katrina.

'They don't seem to be letting up. Captain Truvalor has made arrangements for us to leave tonight, via an underground tunnel,' said Logan.

'There's not much time for preparations. The sun was low in the sky when we left the battlements,' said Nathan.

THE CHANGELING KING

A young alvor led them silently down a ladder to the ground floor. Horses whinnied and nodded their heads expectantly. Salina and Katrina went over to say goodbye to them as the alvor moved a large bale of hay to reveal a trapdoor. A narrow set of stairs led into a small basement. Nathan grabbed a torch and climbed down after the alvor, followed shortly by the others.

Immediately, they could hear the muffled roar of nearby water. The alvor pointed to a second trapdoor. Nathan hauled it open and looked back at the alvor, who indicated that they should go down. Nathan dropped the torch into the hole. The ground wasn't too far below. Logan elected to go first. Salina and Katrina quickly followed him out of sight. Nathan looked to see if their guide was coming. The alvor shook his head.

'The tunnel will eventually be submerged. It is a short swim from there to the river's surface. Be careful, the current will be strong. One of my brothers will be waiting for you on the other side. Now go,' said the alvor.

Nathan dropped inside and found the others anxiously waiting for him. Nathan tried to explain the alvor's directions over the din, but realised the futility of it. Instead, he indicated that they should carry on straight. Soon they were sloshing through ankle-deep water. The water level rose alarmingly fast and the four found themselves treading water. Nathan mimed that they needed to swim under.

One by one, they disappeared beneath the black surface. First Logan, then Salina, and finally Katrina went under. He was alone.

The memory of water filling his lungs and being dragged under bubbled to the surface of his mind. His stomach twisted with fear. He sucked in a deep breath and dove under, kicking blindly, holding out his hands before him, his lungs aching for breath as the undertow pulled him through the tunnel.

Then his head broke surface. Strong hands grabbed him and hauled him out of the river.

Dusk had overtaken the siege. In the distance, enemy campfires flickered to life. An alvor wrapped a warm cloak around Nathan's shoulders and led him to a hidden spot where the others sat shivering, hair and clothes plastered to their skin. The alvor passed them a bottle of dandelion brandy and left them for a second.

NOOR A JAHANGIR

'Everyone all right?' asked Nathan as he tried to control the chattering of his teeth.

'Nothing a hot bath can't sort out,' stuttered Katrina.

Nathan felt too tired to smile. It seemed even a good dunking couldn't wet Katrina's spirits. He took a sip of the brandy then passed the bottle on, sucking in cold air as it created a delicious heat inside his stomach. The bottle went around once more before Nathan pushed the cork back in. By then the alvor had returned.

'It's time to go,' he said, 'your boat is ready, and your provisions and equipment have been stowed inside. Kige watch over you.'

The humans clambered onto the boat and the boys took up an oar each. The alvor pushed them off and then disappeared from sight. Their bodies quickly warmed up as they laboured against the current. After a while the girls took over. They rowed through the night, taking turns at the oars. Time lost meaning as their tired bodies became numbed by exhaustion. The sky lightened from black to grey and then finally a violet-blue, as the sun began its steady ascent.

About midday, Nathan started awake and glanced about in alarm. He had fallen asleep. Salina lay bent over her oar, asleep, as were the other two. Sometime during the morning they must have moored along the riverbank, but he couldn't remember when. After a few minutes of getting his bearings he realised where they were. He shook the others awake.

Ahead of them rose the black, menacing foliage of the Belt.

In the heart of darkness known as the Belt, the air shimmered then slid aside into folds as if something had been thrust through it. In its centre, an oval of liquid silver rippled. A shadow slipped through the opening and slid into the cool darkness. The folds of air flowed back into place and the portal closed. The wraith shifted to reveal eyes the colour of storm clouds and coalesced into the form of a man.

He stood unmoving for an age. At length, stealthy feet padded towards him. A lupine form moved into the circle of the grove. He crouched down to receive the triangular head in his lap, stroking it with a gloved hand. Something imperceptible flowed between them. The man withdrew his hand and the beast rose silently to pad away.

CHAPTER 17: THE GETAWAY
ENGLAND

The warband lay hidden in a copse of trees, which sheltered them from the sun and gave them an excellent vantage point to watch the location of their next target, the local militia's fort.

The raid at the towers of healing had proved successful. One of their targets lay dead and the unit was in high spirits. They barely had time to rest before the orb began to pulse again. It had led them here.

The fort was pyramid-like in shape, with a tower-block rising from each corner. They had witnessed a great number of militia men and women coming and going, dressed in their black uniforms with bright yellow surcoats, marked with blue and white symbols.

The day wore on and nothing much happened. Vasch ordered the troops to rest, setting two sentries to keep an eye out for targets and threats. Then, late in the afternoon, the orb began to vibrate excitedly.

A metallic creature purred up to the fortress and stopped amongst a number of its own kind. Three humans emerged from the belly of the beast. One of them was the boy. Stunned, Vasch failed to order an immediate attack. By the time he regained his wits, the boy and the two women passed into the safety of the fort.

Prodded into action, Vasch quickly called his warriors together to discuss strategy. The militia had more warriors and better weapons. To storm the fortress was a suicide mission. The job called for stealth. None of his comrades stepped forward, so Vasch volunteered himself.

Getting into the fortress proved easier than he would have hoped. The huge, intimidating double-door entrance stood wide open. Immediately within, a glass fronted chamber spanned a wall, where a number of females sat talking, oblivious to Vasch's presence. The second set of doors seemed to be held closed by an invisible force, but Vasch was able to push them open with brute strength. He moved through the corridors quietly, passing room after room filled with humans. Most were busy staring at glowing windows and tapping away on ridged tablets. Others talked animatedly into their palms. None looked up to see him peering in through the rectangular glass panes set in the doors.

Vasch drew the orb out of his belt and let it guide him through the fortress. It led him to a room on the second floor. Vasch looked in through the oblong of glass. The boy and a woman sat quietly inside.

'Oi, what do you think you're doing? Visitors aren't allowed up here unless escorted by an officer.'

Vasch nearly jumped out of his skin at the sound of the sudden challenge. The words were meaningless to him, but his presence had been detected. He turned slowly to face the human, a male with a shiny domed head. The human gasped in horror. Vasch grabbed the man's head with both hands and twisted it violently. An audible snap confirmed the kill.

A scream sounded from down the corridor. Vasch saw a liveried woman running away from him.

An alarm sounded from somewhere within the building. Vasch cursed. He only had a matter of moments left to him.

Vasch kicked the door to the room open and charged in. The boy scampered beneath a table. Vasch strode straight towards him, ignoring the female.

Something exploded against his back. Vasch looked at the woman. She had a chair in her hand. She was white with fear but still threw the object at him. Vasch brushed it aside with a brawny arm. He took two strides and grabbed her by the throat.

Adam screamed as the monster lifted his mother into the air. He scuttled backwards towards Karen's desk. His mother kicked feebly against her attacker's armoured ribs. A single tusk protruded from its thick lipped mouth, its snout furrowing into a sloping forehead. Its round malevolent eyes bore into him.

Karen leapt into the office and pointed her gun at the monster, 'Put her down and turn around with your hands up.'

THE CHANGELING KING

With a roar the thing threw Adam's mother against the wall and stalked towards the detective.

Karen pulled the trigger, emptying the entire clip into the monster. The bullets hit the thing like huge fists, making it stagger. It kept coming.

Ryan pushed her aside and charged at it with a fire-axe from the corridor. The monster parried the blow with its forearm and countered with a backhanded slap that lifted Ryan off his feet.

Karen slid home a fresh clip and fired again. The monster roared in pain. It ran for the window and smashed through it, head first.

Karen ran after it and looked out at the car park below. The monster was nowhere in sight.

Karen turned around and saw Ryan beside Mrs Phelps, who began to come around. Blood trickled down her face from a nasty gash on her brow. One of her arms looked broken. Adam sat huddled against the filing cabinet. When he saw Karen, he leapt up and threw his arms around her neck. He was trembling violently. Karen hesitantly patted his back.

'It's okay, Adam, you're safe now. The bad guy's gone,' said Karen, her own voice shaking from the adrenalin. 'What was that thing?'

'I don't know. In my thirty years of service I have never seen anything like it,' said Ryan. 'Karen, there's no time to waste. That thing may come back. Take Adam and continue with the plan. I'm going to take Mrs Phelps to the hospital. Keep me informed of your movement. I'll call the Met and have them send in the big guns to back you up. Don't argue with me. Just go.'

'Mum?' called Adam.

'Its okay, Adam. Go with Karen. I'll be alright,' said Mrs Phelps. 'Take care of my boy, Karen Rainbow. Keep him safe.'

Adam gazed blindly out of the passenger window. Meadows stretched out on both sides, with sheared sheep dotting the landscape, hemmed in by the Southern Fells. Stone walls, raised without cement or mortar, separated the tilled and fertilised fields.

NOOR A JAHANGIR

Karen slid a disc into the CD player. The sound of violins backed by a piano swelled up from the car's speakers, cocooning them in a mist of sound.

Adam wondered if his mother was okay. That monster had thrown her pretty hard against the wall. It had looked like something out of a videogame, huge, muscular and frightening. Was this the same thing from the lake? Could it be responsible for the disappearance of his sister? Somehow, he knew that there was a link here.

Karen squeezed his shoulder gently. Adam didn't turn around to look at her. He wasn't sure he could hold his tears back.

A sign told him that they were entering Ewes End, welcoming them to the Metropolitan District of Manchester. They drove past a huge factory with seven tall metallic chimneys pumping out thick plumes of smoke. Trees gave way to a short run of terraced houses with tiny front yards. Before long, they were on the high street, a mixture of charity shops, estate agents and fast food places. Karen took a right at a set of traffic lights, past a large public art installation, a bronze hammer balanced precariously on a matching anvil.

Ewes End police station was situated behind a small library, near the town's centre. Karen went inside to pick up some keys whilst he waited in the car. Adam looked through the CD's again to kill time. He didn't have long to wait before Karen came back.

'You're mum's going to be okay, Adam. She's been checked into the hospital but the doctor's don't think there's much to worry about,' said Karen as she climbed back into the car. Adam nodded, feeling relieved but not wanting to show that he had been too concerned.

The sun rode low over the dark silhouette of the moors, setting the steel-dust clouds on fire. It took Adam and Karen almost half an hour to find the farmhouse, a large stone building with a barn that looked ready to collapse. All the ground floor windows were shuttered on the outside. Karen followed the driveway to the back of the house. The moor levelled out into a green plateau and in the distance, a forest undulated in the wind against the blazing horizon.

'Wait in the car, Adam. I want to make sure the house is clean,' said Karen.

'Why, does it matter if it's dirty?' asked Adam, his curiosity finally drawing him out. Karen smiled.

THE CHANGELING KING

'No, I meant that I want to make sure that nobody's waiting for us in there.'

'Oh, I get you now. You're going to go through the house, check every room and shout, "clear", right? Like in the movies?' said Adam.

'Yeah, just like in the movies.'

The backdoor was made from English Oak, solid as a brick wall. Karen unlocked the door and found herself in a large kitchen. The house was warm from the heat of day and smelt of stale air and varnish. It was decorated and furnished in soft neutral tones and monochrome upholstery.

Karen drew her gun and pulled out the magazine clip to see how much ammunition she had left. There were only two bullets in the clip and the spare was empty. Karen sighed and slid it back into place. She checked the ground floor first, going from room to room until she found the study.

The gun cabinet was right where Ryan said it would be. It was stocked with a twelve-gauge shotgun and a bolt-action rifle, ammunition for both and a box of rounds compatible with her pistol. She slipped three slugs into the shotgun and reloaded her spare clip before proceeding to the first floor. The upstairs rooms were also nicely done up, but lacked a personal touch. This house needs a family living in it, thought Karen, bemused by her own turn of mind. Satisfied, Karen went back to the car to fetch Adam.

Vasch was in agony. The female warrior's weapon had cut into his flesh like burning hot pokers. His breastplates had probably saved his life, but the pain was excruciating. Jumping out of the window hadn't been such a good idea either. It felt like he had fractured his ankle and cracked a rib. Luckily, Durke and Tark had been waiting nearby and, between the two of them; they hauled him into the relative safety of the grove. Now his comrades stood arguing around him to decide his fate.

'He failed the mission and now the militia will be aware of our target. It will be that much more difficult to finish it. We should kill him now and consume his flesh,' said Udulf.

'He is our leader and the Trollking's right arm. To kill him will be seen as an attack on the Trollking himself,' objected Haig.

'I agree,' said Sigberd. 'Vasch is a good leader. We will carry him on our shoulders until he is stronger.'

'Do you believe he would think twice if it was one of us laid there instead of him?' asked Udulf with a sneer.

'Agilerd, you have served longest with Vasch. What do you say?' asked Sigberd.

'I will kill anyone who raises a hand against Vasch. But we cannot take him with us. He would slow us down. The mission comes first, am I not right, Vasch?'

Vasch had been listening quietly to the exchange. He had drawn his axe and held it ready, concealed by his leg.

'You must continue with the mission,' said Vasch. 'Agilerd is the oldest amongst you. He will lead in my stead. I will head back to the rendezvous point by myself.'

'I am the strongest. I will lead. That is the troll way,' said Udulf.

'I second Agilerd for leader,' said Sigberd.

'No, Udulf is right. He is the strongest warrior amongst us. It is the troll way. He will lead,' said Agilerd, anxious to avoid a fight that he had no chance of winning.

The rest of the warband thumped their chests in agreement. Sigberd looked to Vasch, but the wounded troll shook his head. There was no sense in fighting amongst themselves. They still had a mission to complete.

'What are your orders, Udulf?' asked Grenld.

'The humans Vasch wounded will go to the temple of healing. They cannot be allowed to reveal our existence to others of their kind. Sigberd, Haig, Tangerd and Chas; return to the temple and kill whoever matches the descriptions Vasch has provided. The rest of us will track the woman and the boy. Vasch, give me the orb.'

Vasch reached into his belt and drew out the orb. He held it to his lips and whispered a name on it before holding it out for Udulf to take. The troll snatched it from his hands and retreated quickly.

THE CHANGELING KING

'Why is it not working?' asked Udulf after turning it around in his hands for a time.

'Throw it to Agilerd,' said Vasch.

Udulf passed the bauble to Agilerd, who held it gingerly at arm's length. The orb began to glow.

'The orb will only work for Agilerd and me. So you better make sure Agilerd survives at least until you have completed the mission,' said Vasch, grinning so that his intact tusk extended to his cheek.

'Try not to become food, Vasch,' replied Udulf.

The trolls slipped out under the cover of night. Last to go was Sigberd and his team.

'Blood and glory, Sigberd,' said Vasch.

The young troll saluted and then led his team out after Udulf's. Vasch lay back and closed his eyes.

Many miles away, Adam lay asleep, tossing and turning, his mind in the grip of nightmare visions. He saw his sister crying alone in a cell. He saw his mother in hospital, the monsters creeping towards her bed. He saw his father lying wounded beneath the rubble of a bombed-out house. He saw himself... dead.

CHAPTER 18: THE CHANGELING

KRYLLON

The Trollking stood motionless, staring into the roiling surface of his cauldron pool. The pool's unholy glow chased crimson highlights along the rusted curves of his armour. Created from lobstered iron plates, the armour was studded with filed bone fragments. His head and face were completely hidden by a tall bucket helm, mounted with the triangular skull of a wivere, its cranial horns flaring out to the sides.

A shadow detached itself from the gloom inhabiting the recesses of the throne room. Like mist, it trickled along the floor towards the Trollking. It stopped before him and coalesced into a cloaked and hooded figure, easily matching the tyrant's height. The ghostly features beneath the hood could barely be defined as a face.

'What is it?' said the Trollking.

'We have finished with the human. We have wracked his mind for answers. He is not the one.'

'Get rid of him. We have no use for the wretch.'

The wraith slid back into the shadows to disappear.

The demon was his ally, but he did not trust it. He did not trust anyone, except Vasch, who had been his comrade right from the beginning. Of all of them, Vasch was most loyal to him. That was why he had been sent through the pool. He did not trust the demon's intentions. Vasch would eliminate everyone, even the boy that the wraith wanted alive.

The pool was unique, the demon had assured him. It could reveal the past if one sought it and even hint at what lay beyond the veil of the future. The wraith had granted him the ability to use the pool for scrying, but withheld the knowledge of activating the gateway between worlds.

The Trollking's alliance with the demon had come at a great price. It had fused his armour and helm to his flesh to grant him mastery over the pool's lower operations. Then there were the blood sacrifices . . .

Things had not always been this way. There had been a time when he had been content to live out his days in the mountains, his foster brothers by his side. But cruel fate had set his destiny on a different path.

'Unveil the past,' the Trollking rasped.

The surface of the pool boiled momentarily before clearing to reveal Ranush as it had been more than a century past, a city second only to Maidenhall in beauty. The harbour full of merchant ships, its market pulsed with colour and the streets bustled with the press of people. But the past prosperity of his city drew no emotion from the Trollking.

The pool focused on one house in particular, the house of an alvorn noble who had once numbered amongst the high and mighty of Ranush.

Within the house, a silver-haired alvor paced outside his wife's room as several healers fought to save her life. The noble's wife had gone into premature labour, something that had only happened twice in half a millennium. The most senior of the healers came out to speak with the noble.

'Fear not, Lord Telemnar, Kige has spared your wife. She is safe. The child . . . well, the child is healthy, but . . . you will understand when you see it. Now, your wife needs a lot of rest, as do we. Please, with your permission?'

Lord Telemnar nodded and thanked them. After they had left, he went to his wife's bedside. Her hair was mussed and her bed sheets were soaked with sweat. She looked as frail as an ancient. He sat down beside her and wiped the glittery moisture from her face with his cloak. She opened her eyes and smiled at him.

'Show me my child,' she whispered.

Telemnar looked around until he saw a bundle wrapped in blankets on a small cot. He lifted the child and brought it over to the bed. The child was unusually large despite its premature arrival. He passed the bundle to its mother's waiting arms. She pulled aside the blanket to look at its face and screamed.

The child slipped from her arms. Telemnar moved swiftly and snatched the baby up. Then he too caught sight of its face. A look of horror came over him.

'Kige be merciful, it's a changeling,' he whispered, his voice reflecting the loathing in his heart.

His wife had averted her face and cried softly into her pillows. Telemnar looked once again at the abomination in his hands then thrust the changeling back into its cot. The changeling began to shriek and wail as if it knew that it had been rejected. The alvor lord pushed the cot out of his wife's chamber and shut the door.

The pool's surface clouded over again and then cleared to reveal a procession moving away from a barge on the river. Ahead of them rose the first knoll of the Pervilheln Mountains. The procession included Lord Telemnar, three Spellweavers and several armed guards. The group stopped at the top of the first knoll and placed the changeling child on a boulder. The elderly Spellweaver who had attended the changeling's birth stepped forward.

'Before we begin, is there anything you would like to bequeath this changeling child?' asked the healer.

'I would give it a name. Bergtatt, the ill-fated,' said Telemnar.

'So it has been noted and so shall we relinquish all responsibility to this changeling and exile it to the Pervilhelns, home of outcasts and rebels. Go forth, Bergtatt. From this day on, you no longer have a place amongst alvorkind.'

As the alvorn procession turned to leave, the changeling raised its hands towards its father.

'Ber-ger-tat?' it crooned.

The alvor lord paused and stared hard at the changeling, torn perhaps between revulsion and paternal instinct to take the child in his arms. The elderly Spellweaver placed a hand on Telemnar's arm.

'You're doing the right thing. The changeling will never be accepted by society. It is evil by nature and will turn on you,

THE CHANGELING KING

regardless of the kindness you may show it. It will become a burden on your family and a mark of shame for your house.'

The alvor lord took in a long, shaky breath, his eyes glimmering silver with unshed tears. The Spellweaver took his hand and led him away, leaving the crooning changeling alone to whatever fate waited for it.

A day passed and the changeling remained on the knoll. Bergtatt's body had already developed enough for him to turn onto his stomach. Soon he began to crawl on his belly. He picked up whatever came in his path and stuck it in his mouth without hesitation. At first Bergtatt only found rocks, which he spat back out. Eventually he caught a beetle from amongst the rocks. By morning, the changeling managed to get up on his hands and knees and began to crawl. When he grew thirsty, he licked at the cuts and grazes he had sustained during his descent. His tongue was unnaturally long and black in colour.

By midday the changeling's body had developed enough for him to walk upright. He began exploring his surroundings. He climbed higher up into the mountains until he located a medium-sized cave. He could hear the sounds of something moving around inside. Bergtatt was hungry; his diet of insects and the odd weed was barely enough to sustain him. Instinctively, he slunk into the shadows and made his way deep into the cave. He soon came upon the source of the sounds.

A litter of troll cubs fought over the carcass of a small creature. The changeling left the safety of the shadows and crouched down by the remains. The cubs stopped eating and gazed at him fearfully, unsure whether this strange creature was predator or prey. Bergtatt kept one eye on the cubs and tore a scrap of flesh from the carcass and began to chew. The cubs watched for a few moments before they resumed feeding. Once the changeling had eaten his fill, he lay down beside the cubs and went to sleep.

When the mother of the litter returned to her den, she sat puzzling over the appearance of this strange-looking troll. Then, with, a shrug she picked up the changeling and her three cubs and held them to her teats. Still asleep, Bergtatt and the cubs began to suckle.

NOOR A JAHANGIR

Over the next few months, Bergtatt grew and began to hunt with his new family. His body continued to develop rapidly and he grew as large as his foster brothers and sister. They quickly learnt to be wary of their vindictive fosterling.

Bergtatt lay on his stomach and peered down from his vantage point at a group of approaching trolls. At ten, Bergtatt was almost seven feet tall, bull-necked and wide of chest. His head was shaved clean and his arum-shaped ears had been bitten off at some point. Crouched behind him were his foster brothers, Thark and Noont.

There was a shortage of meat in the mountains and the winters had been getting harder and harder. Their sister had perished the previous year from starvation and the family had barely survived on her flesh. In the following spring Bergtatt and his brothers joined the hunting party of an old troll called Bakwas.

In the summer season, a rival hunting party began making incursions into their territory. Bergtatt, as the most proficient hunter in the pack, was given the honour of leading the attack against them.

The trolls were only a few feet away from the ambush point. Bergtatt counted ten. Their spears were lowered and they moved along at a lazy pace. Bergtatt signalled his brothers to ready themselves. When the trolls were directly beneath them, Bergtatt leapt to his feet and cast his spear at the leader of the pack. The spear took the troll high in the back. This was the signal for his brothers to cast their own spears. Bergtatt grabbed his club and leapt down with a roar onto the panicked trolls beneath.

A stocky troll broke his fall. Straddling his victim's body, Bergtatt smashed his club down on the fallen's skull. His brothers joined him as he turned to face his next target. Bergtatt swung again and again, breaking the troll's ribs, collarbone and shoulder. Two dropped their spears and tried to run. Bergtatt unsheathed a pair of daggers, taken from a human killed three winters ago, and leapt on the deserters, bearing them down to the ground. Savagely, he thrust his daggers into the trolls beneath him, covering himself in their blood.

Finally, he returned to deal with his previous quarry, who lay clutching his broken shoulder. Bergtatt flipped the troll over with a kick and grabbed it by the topknot. He yanked its head back and began to saw through the troll's scalp, ignoring its screams.

CHAPTER 19: THE BELT

KRYLLON

The Belt lacked the coolness and the tranquillity of Alvorn Reach. Instead, humidity pressed down on Nathan like a physical presence, and yet his sweat ran cold.

The river had turned a dirty brown; its surface clogged with lifeless vegetation and winged insects skating on the surface. The four looked about themselves as they rowed, their eyes trying to see past the dark trunks with their near black foliage. Strange muffled sounds carried to them from all directions.

'I feel like that guy in Heart of Darkness, sailing up the Congo with cannibals shadowing him,' said Katrina in a hushed voice.

'Why do you have to talk about cannibals? This place is creepy enough without filling the undergrowth with cannibals,' said Salina.

'You've got that right. Besides, the cannibals weren't shadowing them, they were serving as the crew on the boat,' said Nathan.

'Yeah, whatever,' replied Katrina with a sour look.

An hour passed and the jungle pressed ever closer as the river narrowed and brooding willows blocked out most of the natural light. Salina lit a storm lantern she had found in the boat's chest and stuck it on the end of a staff she had cut from some deadfall. She held it out before the vessel to light the way ahead. Nathan and Logan continued to row silently. Katrina sat in the aft with her bow across her lap. Ripples on the river's surface disturbed their dark musings.

'Did any of you guys see that?' asked Katrina.

'See what?' said Nathan.

'Ripples in the water. A little ahead of us, to the right.'

'We're on a boat, Kat, there's bound to be ripples,' said Nathan.

NOOR A JAHANGIR

'I know that, idiot. But the boat causes ripples to go away from us not towards us,' said Katrina quietly.

The others all stared in alarm at the place that Katrina had indicated. Katrina nocked an arrow to her bowstring. Nathan and Logan pulled harder at the oars.

The river wildlife exploded into cacophony as the ridged spines of a large reptile cut through the water and smashed into the hull. The boat teetered to one side before falling back with a slap. Nathan signalled to Logan to make for the bank. The boat was hit a second time, sending Katrina headfirst into the murky water.

As soon as the boat levelled out, Logan leapt in after her. Salina slid into his place and took up the oar. Water was pouring into the boat from a sizable rent in the hull.

'Logan, Katrina, where are you?' yelled Nathan.

Logan surfaced first. He looked about for Katrina before diving back under. He resurfaced a few feet away.

'I can't see her. Where is she?'

The boat neared the bank when Salina spotted Katrina. 'There she is.'

Katrina pulled herself up onto the river bank.

'I'm okay. Logan, get out of the water,' said Katrina.

Nathan and Salina brought the boat to a rest near Katrina and clambered out onto the bank. Katrina recovered her bow and took up position to cover Logan. She screamed as he suddenly dipped beneath the surface. Nathan drew his dagger and leapt in after him.

The girls watched anxiously. The combatants reared out gasping for air. The boys were grappling with a scaly creature with a sinuous body and short, powerful limbs that protruded from its trunk. Logan straddled its back and held the elongated, triangular head by its cranial horns, to stop it from biting his face off.

'It's a nicor,' Nathan said as he struggled to hold on to the dragon's barbed tail.

Salina drew and shot, her arrow punching into the reptile's gaping mouth. The nicor chomped its jaws, smashing the shaft into splinters. Logan hauled back on the horns with all his might. Nathan moved around to hack at its exposed neck, chopping through scale and sinew and covering himself with blood. The nicor writhed and thrashed until Nathan was forced to fall back. Logan and the reptile disappeared once again beneath the surface.

Nathan wiped water from his eyes and cast about desperately for his brother. It seemed like an age had passed since he had gone under. Nathan tried to recall Logan's record time for holding his breath. He wasn't prepared to lose Logan. Not to this lizard, not in this world.

Logan exploded out of the water, gasping for breath. Nathan grabbed him in a fierce hug from behind and then drew him to shore. The girls, in tears, reached out to pull them up. Behind them, the carcass of the nicor floated to the surface and drifted away.

The boat was taking on water. They pulled it up on to the river bank and secured the painter to a tree. They would have to try and repair it in the morning.

'What do you guys want to do? Shall we find somewhere better to make camp?' asked Nathan through chattering teeth.

'I vote we stay right here until you guys have dried off properly,' said Salina.

The others nodded in agreement. Salina scrounged around the forest floor whilst the others huddled together for warmth. She quickly found a few thick branches and plenty of kindling to get a decent fire going. She formed a small pyramid with the kindling and lit it up with a bit of tinder, then pushed four thick branches into the fire, forming a cross. Soon she had a decent fire going. Nathan passed around some dry rations, which they ate in silence, listening as the nocturnal creatures struck up their broken chorus. It was going to be a long night.

The next morning, Katrina found their boat littered across the opposite bank. She exploded into a string of curses, alerting the others.

'I don't get how the hell this happened without any of us waking up,' said Logan.

'We were exhausted,' said Nathan.

'If we ever come across whatever did this, I'm going to give it a piece of my mind,' said Katrina.

NOOR A JAHANGIR

'I for one hope we don't ever come across whatever did that to the boat. It was made by the alvor, with spells and everything, and it turned it into matchsticks,' said Salina.

'Point taken,' said Katrina.

'We're going to have to continue on foot,' said Nathan.

'Through the Belt? Isn't that like the last thing we should be doing? I mean Gillieron was very clear in stressing that we should avoid walking through the Belt,' said Katrina.

'Kat, it's not like we have many other options,' said Nathan.

'Couldn't we make a raft or something?' said Salina.

'With what? Even if we had an axe and a saw, we wouldn't be able to make something as strong as the alvor boat.'

'I'm with Nathan on this one,' said Logan.

The Belt stank of death and decay. Nathan's eyes flitted back and forth, trying to see through the unnatural twilight created by the thick canopy. The tight press of foliage forced them to move slowly. The muggy air left a greasy residue on their cloaks and armour. The inhabitants of the jungle were silent today and only the mosquitoes seemed active. Katrina swore constantly as she slapped at her exposed skin. They rested when they needed to; but never for long. They ate quickly, always keeping a wary eye out for signs of danger. Nathan wondered how long they would have to endure the Belt.

Over the next few days Nathan tried his best to keep an account of how much time had passed, but his only way of measuring it was Logan's stomach. He also kept a close eye on their rations. The unplanned trek meant they had to use more of their food to keep their energy levels up. The forest was rich in fruit and nuts, but all of it was too high up in the jungle canopy. There didn't appear to be much game either. The Belt continued to wear on their frazzled nerves and soon they were snapping at each other. By the fourth day, they had fallen into a sulky silence. Nathan felt that as the leader he should be doing something to motivate them. But truth be told, he was sick of bickering with Katrina and waiting for Logan's stamp of approval on any decision he made. Even Salina's attempts at being peacemaker had started to annoy him.

Something else was bothering him too.

THE CHANGELING KING

He had the uncanny feeling that they were being stalked. Maybe it was another nicor, or perhaps the enemy troops that had laid siege to the watchtower? Whatever was out there, he didn't fancy finding out.

'Let's pick up the pace a little,' said Nathan.

'You feel it too?' asked Logan.

Nathan nodded tersely. The girls didn't ask any questions, but lengthened their strides to match the boys. They could all feel it now. It was as if someone had hit the mute button, silencing the cacophony of the jungle's residents.

The undergrowth came alive with amber eyes.

Panic overcame their training and soon they were crashing through the jungle at full run. But the eyes overtook them and quickly surrounded them. The four stood back to back and drew their weapons.

The eyes coalesced into feral silhouettes, which melted together to form a single wolf the size of a Spanish bull. It sat back on its haunches, revealing a shaggy grey mane covering its neck and shoulders.

'We mean you no harm.'

'What? Who was that?' exclaimed Katrina. 'Did any of you guys hear that?'

The other three nodded as they searched the shadows.

'We mean you no harm, put up your weapons.'

Nathan looked deep into the wolf's unblinking eyes and saw something there that caught him off-guard; intelligence.

'Guys, it's the wolf. It's bloody telepathic,' he said quietly.

'Your weapons cannot harm us. Put them away. We would have killed you when you entered the forest if that was our intent. You are not our prey.'

'Do as they say,' said Nathan as he sheathed his sabre.

'They?' asked Logan.

'What do you want from us?' said Nathan.

'We were sent by the Dark Man to guide you to him. You must comply.'

'Who are you and who is this Dark Man?'

'We are the Shadow Pack. We serve the Guardian of the Void, the Dark Man. You must follow. There is danger in these woods. The Dark Man waits.'

'How do we know that we can trust you?' asked Katrina.

'Without our help you will wander here forever until you die. Then you will only be food for scavengers.'

'Then we have no choice,' said Nathan.

'There is always a choice. You can choose to comply, or you can choose to fail.'

Nathan looked at the others. They looked back at him, happy for him to shoulder the responsibility, to take the blame.

'Okay, lead on.'

They travelled into the night in the company of the Shadow Pack. The great wolf had split into five regular sized wolves shortly after their conversation. The companions jogged along at a steady pace, unnerved by their silent escorts.

Nathan was beginning to understand now that the Belt was more than what it seemed. He could feel it insinuating itself into his mind, praying on his darkest thoughts and fears.

'All things that grow have a life force. The Belt is a sentient extension of the Void, as are we.'

'Do me a favour. Stop talking. You're making my head hurt,' said Nathan aloud, hoping he sounded brave to his friends.

The wolf pack did not speak again to them.

At some point, Nathan realised that the pack had melted away into the forest. They searched the area around them tentatively, keeping together; careful not to draw the attention of anything else that lurked out there. When their search came to naught, they sat down and chewed on stale water-biscuits. Lost, hungry and tired, they rolled themselves up in their bedrolls. Cold vapours rose from the damp ground.

It had gotten colder, reflected Nathan, wiping his dripping nose with a rag. The wolves were probably still out there, keeping an eye

THE CHANGELING KING

on things. He couldn't be too sure though, so he decided to sit watch for a while. Maybe when he felt sleepy, he would wake Logan to take over. Nathan's eyes closed, his head slumped forward, unconscious.

The forest drew away from him and a grey fortress sprouted from the soil, a chasm opening up at its base. A bridge branched out from the solid rock walls to span across the breach. Nathan glanced back to see where the others were, but found that the forest lay far behind him and the sky had disappeared into a colourless void. The chasm gaped on either side of him as he found himself standing before a huge portcullis. Then the portcullis slammed shut behind him and he stood in a courtyard. His eyes were drawn to an open door through which he could see a fire blazing in a hearth. Two chairs were set beside the fire. Abruptly, he found himself seated. The flames flared up, shedding neither light nor heat. The world disappeared and all that remained were the two chairs and the fire.

Someone sat in the other chair. A cloaked and hooded figure filled his vision. When the hood fell back, there remained only storm-grey eyes.

'Remember.'

CHAPTER 20: CALLERS AT THE DOOR
ENGLAND

The kitchen clock read 7.30 pm but it was still light outside. Adam had picked a room upstairs and was having a lie down. Karen was trying to get through to the hospital from the kitchen phone but the lines were busy. She tried Ryan's mobile. The phone rang for ages before there was a crackle of ambient sounds.

'Hello?' said Ryan.

'Hello, Ryan, it's me.'

'Karen. Are you and Adam okay?'

There was a sense of urgency in his voice that surprised Karen.

'Yes, we're completely fine. What's the matter?'

'Karen,' Ryan lowered his voice, 'the hospital was hit again late last night by those things.'

'Oh my God,' whispered Karen in shock.

'They killed about fifteen people. I would have been amongst them too if Mrs Phelps hadn't woken up and insisted we get out of the room that very instant. The special arms unit was on standby and they got here pretty quick. They took out two of those things, but they managed to escape and haul their dead away with them.

'Karen, you better stay alert. The CID officers from the Met have taken complete control. Everything has to go by them now. You're on your own, Karen. I wish I could come and help you, but I've been suspended and placed under guard, with an inquest pending.'

'Do they have the authority to do that?'

'I don't know. Karen, stay alert.'

'Goodbye, Ryan.'

THE CHANGELING KING

Karen put the telephone receiver back down into its cradle. Her head was throbbing with anxiety. She took out some pain-killers from her bag and filled a glass with tap water. The image of the monster's face rose up in her memory and again she felt paralysed.

Karen heard the sound of feet thundering across the creaky floorboards above and then clattering down the service stairs. Adam appeared in the doorway.

'They're here,' he yelled.

Karen grabbed her handbag and together they ran back up to the bedroom. She knelt by the largest window and searched the fields. Running through the tall grass toward the house, in a staggered line, they came. She pulled away from the window. All her strategies were forgotten as terror took hold of her. They were going to die.

CHAPTER 21: REMEMBERING
UNKNOWN

The darkness receded from Nathan's mind. Logan, Salina and Katrina were lying close by, still unconscious. They were in a courtyard of a large citadel. An oily black sky curved above them; completely starless and yet still conveying a physical presence. Gazing at it made Nathan queasy, so he looked away. He shivered as his bare skin pimpled with goose-flesh. His swimming trunks were still slightly damp and provided scant protection from the clawing cold. Nathan rolled onto his stomach and crawled over to Salina. His body felt like it had been pummelled by a heavyweight boxer. Gently, he shook her shoulder until she opened her eyes.

'Are you okay?'

Salina nodded but she looked disoriented and wide-eyed. Nathan pointed to Katrina and then moved over to Logan to wake him too. It took a while for them to recover from the shock of their traumatic passage. They huddled together for warmth and looked about at their surroundings.

'What is this place?' asked Katrina. 'How did we get here?'

'Don't you guys remember what happened at the lake?' said Nathan, rubbing his arms briskly.

'Oh my God, we drowned. We can't be dead, can we?' asked Salina, her lower lip quivering as tears spilled from her eyes.

'If we're dead, then this must be purgatory or something,' said Katrina staring up at the viscous sky.

'We're not dead, alright?' said Logan. 'We wouldn't be freezing our butts off if we were dead.'

'Maybe we're in a coma, then?' Katrina sounded hopeful.

THE CHANGELING KING

'Oh, okay, so we're all lying in our hospital beds somewhere, and this is all just a mass hallucination? Perhaps its collective dreaming or something,' said Nathan with a sneer.

'Shut up, Nathan. Don't be an ass. It's not helping,' snapped Logan.

Nathan glared at his brother. He hated it when Logan put him down like that in front of other people.

'We're not dead and we're not in a coma. Despite this acid trip sky and the Hammer Horror castle here, this is all real. Just because we can't explain the how, doesn't make this place any less real,' said Logan.

'Great, bro, where the hell did you get that from? Freud for Dummies? The Idiot's Guide to the Incomprehensible?'

'Nathan, shut your pie hole or I'll shut it for you. You're scaring the girls, okay? If you have a better explanation, share it, otherwise shut the hell up.'

Nathan felt his cheeks burning and he considered jumping his brother. Past experience had taught him, however, that he would be the one ending up getting his arse handed to him. The uncomfortable silence went on for several minutes before Nathan decided it had gone on for long enough.

'How about we have a look around, then? If we don't find anything, at least it'll keep us warm.'

'Good, now you're thinking straight, bro.'

They trotted over to the nearest wall and patted it. It felt rough, damp and comfortably real. The moss in the mortar was springy and came away easily as Nathan picked at it. They followed the wall around to one of four doors and gave it a push. The door swung open smoothly. They entered the castle and immediately felt more at ease than they had under the strange sky.

A long corridor stretched ahead of them. Doors led off from it to the right and lockers ran down the left. The corridor wouldn't have looked out of place in their school. It smelt of the same concoction of disinfectant, books, cheap perfumes and gym socks – just like school. They walked along the corridor, trying each of the doors as they went. They found four lockers open, side-by-side. A quick examination of the lockers revealed clothing in their exact sizes. They pulled on the belted knee length tunics, trousers and hooded cloaks over their swimwear.

Dressed and finally warm, they continued along the corridor, trying out every door they passed. Eventually they found one that wasn't locked.

They stood in a library with rows of bookcases extending as far back as they could see. Chandeliers hung on chains from the vaulted ceiling, shedding pockets of light on the polished, tiled floor. They spent a while looking at the books and scrolls for clues to where 'here' was. The texts ranged in age and languages, some of which Nathan suspected weren't even human. They replaced the books and headed back to the door they had entered through.

When they passed through the door, they found themselves on a stairwell. Nathan closed and opened the library door again and this time found that it led back to the courtyard.

'What kind of a weird place is this?' said Katrina.

'Let's get out of here. One of those doors is bound to be the exit or lead us to the exit,' said Nathan.

He led them out into the courtyard and made for the next door along. When they got there it opened to an identical set of stairs. They moved along to the next door and then the next, until they had opened every door in the courtyard. All opened on to the same set of stairs.

'How is this possible?' said Nathan.

'I guess we're taking the stairs then,' said Katrina.

The steps were wide and easy to climb. In fact, the further they climbed, the easier it became. Katrina counted the stairs aloud and at step one hundred and twenty-three they came to a landing with a single doorway. A feeling of expectancy passed through them. They counted to three and pushed the door open.

They were in a brightly lit room. Two paned windows on either side offered views across the castle. A smokeless fire burned in a huge, mantled fireplace. Five armchairs were arrayed around the fire.

'Come in,' said a rich, masculine voice from the chair closest to the fire.

THE CHANGELING KING

The door closed behind them of its own accord, making them jump.

'Please, do not be afraid. Join me by the fire,' said the voice.

They walked to the chairs and sat down without knowing why they were complying. The fire wasn't giving off any heat and yet they felt warm and at ease. Nathan looked at the person who had spoken. A young man, of an age with them, occupied one of the chairs. He was dressed in an elegant grey tailcoat and wore a cravat around his neck. His hair was long and black, parted from the left. Nathan found himself drawn into the youth's storm-grey eyes.

'Who are you?'

'I am Shadel'ron, Guardian of the Void.'

Nathan sat in a cushioned chair with a swinging desk attached to the arm, in a familiar class room. Logan, Salina and Katrina were sitting in similar chairs to either side of him. A tall man in a black academic gown, complete with hood and mortarboard, stood in front of them. Nathan's mind felt ready to explode as memories clashed. He wanted to scream. He knew he should be in Kryllon and yet the room was identical to the one he had sat in so often in school.

'Where are we? Who are you?' he asked.

'You know the answers to your questions now,' said the man.

Thoughts and ideas that Nathan seemed to have developed some time ago conflicted with what he remembered of his more recent past. A name popped into his head.

'Shadel'ron?'

'Good. What else do you remember?'

'Everything seems confused in my head,' complained Katrina.

'Let me help. You were swimming in a lake on Planet Earth. Then something happened. Do you remember what it was?' asked the man called Shadel'ron.

'I know this one,' said Salina, 'something below started to glow and then sucked us down into it.'

NOOR A JAHANGIR

'Those lights are runes carved into the stone circle that sits at the bottom of the lake. The circle was activated by a surge of energy in the lay lines that connect the circle to the rest of the world.'

'What the hell does any of that mean?' asked Katrina.

The others nodded, equally confused.

'I've already explained this to you before. It seems your memories are going to need a little more encouragement. I'll give you the short version this time.

'A long time ago, the Guardians were at war with demonkind. The Guardians are the mortal agents of the Most High, each with responsibility for a system, a planet or a land. Our war spanned many worlds and star systems. We fought the demons wherever we found them. Big, small, male, female, it didn't matter. Eventually, the powerful amongst them were captured and imprisoned in the farthest reaches of existence. The lesser demons went to ground and scattered through the universe, fearful of being found.'

'No offence, but this is still going right over our heads,' said Katrina.

'Bear with me a while. The greater demons, from time to time, attempt to break free of their prison, utilising the aid of their minions. One such minion on Earth harnessed the power of the land and succeeded in opening a gateway to Kryllon. The same power flux activated the stone circle beneath the lake; a second gateway.

'At one time it would have led to another planet. Now all gateways lead to one place alone; the Void. All the gateways were sealed, but there are still some who try and use the Void as a corridor to other worlds. Then there are others like you who accidentally fall through. Lucky for you that I was in the area, otherwise you would have floated around in stasis for millennia.'

'So, you're saying that you found us by coincidence?' asked Salina.

'No. I believe I was meant to find you. About a hundred years ago, in the Kryllon timeline, a goblin shaman by the name of Vermin opened up a dead gateway. The fool summoned a demon so powerful that it can project its presence across space and time. He paid with his soul. The demon now rules Kryllon through the Trollking.'

'That's stupid. If the demon is that powerful, why does it need the Trollking?' said Katrina.

THE CHANGELING KING

Shadel'ron took a deep breath.

'The demon is stuck on the far side of the universe. It's using most of its prodigious power to maintain its projected essence, and, even then, it has to replenish itself by consuming more souls. Any use of additional power drains it so low that it risks killing itself. Therefore, it resorts to coercion. And if I'm right, it's not working alone either.'

'Why Kryllon? And what does this all have to do with us?' asked Nathan. His head felt like someone had tightened a vice on it.

'I've traced all the timelines in all of the worlds protected by Guardians.'

Nathan and the others straightened in their chairs and leaned forward anxiously.

'A thousand years ago, on a distant system named Thoraxus Major, a Guardian was taken from her home-world. A few hundred years later, on the other side of the universe, a second Guardian was snatched. Then, seemingly randomly, Guardians began to disappear without any consistent pattern emerging. The only thing they had in common is that none of them had yet come into their power. The next Guardian on the demon's list is on Earth.

'Now, pay special attention, because this is where you come in. The demon has sent a small force of trolls to Earth to capture the Guardian. When the gateway was open, I became aware of it and went to investigate. Then you four came tumbling through.

'At first I wasn't sure what you were doing in the Void, or whether one of you is the Guardian. I brought you to my home to learn which of you the demons are searching for. After that, I was going to send you back and seal up the gateways again.'

'We were your prisoners then?' said Logan.

'Not quite, but maybe I should had locked you up instead of letting you wander around,' said Shadel'ron sourly.

'Holy crap, I remember what happened,' said Nathan suddenly, his eyes flitting back and forth. 'We were exploring the castle and found a room full of doors.'

'Yeah, I remember that too. Freaky,' said Katrina.

'That's right. Nathan and Katrina started to try out the doors, but they were all locked,' added Salina, excitedly.

NOOR A JAHANGIR

'Except one,' said Logan.

'The Wayward Hall, that explains a lot,' said Shadel'ron. 'You should never have gone in there. That room was locked and sealed. The Wayward Hall is a junction between many gateways. I do not understand how you got in there, or why the door to Kryllon opened for you, but it does explain why you suffered memory loss. It's a safety feature. If by any chance a doorway is breached, anyone who walks through it instantly forgets ever having visited my home or entering the Wayward Hall.'

'That's a stupid feature,' said Katrina sullenly.

'That's your opinion. But I'm sure you appreciated the other special feature. Well, at least now I know it works. The same seal that wiped your memories also enveloped you in a protective bubble that lowered you to Kryllon's surface.'

'Can I ask a question?' asked Logan, raising his hand. Shadel'ron nodded. 'How is it that we knew how to speak the language of the alvor, right away?'

'That was a part of your neural programming,' said Shadel'ron. 'I had to keep your minds occupied. Otherwise fifty Earth years in the Void would have made you into vegetables.'

'Are we in the Void now?' asked Nathan. 'Does that mean we don't have to go to Ranush? You can send us back to Earth?'

'I am so sorry,' said Shadel'ron. 'This is not the Void. You are lying in a clearing in the Belt. This room is a construct of your own making, to cushion your mind from what it cannot comprehend. You are no more here than I am in the Belt. Reality has eroded here enough for me to project my own essence into this world. I am afraid I cannot help you yet.

'You must continue your mission. The old alvorn sorcerer was right. Your only way home is through the cauldron pool in Ranush. Once you enter the Void, I will be waiting to guide you home.'

The walls of the classroom shimmered and began to fragment. Nathan looked to see if the others had noticed.

'It is time for you to wake. Good luck, my friends. I'll be waiting.'

***

THE CHANGELING KING

Nathan opened his eyes and saw the sky above him. It took him several moments to realise that he wasn't in the forest anymore. He sat up and found the others sleeping beside him on a grassy bank. Before him he could see blue-grey mountains, rearing up high above the clouds. Behind him he saw the unwelcoming silhouette of the Belt. Shadel'ron had somehow delivered them to the foothills of the Pervilheln Mountains.

A flock of wild geese flew by overhead. Katrina shot down a couple for lunch. Nathan cleaned the birds whilst the girls fetched kindling for a fire. Logan volunteered to cook again. They ate quietly, each lost in their own thoughts.

They had thought that they had lost a year of their lives, but now they knew it had been more than fifty. It made Nathan question whether he was the same person he had been before Kryllon, rather than a middle-aged stranger with memories he couldn't remember creating.

The River Caprice glimmered like a silver chain carelessly cast down amongst the rocks. Nathan decided it would be best to continue following the river as planned. The sun was out in full force and a brisk breeze blew from the mountains. The others seemed to be in better spirits, but Nathan could still feel tendrils of the cursed forest swilling in his mind. They laughed and argued about things they were only beginning to remember. The conversation eventually turned to older memories. They talked about favourite pizza toppings, movies and celebrity eye-candy. Nathan didn't join in. The brevity began to grate on his nerves. It was not like they were home and free yet.

A few hours before sundown, they stopped by a large flat-topped rock and made camp. They whiled away the remaining hours of the day catching fish with improvised fishing rods and then roasted them over an open fire, watching the sunset over the mountains. They talked well into the night, their laughter carrying miles around along the crisp mountain air. Nathan didn't join in. He lay down by the fire and covered his ears with his forearms, pretending to be asleep.

The next morning their route led them to a point where the river disappeared into a wide, natural tunnel.

NOOR A JAHANGIR

'Wow, it must be at least a mile long. I can just about see the other end,' said Katrina as she leaned dangerously far out with Logan gripping her belt. 'Do you think we could swim it?'

The current proved too strong and the water almost glacier cold. They worked their way back along the mountain. The further they went in, the more they began to despair of ever finding a way through. Once again the sun started to set over the mountains. The day lay wasted and Nathan's persistent silence only added to the groups sinking spirits.

'What are we going to do tomorrow?' asked Katrina, pointedly at Nathan.

'I don't know. I guess we'll just have to carry on going,' said Nathan.

'You don't know? I think carrying on is a stupid idea,' said Katrina.

'Come on, Kat, give Nathan a break, you can't expect him to have all the answers,' said Salina defensively.

'Well then I don't think he should be in charge anymore. One of us should have a go. You're too soft, so it's between me and Logan,' said Katrina.

'Shut your face, you stupid cow,' said Nathan. 'All you ever do is moan.'

'Hey, that's enough. Both of you apologise immediately,' said Logan firmly.

Before Nathan could retort, Katrina launched herself at him and began to claw at his face. Nathan grabbed her hands by the wrists and flung her off him. Katrina landed hard but rolled to her feet and rushed at him again, pounding his torso and head with clenched fists. Nathan tried to grab her hands but she caught him with a blow to the chin. Without thinking, Nathan punched her back and knocked her down.

'Nathan! How could you?' said Salina in horror.

Nathan froze, shocked by his own actions, but rankled beyond his limits to the challenge to his authority.

'The hell with you all. If anyone thinks they can do better, go ahead, you're bloody welcome to it,' said Nathan.

THE CHANGELING KING

He stormed out of the camp and continued walking until the glow of the campfire was out of sight. Then he sat down with his head in his hands and began to cry.

Nathan awoke feeling stiff. His eyes were gummy, his nose bunged up, and he had a sore throat. He looked up at the sun and decided it was about two hours to midday. Typical, without him to wake them up, they had slept in. Stuff them, he would return to the campsite and make himself some breakfast. He had only gone a few paces when he heard someone up ahead, coming his way.

The footsteps were too heavy to be one of the guys. Nathan hid behind a rock. He cursed in anger, realising that he had left his sword at the camp. All he had was his dagger. He slid it out from his boot and held it ready, waiting for whomever to walk past. The footsteps stopped several yards short and turned back again. Nathan waited a whole minute then he stepped out and made his way to camp, keeping low and using all the cover he could find. When he was close enough, he heard gravely voices speaking in a slurred, guttural tongue. Goblins.

CHAPTER 22: SECOND FLIGHT
ENGLAND

'What are we going to do?' asked Adam.

Karen took a few slow, deep breaths to quell the hysteria she felt clawing its way up her throat.

'Alright, Adam, I want you to watch how I do this,' said Karen as she grabbed the rifle and took out the magazine clip. She opened a box of .22 calibre bullets and began to load the clip.

'Do you think you could do that for me?' asked Karen.

Adam nodded. He looked very scared. She wondered whether she was doing the right thing by letting him help her. It wasn't exactly high on the constabulary's agenda to teach school kids how to load a gun. A glance out of the window convinced her that this was a genuine exceptional situation. She passed Adam two spare clips and then pushed the magazine she had just loaded into the rifle.

Karen lifted the weapon so that the stock rested against her shoulder and drew back the bolt. She could see out of the window that the monsters were getting closer. They were cutting a straight course through the heather and the tall grass. Karen sighted down the .22's barrel, the smell of gun-oil making her nose wrinkle. She drew a bead on the front runner.

The rifle cracked and, a moment later, the beast bucked as if hit by a sledge-hammer.

Karen pulled back on the bolt and then tracked another monster before taking her next shot.

THE CHANGELING KING

Dirt kicked up near its feet, letting her know that she had missed. Karen reloaded and fired again. It staggered but continued to run. A third bullet to the head stopped it dead.

'Damn, what the hell are these things?'

'They're trolls and they're coming to kill me,' said Adam, his voice flat.

Karen looked sharply at Adam.

'Hey, no one is going to kill you, not as long as I'm breathing,'

Karen turned back to the window. Trolls. For some reason, the name fit. The 'trolls' started to zigzag from side to side, their feet creating clouds of dust as they changed directions. The rifle was heavy and Karen's arms were tiring quickly. She shot off another six rounds before the rifle clicked empty. She had only managed to take out one more troll.

Karen ejected the used clip and took a fresh one from Adam. The trolls were close now. She tried to recall what she knew of the folklore about them, but the image of a troll leaping out from under bridge to menace the billy-goats kept coming to mind. The only other thing that seemed to stick was that trolls were meant to turn to stone when the sun came up. Or was it dust? Whatever they were, they bled and they died and that was all she needed to know at present. She shot off all ten rounds in quick succession. Two wounded and one more dead.

'It's time to move, Adam. I need you to carry my handbag. Stay close to me,' said Karen.

She slung the rifle over her shoulder and instructed Adam to empty the ammunition into her handbag. Then she filled her trouser and jacket pockets with shotgun shells. Karen fed three rounds into the shotgun's receiver before moving to the bedroom door.

A loud crash from below suggested that the trolls had smashed through the front door. Karen and Adam ran across the landing to the service stairs. They descended cautiously, their backs to the wall.

The door that opened into the kitchen was ajar. The room beyond lay empty. Together they got down on to their hands and knees and crawled to the backdoor. Karen went to the sink and peered over it through the window. Her Ford sat in the driveway without a troll in sight.

NOOR A JAHANGIR

Adam turned the key in the lock and pulled the heavy oak door open but Karen signalled for him to wait. She wanted to take a proper look first. She stepped out with the shotgun raised and screamed as a troll appeared as if from thin air.

For a second all three stood frozen.

The shotgun boomed.

The troll flew back several yards.

Karen stalked forward as the troll shook its head and tried to get up. She fired again. The troll's body spasmed once and then lay still.

'Get in the car,' said Karen as she fumbled for her keys and pushed a button on her key-fob.

The car flashed its hazard lights in welcome. Adam pulled open his door and leapt in.

A roar sounded from inside the house.

Karen turned and fired blind. She didn't wait to see if she'd hit anything. She got into the car and started the engine.

'That was awesome,' said Adam breathlessly.

Gravel flew into the air as Karen jammed the accelerator to the floor. She pulled the handbrake up and spun the wheel, sliding the car through a hundred and eighty degrees before racing to the front of the house.

'Watch out,' yelled Adam.

A couple of trolls, armed with crossbows, blocked the driveway. Karen pulled the handbrake again and twisted the wheel to the left. The Ford's back end slid out spraying the trolls with gravel as the front wheels clawed for purchase. Then the car shot off across the lawn. Something hit and cracked the rear windscreen.

'Whoa!' cried Adam.

'Get your seatbelt on,' said Karen. 'It's going to get a little rough from here.'

Karen smiled grimly as she heard Adam's belt clicking shut. A picket fence loomed up in front of them briefly before they smashed through.

THE CHANGELING KING

The ride grew bumpier as they drove onto a neighbouring field, slowing them down. Karen glanced at her rear-view mirror. The trolls were catching up.

'Here, hold the wheel as straight as you can,' said Karen.

Karen waited until Adam grabbed the wheel before opening her window. She grabbed her pistol and leaned out to fire in rapid succession. The trolls slowed and dropped behind. Karen slid back into her seat and took control of the car.

'Where did you learn to do that?' asked Adam.

'I'm improvising.'

Risking damage to her car, Karen pushed the Ford harder. The trolls receded in her mirrors.

A few miles on, Adam noticed the fuel gauge plunging towards empty at an alarming rate, causing his already racing heart to lurch again. The Ford got them within a mile of the wood before giving up the ghost.

Adam put Karen's handbag around his neck and grabbed the rifle. He watched as Karen reached for the shotgun on the backseat, finding it difficult to reconcile his previous image of her with this action-woman.

'Adam, grab the torch from under your seat. There's a town on the other side of the wood, but I don't know how far it is. It may get dark before we get there,' said Karen.

Adam did as he was told. His fingers brushed something hard and leathery.

'There's something else down here, too. It looks like some kind of a weapon,' said Adam, pulling it out.

'Weapon? The dagger. I completely forgot about that.'

'Are you sure this is a dagger? It looks more like a sword or machete,' said Adam, it was as long as his arm.

'We might as well take it along with us. It may be useful. I don't know, maybe we can chop some wood with it or something.'

They got out of the car together and began to walk.

NOOR A JAHANGIR

'Do you think there'll be wolves in the forest?' said Adam, as the woods loomed large ahead.

'This is England. There haven't been wolves here for a while.'

'Yeah, there haven't been trolls here for a while either. Someone should go tell them.'

'Why don't you?'

'Nah, I don't think so. What are you so grumpy about?'

'I don't like being shot at or being chased by mythical creatures. They've killed my car with arrows and hospitalised my partner. And for the icing on the cake, I've got a banging headache.'

'Sorry. I'll be quiet now,' said Adam meekly, wondering whether he'd done something to make her mad at him. Salina used to do that. 'You were pretty awesome back there.'

Karen sighed.

'Listen, I didn't mean to snap at you just now. But I need to think of a way of getting us out of this mess.'

Adam nodded his head, feeling dumb, realising for the first time that she wouldn't be here if it wasn't for him. The trolls were after him. Maybe it was up to him to figure out a way of making things right. He pictured himself standing up to a bunch of those trolls, blasting one with the shotgun whilst side-kicking the other. Karen would have his back with the pistol, keeping them at bay long enough for him to reload again. He snapped back to attention as he stumbled over something. He was falling behind Karen. Ahead, the forest looked dark and sinister. Not for the first time, Adam wished his father was here.

Vasch threw his hands out to break his fall. He was tired and hungry and his ankle throbbed with every step he took. He had slept awhile in the copse outside the militia fortress, not caring if he was discovered. Once it grew dark, he gathered some dry branches from the ground around him and made a splint for his ankle. Agilerd had done a fairly good job of removing the bits of metal projectile lodged in his thick skin and had bound the wound. He hoped the old troll survived Udulf's leadership.

THE CHANGELING KING

Vasch hobbled out of the grove and headed in the general direction of the tower. In his current state, it would take him days. Hopefully, by then the others would have completed the mission. The black roads were quiet. Hills rose steeply ahead of him. He glanced to the right where, in the distance, he could see the multiple towers that marked the temple of healing. He wondered briefly how Sigberd and his team had fared in their assignment.

The occasional metal beast roared along the road, but Vasch was in the hills now and was confident that he wouldn't be noticed. He took frequent breaks to rest his ankle. The deeper he went into the hills, the more uneven the ground became.

A few hours before dawn, the sound of hoof beats alerted him to riders rapidly approaching. Vasch pressed himself to the ground and unhooked his axe. He had little chance of outrunning a horse. If they were after him, they wouldn't take him without a fight.

Over the hill, two riders appeared, leading half a dozen horses behind them. Vasch squinted then whooped in delight. It was Sigberd and Haig. He raised his axe and waved at them. The trolls spotted him and rode towards him.

'Well met,' called Sigberd, he looked as weary as Vasch felt.

'Where are the others?' asked Vasch.

'Dead,' replied Haig.

'What happened?'

'We killed a number of the guards, but the militia were waiting for us. They got Chas first. Nearly took his head right off. Tangerd they shot as we were escaping. We managed to carry their bodies out with us. We fed from them before burying them. They deserved that much,' said Sigberd.

Vasch swore.

'Udulf shouldn't have split up the warband. You should all have gone after the primary target. The others were just a bonus,' said Vasch. 'Where did you find the horses? They're bigger than any I've seen on Kryllon.'

The smallest of the horses was at least sixteen hands, a few black and the rest bays. They had muscular chests, arching necks and broad backs, too wide perhaps for a human to straddle. The horses had long, powerful legs, with fine white hair growing from their hocks, covering their hooves. Their eyes were shielded with leather blinders.

'A farm a few miles from here. They went wild at the sight of us until we got them blinders over their eyes,' said Haig.

'If we ride hard, we may be able to catch up to Udulf and the others,' said Vasch as he mounted up.

Karen and Adam had been walking for several hours. Adam's feet were sore and his shoulders ached from the ammunition laden handbag. He had a feeling that they were completely and utterly lost. According to Karen, they should have reached the town ages ago. The shadows beneath the trees had deepened considerably and all directions looked the same.

'We might as well make camp, Adam. It looks like we're going to have to wait till morning before we carry on. I don't feel like stumbling around in the forest at night,' said Karen. 'Adam, what's wrong?'

The thought of spending a night in the wood filled him with dread. A half remembered dream teased his mind with images of himself lying dead at the base of a tree. 'Nothing,' said Adam eventually. 'Can we have a fire?' said Adam.

Karen looked like she would object, but then she pursed her lips together and nodded. It didn't take them long to gather enough wood for a small fire. The forest floor was littered with twigs and branches. Karen built the fire in a spot sheltered from the wind and lit it with a lighter from her pocket. Feeling a little spooked by the strangeness of the silhouettes of the trees against the night sky, Adam sat down beside Karen. She smiled at him.

'You know, you look really pretty when you smile,' said Adam without thinking.

Karen burst out into laughter.

'Did I say something funny?' asked Adam, his cheeks burning red with embarrassment.

'I'm sorry, I'm not making fun of you. The last time I heard that, a senior detective was trying to hit on me,' said Karen.

THE CHANGELING KING

Adam smiled to cover his confusion. Karen reached out and ruffled his hair. They sat in companionable silence.

The silence was broken by the howls and hoots of their hunters.

CHAPTER 23: THE PRISONER
KRYLLON

Deep down within the bowels of the Trollking's stronghold, a lonely prisoner lay lost in fevered dreams. Filth covered his battered body and his hair was matted with unnameable gunk. He lay in the corner farthest from the door. His hazel-flecked brown eyes stared unblinkingly at something that he alone could see. From time to time he would smile and cackle. The rats were content to ignore him, feeding instead on the festering gruel occasionally left for him by a guard.

In his mind, he wandered far away from pain and hurt, in a mango orchard, in the westerly gardens of his father's palace. Beside him pranced a tiger cub. A cool and sweet breeze blew from the direction of the Bengal Mountains.

A key rattled in the door and a troll barked something at him. The prisoner cringed and curled into a ball. The troll struck him with a whip and then dragged him out of the cell by his painfully thin ankle. When the prisoner saw who had come to visit him, he screamed in fear and fell to the floor in a swoon. The troll looked nervously at the apparition that accompanied it, cloaked in darkness and towering a head taller than the troll. Its chitinous features were thankfully hidden in the deep recesses of its hood.

The spectre signalled to the troll to lift the prisoner up and to bring him along. The troll wrinkled its nose and continued to drag him. The wraith whirled around and hissed like an angry marsh-viper.

The troll, sweating profusely despite the biting cold draft, threw the prisoner on to a brawny shoulder. The demon led them through an antechamber, where three goblin guards sat drinking gut-rot and gambling. They jumped up in fear as the spectre glided by. A door from the antechamber allowed them access to the sewers. The troll

THE CHANGELING KING

stumbled along behind the wraith in the darkness, until they left the stench of the sewers behind for an earthy smelling tunnel. All the while, the prisoner remained silent. Noise and movement usually resulted in a beating. The tunnel grew brighter as they climbed, until they stepped out from the earth and into the marsh. The prisoner could see the dark outline of the city walls some distance behind them.

The troll's pace slowed as it struggled against the suck and pull of the thick marsh mud. The air was oily and heaving with meat-flies. The prisoner quietly reached down to the troll's belt and worked loose its dagger. The troll continued to trudge along, oblivious to its prisoner's activities.

When the city was no longer visible, the wraith signalled the troll to wait and then continued on ahead, alone. The troll threw the prisoner to the ground and sat down on a rare patch of moss. Tall reeds and thorny brush surrounded them on all sides. The prisoner rolled over and looked about. The troll sat facing away from him, confident that the emaciated madman posed no threat.

The prisoner scuttled forward on all fours and rose up behind the troll, drawing the pilfered blade across its exposed throat. The troll clutched its throat in surprise. It staggered to its feet trying to call out to the wraith, but its vocal cords had been severed. After a fewsteps the troll toppled sideways into a bog. The prisoner watched with great fascination as the body sank beneath the glutinous surface.

The emaciated rogue fancied he could see mountains on the horizon, far away to the west. Memories of a large house amongst snow clad peaks beckoned to him. He lay down on his stomach and began to slide away, hissing and spitting like a large reptile. A startled marsh viper slithered out of his way.

The day passed quickly as he made his way through the marsh, pretending to be various creatures from the jungles that had once surrounded his home. At one time he played an elephant, trumpeting and swinging his arm in front of himself as if it were a trunk. Then he was bear, walking on his hind legs and dancing a jig for invisible onlookers. Now he was a wolf, running swiftly and howling at the moon. He continued to play this game until he left the marsh behind and came upon a river.

NOOR A JAHANGIR

A cloud parted briefly in his mind as he saw his own bedraggled reflection. He leapt into the river and scrubbed the mud and the filth off himself, before swimming over to the west bank.

His mountains were a lot closer now and he could make out the snowy peaks. But then the fog returned again to cloud his thoughts. In his mind, he was with his father and some other men. They were hunting a tiger that had become a man-eater. The party had tracked the beast all the way to its lair. The boy watched from a safe distance as the hunters cornered the tiger.

The beast leapt on the nearest hunter and tore his throat out. His father charged in and speared the tiger through its white, fur covered breast. Suddenly, the fight went out of the feline and it began to crawl away from its lair.

The prince saw something small slink along, amongst the rocks above the hunters. The tiger was trying to lead the party away from its cub. As the hunters closed in around the wounded beast, the cub leapt down in front of them and growled.

The boy sprinted up the mountain.

The mother's strength had given out and she lay panting as her blood pooled beneath it. The boy pushed through the hunters and snatched the cub up into his arms. He looked up at his father pleadingly.

'A tiger cub for my Sultan? What shall you call it?' said his father, smiling that gentle smile that he saved for his children.

'I shall call him Bahadur, the brave, for he stood up to your hunters.'

'Then Bahadur it shall be. Come, my wonderful boy, let us go home.'

Home, thought the fugitive, I must go home. He got up onto his feet and began to run, the wind streaming through his hair.

Night fell and Sultan grew tired. He had run all day and still no sight of his uncle's palace. Exhaustion overtook him. He stumbled and fell to the ground, his cheek pressed against the cool grass listening to the wild rhythm of his heart. Content to lie where he fell, Sultan closed his eyes and slept.

THE CHANGELING KING

In his dreams he strolled through his father's gardens. There were fountains, streams, ponds and small waterfalls everywhere amongst the flowerbeds and trees. Each garden was arranged in symmetrical, geometric designs; intricate as the gold latticework that covered the windows of the royal palace.

A familiar voice called to him.

The fugitive walked into a small apricot grove and found his father waiting for him. Suleiman was dressed in a long white tunic, belted at the waist with a sash. There was something wrong with the Shah's eyes. They were grey instead of the deep mahogany that he remembered. His father took him by the hand and led him from the grove onto an avenue lined with pools on either side.

'Shelter is not far, my son. Follow the river and you shall come upon your destination before night falls again. Now wake up, my wonderful boy, for morning is here.'

Sultan rolled over and looked up into the sky. The sun had begun its ascent. He looked around for his father. There was no sign of him. Perhaps he would be waiting for him at uncle's home in the mountains.

At midday, Sultan came to a point where the river branched off to his left and right. He waded across the left branch and continued to follow the wider northerly route. Along the way he found some bushes that were still bearing berries. There were several kinds to choose from. The fugitive picked one off and put it into his mouth, then spat it out when the juices turned his stomach. He tried the others until he found some that he could keep down. At dusk, he saw something sparkle in the distance. As he drew closer, it resolved into a city sat poised on the horizon, its minarets, spires and domes beckoning him home.

CHAPTER 24: PERVILHELN

KRYLLON

There were goblins in the camp.

This was the first time Nathan had seen a goblin up close. They stood upright, but hunched forward as if their large heads were too heavy for their thin necks. Their limbs were gangly, with long, articulate fingers. The goblins' features were in proportion to their big heads, with bat-like ears, bulbous eyes, hooked noses and lipless mouths, full of teeth filed down to points. Tribal tattoos covered their faces and what could be seen of their hairless bodies. Some of them supported various kinds of facial piercing, mainly odd shaped bones and a few bronze rings.

There were three goblins arguing around the camp fire. Two more were marching away from him. A further two were positioned on the ridge above him, armed with crossbows. He might have been able to take out the sentries, perhaps even the three in the camp, but the crossbow bearing goblins were too well positioned for him to sneak up on.

After a few frantic moments, he spotted Logan and the girls, squatting unhappily in iron-mesh cages. Why hadn't they set a watch? Maybe if he hadn't stormed off last night, this wouldn't have happened. Or maybe, if he had, he too would have been cooped up with the others.

Nathan snuck back to where he had slept and began to climb up the peak. He edged towards the camp until he spotted one of the goblins urinating down the mountain side, above his unsuspecting comrades. The terrain between them was unforgiving and treacherous. He was unable to get close enough to take out the goblin without giving himself away. Nathan clambered up higher and found a decent vantage point.

THE CHANGELING KING

It was cold on the side of the mountain, with little to shelter him from the wind. He unfurled his cloak and pulled it over his head to keep his ears warm. He could see all the way to the dark canopy of the Belt to the south, the Higard Hills to the east and, to the west, the sea, a silvery glimmer above the jagged peaks of the mountains.

The goblins were on the move. A sixth goblin that Nathan hadn't noticed before had joined them. He fancied he could hear Katrina complaining and swearing at the goblins in English. Whilst he had been gawping at the view, the crossbow-goblins had also moved, to a spot just a few feet below him. If they were to look up now they would see him. He held his breath and willed himself to blend into the mountain itself. They passed on by without spying him.

The goblin party proceeded up the trail. Nathan followed them for the rest of the morning. There must be a concealed tunnel entrance in the mountain that we missed, thought Nathan. That must have been how they chanced on the camp. He needed to get closer.

The party disappeared around a large outcrop. Nathan sprinted along a narrow ledge, his eyes fixed on the uneven ground. He slowed near the projection to get a fix on the goblins. They were just around the corner. A tunnel lay concealed behind the oblong protrusion, rendering it impossible to see from the path below.

Nathan counted to a hundred and then took another peek.

The goblins had gone inside.

Nathan got down on his hands and knees and crept forward towards the entrance. They were just a little way ahead of him. He waited until they were out of sight before swinging down inside. The walls were rough and pitted as if the tunnel had been dug out with tools. He tripped a few times in the dark, until his knees and hands were grazed raw. The more he thought about his footing, the more unbalanced he felt. Each time he stumbled, he froze to listen for sounds of alarm, before getting up and moving on.

Soon he had lost all sense of time and direction. Right now he would happily have walked back out of the tunnel if he could just find the way. But then thoughts of Salina, his brother and Katrina made him push on. Guilt settled like a rock in the pit of his stomach. What if he never saw any of them ever again? They would think he had abandoned them.

NOOR A JAHANGIR

After what felt like hours, he came to a dead end. Despair filled his heart and he considered calling out for help. If the goblins found him, he wouldn't have to worry about where he was. Get a grip Nathan, he scolded himself. The tunnel must have split somewhere along the way. All he had to do was feel his way back along the opposite wall until he came to the branch.

Nathan's fingers brushed against the lip of another ledge. He felt along it to see how far back it went. Carefully he pulled himself up. He continued his exploration of the rock-face ahead of him and soon found a crevice that was barely wide enough for him to slide through sideways.

The sound of goblin speech echoed from a distance from the other side of the fissure.

Nathan pushed himself into the crevice, sucking his stomach in and inching forward. Soon he had to turn his head to one side as the fissure grew narrower. It seemed to go on forever. Just as Nathan was considering turning back, his leading hand found open air. With relief he pulled himself out of the crevice.

The voices grew louder.

Nathan found himself on a balcony of sorts, overlooking a large cavern, lit by a phosphorus substance dribbling down the walls. The goblins were pushing towards a bottleneck opening on the far side. They were hemmed in on either side by a jagged maze of stalactites. Thankfully, his brother and friends were still safe and alive in their cages.

Stealthy movement amongst the limestone spikes caught his eye. A third party was moving in on the goblins. Nathan cursed under his breath. Why did everything have to get complicated?

The newcomers drew their weapons.

The goblins were completely unprepared for the ambush. Several fell dead, riddled with arrows, before they even realised they were under attack. The goblins scattered in panic, the caged prisoners forgotten. Nathan leapt down to the cavern floor. Katrina lay closest to his position and was the first to spot him. She knew well enough to stay quiet. Nathan scrambled the short distance between the rocks and the cages. The newcomers had the goblins pinned down. Nathan drew his dagger and cut through the grimy leather bindings on the cage door. The door swung open but Katrina didn't move.

THE CHANGELING KING

'What are you waiting for?' asked Nathan.

'I can't move. My whole body is completely numb,' said Katrina, her eyes swollen from crying.

Nathan glanced around quickly and then nodded. He grabbed a hold of Katrina's arms and pulled her slowly out of the cage. Then he lifted her in his arms and sprinted to a nearby cluster of stalagmites. He put her down gently and then ran back to the cages. Salina covered his face with kisses as he liberated her next. The girls hugged as Nathan went back for Logan.

'Hey, Nate, I'd started to wonder where you'd got to,' whispered Logan.

Nathan didn't reply. He cut through the bonds and opened the door. Nathan hooked his hands under Logan's arms and pulled. Nothing happened. Nathan pulled again, but Logan wouldn't budge.

'Try cutting the bindings holding the cage together,' said Logan.

Nathan moved around to the side of the cage and began to saw through the tough leather.

'Watch out, bro, one of the goblins is heading our way. And he's got your sword,' said Logan.

Nathan rose and reversed his grip on his dagger. The goblin was nearly two feet shorter than him but its thin arms seemed to be all muscle. Nathan moved in, the dagger flickering in the torchlight as he slashed the air in intricate arcs. The goblin's eyes tried to follow the movement of Nathan's hand even as Nathan lunged forward and cut the goblin's forearm.

The goblin howled in pain and swung the sabre at Nathan. Nathan rolled on his shoulder and slashed the goblin's calves.

The goblin turned to decapitate Nathan as he came to his feet, but its legs gave out. Nathan kicked the sword from its hand and lay its throat open. Its blood looked black in the dim light.

With the goblin dead, Nathan retrieved his sword and returned to Logan's cage. The sabre made quick work of the bindings. Logan toppled sideways still curled up in a ball. Nathan grabbed his brother's ankles and dragged him to the safety. Katrina had recovered enough to sit up and now she was rubbing life into Salina's legs. Nathan passed his dagger to her.

NOOR A JAHANGIR

'Where are you going?' asked Katrina.

'To get our stuff back.'

Nathan strode out from behind the stalagmites, psyching himself up with dark thoughts, letting his anger and fear strengthen his resolve. The crossbow-goblins lay dead, their bodies bristling with arrows. The remaining five were engaged in close quarter combat with the newcomers.

Nathan didn't bother giving the goblins the benefit of a warning. He cut the throat of the first goblin with a back hand slash, then reversed the blade and plunged it under the second goblin's arm. He pulled the sabre clear before the goblin collapsed. A third goblin fell to the ambushers as Nathan moved onto the fourth. The goblin stabbed its opponent in the thigh and then turned to face Nathan. Its dark serrated blade clashed against Nathan's sabre. Nathan stepped in close and shattered its knee with a well aimed kick, before spinning away from the goblin. His sabre came round in a full circle and separated the goblin's head from its shoulders.

'Nicely done,' said a deep voice in Common.

Nathan looked up from the body as the ambushers walked over to join him. The last of the goblins lay dead from multiple stab wounds. The ambushers were dressed in blackened leather armour, their faces hidden by lacquered masks. They all had their swords out, but held them relaxed at their sides. The masked men were much too tall to be goblins or even alvor and too short to be trolls. Nathan lowered his own sword, letting its tip rest on the ground. There were seven in total.

'Show your faces,' said Nathan.

The tallest of the ambushers nodded his head to his comrades and pulled off his mask.

'You're humans,' said Nathan, his jaw dropping in surprise.

'I am Captain Haldrin of the Erskine Rangers,' said the ambusher.

CHAPTER 25: ERSKINE

KRYLLON

After patching up their wounded and disposing of the dead goblins, the rangers led Nathan and the others out of the caves and into crisp mountain air.

Nathan took the opportunity to study their new friends. Captain Haldrin was tall and athletically built, like a sprinter; narrow of waist and broad shouldered. His face was thin and angular, accentuated by close-cropped blond hair and arching eyebrows. His cheeks and upper lip were clean shaven, but his chin supported a long goatee, shaped into a point. There was a woman amongst his rangers, whom he had introduced as Kira. She had the same no nonsense I as the others.

'We live under the shadow of the Trollking. His spies are everywhere. Though Erskine remains an independent township, it is only because of the high taxes we pay to the Trollking,' said Haldrin.

'Why not force them out of Erskine? You guys seem handy enough in a fight,' said Nathan.

'The Trollking's horde numbers many – enough to take Erskine apart, stone by stone. Be mindful of what you say in Erskine, you never know who is listening.'

'But what about the skirmish back in the caves? Won't the Trollking retaliate?' asked Katrina.

'There are lots of rebels and brigands in these mountains. We do what we can to root them out, but now and then a goblin unit or a small pack of trolls will fall prey to an ambush. You understand, of course?' replied Haldrin with a grin.

The rangers led them up a narrow trail through a niche in the mountain and out onto path that ran along the base of a ravine. When they emerged from the gully, Haldrin pointed down the mountainside. Nestled between the snowy peaks was a grassy valley, sheltered from the harsh winds by the peaks. Erskine was no more than ten or fifteen large buildings surrounded by smaller dwellings. High walls of napped flint ringed the town. Tilled fields flanked the path, worked by a handful of farmers. They looked up from their work to greet the rangers by name.

The town gates were open and, judging from the tracks on the ground, had been that way for some time. They were manned by guards in yellow and white tabards, who let the group pass with only a perfunctory glance. The four companions looked at each other with raised eyebrows as they stepped on the cobbled streets of Erskine. Then the smell hit them.

The streets were littered with rotting scraps of food and human waste. Dogs and rats fought in the alleys over bones and other unnameable objects, eyed by hungry street urchins. A rodent tumbled in the direction of the children. The urchins pounced on it and a scrap ensued to decide who would take it home. The houses were mostly double-storied. The upper floors projected out over the narrow streets, supported by wooden struts. The stonework was covered with flaky plaster. A pack of goblins sat drinking and arguing outside a tavern.

Nathan reached for his sword. Haldrin placed his hand over Nathan's and shook his head. Just then a troll walked out of the tavern. He paused when he saw the humans. For a second, Nathan found himself looking into the troll's little black eyes. It looked away first and grabbed the nearest goblin and whispered something in its ear. The goblin looked in their direction then stood up and ordered the others inside with the aid of a whip.

'You allow entry to trolls and goblins?' said Katrina.

'As I told you before, the Trollking's emissaries are everywhere,' said Haldrin.

'Who was that troll? It looked at me as if it knew me?' asked Nathan.

'That was Captain Dross and the goblin his second-in-command. They've been asking around about newcomers and strangers,' replied Haldrin.

THE CHANGELING KING

'If I were to say that despite the apparent beauty of your lovely town and the warm hospitality of its citizens, we want to leave right away, what would be your response?' said Nathan.

'You are not prisoners but I would advise caution. Dross has his mercenaries watching all the routes going out. Besides, if you don't make an appearance before the Lord Mayor, it would raise suspicions.'

'Why do people keep saying we're not prisoners and then tell us we can't go anywhere,' muttered Katrina.

'One other thing, do not mention the alvors. There is a long standing feud between humans and alvors.'

Nathan looked at the others. Their argument last night was still on his mind and he was reluctant to stick his neck out again.

'Lead on, Captain,' said Logan.

Haldrin guided them through the haphazard streets to the town's centre, a square dominated by large buildings. Most of their escort broke off and took their gear into the first of these buildings. Nathan assumed that this was the barracks. Haldrin, Kira and a ranger named Flinn, continued on with them.

They passed a guild hall, then a grain house and a number of other buildings, before stopping in front of an official-looking building, flying a dirty white flag, emblazoned with a yellow shield and a white mountain-goat chewing on brambles. Haldrin walked up to the doors and threw them open. A startled man scuttled over to intercept them.

'Captain Haldrin, what business do you have with the Lord Mayor?' asked the man as he ran his hands down his tabard.

'That is between the Lord Mayor and me. This is urgent business. Where is he?' asked Haldrin as he continued to stride forward.

The seneschal was hard pressed to keep up with him.

'He is in council. Who are these strangers?'

Haldrin suddenly came to a halt, causing the man to stumble.

'That tabard you're wearing seems rather tight. Perhaps I should ventilate it to help you to breathe easier?' said Haldrin.

NOOR A JAHANGIR

'No no, it's fine. Please, don't let me hold you up. I've got some paperwork to take care of anyway,' said the man, teetering out of the way.

Haldrin led them on through the building. Nathan did his best to memorise the placement of windows and doors, to map possible escape avenues. The walls were clad with wooden panels, shedding a whiff of orange oil polish that tickled Nathan's throat. Paintings of men dressed in fur-lined velvets hung along the length of the corridor.

'Who goes there?' asked one of two guards, stood outside the council chamber.

'Do we have to do this every time I come through? I'm Captain Haldrin of the Erskine Rangers, as if you didn't know,' said Haldrin, not hiding his irritation at the requisite ceremonial pomp.

'State your business,' barked the same guard.

'I am escorting these pilgrims from the South to pay their respects to our Lord Mayor.'

The second guard opened the door a crack and slipped through. He returned within a few minutes and whispered something to his fellow.

'The Lord Mayor will see you and the emissaries now. Please remove your weapons,' said the first guard.

'Kira, Flinn, you two wait out here with these two jesters. This is one of Brand's swords. It cost me a good pile of gold. I'm not leaving it with them.'

Haldrin removed his sword belt and dagger and handed them to Kira. He indicated to Nathan and the others to do the same. Then the second guard led them through the doors into a long, rectangular room.

The chamber was tiered with high-backed benches of lacquered wood, upholstered with yellow dyed leather. A podium, mounted with an ornate chair, stood at the far end of the room. The podium was embossed with a relief of the town's coat-of-arms.

'Captain Haldrin of the Erskine Rangers requests an audience with his worship, the Lord Mayor,' announced the guard.

THE CHANGELING KING

'You have permission to approach,' replied a clerk, standing to the right of the podium.

Nathan looked towards the benches. The seats were mostly occupied by men, as well as a disconcerting number of goblins and trolls. The latter glared down at them with undisguised hatred. The delegation stopped several feet short of the mayoral seat.

A heavyset man sat atop the chair, his large head crowned with a wig of grey curls. Bushy eyebrows and a thick droopy moustache framed a surprisingly thin nose. He was dressed in the velvet and fur robes of his office, with the gold mayoral chain resting on his chest. The mayor leaned forward over the podium to get a better look at them.

'Haldrin, please introduce the Emissaries,' said the Mayor.

'It would be an honour, Lord Mayor. These are the brothers Sir Nathan and Sir Logan, and their companions are Lady Salina and Lady Katrina.'

'All children of men are welcome to our hallowed halls,' replied the mayor. 'What business brings you hither?'

Nathan furtively glanced at the others. They nodded imperceptibly for him to speak. He took a deep breath, stepped forward and bowed to the Mayor. His mind raced to construct some plausible fabrication that would alleviate any suspicion. He straightened and looked the Mayor in the eye.

'We come from a settlement on the south coast. My brother and I are making a pilgrimage to Maiden's Lake. Alas, we have been unable to have children and have heard that the waters of Maiden's Lake possess healing powers that will make our women fertile again.'

'It is true that this Lake is a blessed place,' said the Lord Mayor. 'Our ancient ancestors, who once ruled this land, venerated its waters for their healing properties. This is a worthy cause and I commend your women for accepting their shortcomings. You are most welcome guests, for it is also known that there is much virtue in aiding pilgrims on their journey. You will, of course, do us the honour of residing in Erskine before you press on with your journey.'

'I must beg your leave, your worship,' interjected Nathan, 'but we do not intend to linger in Erskine beyond the time it will to take to resupply. It is our humble desire to complete our pilgrimage and return home before the harvest.'

'Will you be passing this way on your return?'

'We intend to buy passage home at one of the small fishing villages on the northern coast,' said Nathan.

'Ah, it's a pity. May I press upon you to at least honour me by having dinner with me tonight, at my home? Captain, you will escort the pilgrims this evening?'

'Your lordship is most kind,' said Haldrin, bowing once more to the Mayor. The companions bowed with him and then followed him out of the council chambers.

They collected their weapons from the rangers and then continued out the way they had entered. Haldrin did not speak until they were outside the town hall, in a quiet corner of the square.

'You did well in there, southerner, although it was quite clearly a big, steaming pile of horse manure. The council may have bought it but not the mayor. Lucky for you his curiosity won out. He'll be expecting to hear the truth tonight,' said Haldrin.

'We'll worry about that tonight. Right now we need to buy supplies and find rooms for the night,' said Logan.

'The inn across the square is owned by a friend of mine. It's called The Silver Penny and it is quite a respectable establishment. My friend's name is Justine. Tell her I sent you. There is a trading post opposite the inn, which is owned by Justine's son. You will be able to purchase whatever you need from him. I need to report in at the barracks. Even captains have superior officers. I will see you an hour before sunset,' said Haldrin and with that departed for the barracks.

'Guys, I owe all of you an apology for my behaviour,' Nathan began to say as they were finally alone.

'Save it, bro. We'll talk once we've all had a bath and some hot food in us,' said Logan.

The girls nodded quietly in agreement. Nathan felt his stomach drop in discomfort. He had hoped they would have let bygones be bygones, but it seemed a quick apology wasn't going to set the matter straight.

THE CHANGELING KING

The inn was a two-storey building, as seemed to be the norm in Erskine. The flint walls were bare and the exposed beams and shutters looked freshly painted. A painted sign read, 'The Silver Penny – we do not serve non-humans'.

Inside, the floors were varnished and recently mopped. The tables were covered in yellow and white chequered cloth and bore fresh flowers in small clay vases. The clientele, a mixture of well-to-do people and uniformed officers, sipped drinks and engaged in animated conversation as they ate. A bar ran along the length of the common room, with a staircase in the far corner by the hearth. A dark-skinned lady stood watchfully behind the bar.

'Would you be Justine?' asked Nathan. 'We're friends of Haldrin. He recommended you,' replied Nathan.

'Of course he did. You wouldn't want to stay at one of them goblin grog-pits, now would you? But first you'll need to scrub up. I don't want lice in my inn. There is a bath-house round the back. You'll find hot water and separate facilities for the ladies. I'll send someone over with clean clothes. When you're done, come back here and we'll have a nice meal ready for you.'

The four deposited their belongings behind the bar and headed out to the bath-house, via a back door. There were two outbuildings. A chimney pipe pumped out huge puffs of steam from the smaller of the two. The equine sounds coming from the longer building, identified it as the inn's stables. Logan stopped Nathan before they entered the bath-house.

'Take a look back across the square, but don't make it obvious,' Logan whispered in his ear.

Nathan held the door open for his brother and surreptitiously glanced over his shoulder. A goblin in a long coat stood idly scuffing his clawed feet on the cobbles. His gaze was fixed on Nathan and his friends.

CHAPTER 26: THE WOOD

ENGLAND

Karen's lungs burned and her legs felt like they had turned to lead. They had been running for fifteen minutes now and had lost all sense of direction. Adam had dropped her handbag spilling most of the contents out into the underbrush, including the .22 ammunition. With no time to look for them, Karen threw the rifle into the bushes too. There was no point in keeping it. She still had the twelve-gauge and the Glock, as well as the troll-dagger tucked into Adam's trouser belt like a sword.

The monsters were getting closer. Karen could hear them thrashing about nearby. Adam stopped running and bent over gasping for breath.

'I can't run anymore, Karen, I just can't.'

Karen tried to get a fix on their location. Then she spotted the remains of the campfire they had made earlier and groaned.

'Hey, Karen, look, it's your rifle. How did that get here?' said Adam, 'Wait this place looks familiar. Oh no, we're back here again.'

'You're right; we're not going to be able to outrun them. We're going to have to climb up that big tree there and hold them off.'

Karen fished in her pockets for some shotgun slugs and slid them into the breach, before securing the weapon with a strap over her shoulder.

'Quickly, Adam,' she said as she laced her fingers together and cupped her hands, 'Come on, I'll give you a boost up.'

Adam reluctantly came over and put his right foot in her hands. Karen counted aloud to three and pushed upwards. Adam grabbed the lowest branch and began to clamber up. Karen jumped and grabbed the branch, too, and then pulled herself up. She worked her way up to a point where the tree formed a natural crook. Adam passed her the dagger and then quietly began to climb higher.

THE CHANGELING KING

Karen wedged the shotgun between several branches until it was secure then checked the Glock's magazine. Once she was comfortable she settled back to wait for the trolls.

The trolls passed their location several times. They were looking down at the tracks Karen and Adam had left, confused, perhaps, by the number of times they had passed that way. Karen glanced up to see how Adam fared. He looked up at the night sky. His face was smeared with grime but she could see that it was drawn with exhaustion.

'What's up?' whispered Adam.

'Nothing. I was just thinking that you shouldn't have to go through this,' replied Karen, her voice quivering with passion.

'Millions of other kids in the world shouldn't have to go through what they do, every day. The only difference between them and me is I've had a good life up till now. That and the fact that it's trolls trying to kill me, not malaria or HIV,' replied Adam.

'You're a pretty amazing boy, Adam.'

'You're not too bad yourself, for a girl.'

Karen smiled.

Karen looked at her watch. 3.30 am. The sky brightened and a filmy mist had begun to rise up from the ground. She straightened and wrapped the shotgun strap around her hand. Quietly, she raised the weapon to her shoulder.

The boom of the shotgun reverberated through the forest.

A troll shouted out in pain. It staggered into sight and threw an axe at them. The weapon struck the tree with a solid thwack and thrummed from the displaced force. Karen pumped another slug into the chamber and fired again. The troll took the shot to its face and fell. Amazingly, the thing was still alive and struggling to get up. Karen drew the Glock and shot it twice in the head.

The forest erupted with movement and war cries. Karen loaded two more rounds into the shotgun and then wedged it back between the branches. She gripped the pistol's butt in her right hand and braced her wrist with the other hand. There was movement to the left. Karen squeezed the trigger again and again, counting the shots under her breath. When only one bullet remained in the magazine, she ejected it and replaced it with a fresh one.

A troll charged at the tree and struck it at full tilt, dislodging Karen. A lower branch broke her fall but knocked the pistol from her hand. Something grabbed her ankle from beneath and yanked hard. Karen kicked out with her free leg and felt her foot connect with something solid. Her leg was free. Karen dropped to the ground.

'Adam, throw me the shotgun,' said Karen, with desperation in her voice.

Adam began to descend slowly to where Karen had left the gun, carefully probing with his toes for footholds. The troll loomed up before her, its face covered with old burns. It sent her reeling with a backhanded blow.

Adam shouted her name.

The left side of Karen's face felt numb and her ears were ringing. The troll stalked towards her. Karen ran behind the tree. She needed a weapon. The rifle jutted out from the bush she had thrown it in. She grabbed the rifle's barrel and turned around to face the troll.

Adam screamed, sending jolts of cold through her veins as her mind conjured images of the troll tearing off the boy's limbs. Karen charged back around the tree brandishing the rifle like a club. Adam lay motionless amongst the tree's roots, the shotgun still clutched in his hands. Burn-face stood over him.

Suddenly Adam was every murder victim she had cried over in her past, wondering how anyone could be so cruel. She had spent years having to live with the impotent rage of knowing murderers of children had escaped justice, never having known the pain and fear their victims had suffered. She couldn't let it happen again. She wouldn't let it happen again.

Karen shrieked like a banshee and swung the rifle at the troll's head. Burn-face rolled with the blow. Karen swung again and again, each time drawing blood, until the troll caught the rifle and twisted it out of Karen's grip. Thick muscles bunched in its thick arms and twisted the .22 into a boomerang.

Burn-face threw the rifle aside and grabbed Karen by the throat. Karen struggled to pry its fingers loose as it forced her head back.

THE CHANGELING KING

Darkness closed in around her vision. The dagger was just above her, stuck in a branch of the tree. Karen reached for it, her fingers brushing its pommel. The troll shook her until it felt like her teeth would start rattling. She closed her eyes as they bulged, crazily wondering whether they would explode out of their sockets. Her fingers brushed the dagger's hilt again and closed around its grip.

Karen yanked the blade free and stabbed the troll's hairy forearm. The troll howled in pain and let her drop. She lay in pain, gasping for air through her bruised throat.

She crawled over to Adam and wrapped her fingers around his thin wrists. He had a nasty gash on his forehead. She whispered a prayer of thanks as she felt a strong pulse. A twig snapped behind her.

Karen snatched the shotgun from Adam, whipped around and squeezed the trigger.

The troll roared as its wounded arm fell to the ground.

Karen pumped the action and aimed again.

The troll turned and fled.

Karen slumped down beside Adam, for the moment beyond caring of what happened next. Far in the distance, an alien horn sounded.

NOOR A JAHANGIR

CHAPTER 27: SINS OF THE FATHER
KRYLLON (AGE OF THE ALVOR)

Many of Bergtatt's hunting party did not make it through the winter. Bakwas, the leader of the hunting party did not survived either. Unlike the others, he did not died of the cold or hunger.

Still drenched with hiS predecessor's blood, Bergtatt declared himself the leader. One troll had challenged his right to lead. Soon, he too lay with Bakwas at the bottom of a ravine. The other trolls quickly learned to fear Bergtatt and his lieutenants, Thark and Noont.

In spring, fresh game came to the mountains and another party were making incursions into Bergtatt's territory. Bergtatt sent out a warband under Thark to discourage the insurgents. Several days passed and the warband did not return. Bergtatt decided it was time to take more direct action. He formed a second warband and led them himself, with his brother Noont as his second in command.

They ranged into the eastern region, tracking Thark's party. The trail led them to a canyon where the warband found signs of ambush. Thark's trolls had been surrounded on all sides and slaughtered. Bergtatt vowed he would find those responsible and avenge his brother. Several rocks skittered down from the ridge to the party's left. Bergtatt scanned the deep shadows that pockmarked the incline. His keen eyes picked out furtive movement where most would have missed it.

'Ambush,' he roared.

The warband dashed for cover as dark figures rose up from hiding and hurled fist-sized rocks at them. Bergtatt squatted behind a boulder beside Noont. He cursed himself for a fool. If he had been thinking instead of getting angry, he would have seen this for the trap it was. He had walked in, blind as a mewling pup. The enemy had them pinned down.

Noont suddenly dashed out from cover to charge up the side of the gorge. He made ten yards before a thrown rock cracked open his skull. Rage ripped through Bergtatt's veins and pounded in his ears. He signalled for his warband to charge. Panicked, the trolls ignored the order. Several of them made a dash for the safety of the canyon's mouth but were cut off by a landslide. They didn't make it back to cover. The bombardment continued for several minutes.

Bergtatt sneaked a quick look up the slope as the final rock clattered to a halt. The enemy had begun their descent.

Bergtatt didn't need to know how to count to realise that the odds were against him. Cold reason doused the flames lit by his need for vengeance. It was time to leave. Bergtatt leapt out from behind his boulder and sprinted towards the other end of the chasm. His comrades followed suit. The injured amongst them quickly fell behind. Their gurgling death screams urged the others on.

A troll who had kept pace with him went down with a spear in his back. Bergtatt swerved to avoid the body as it fell into his path. Pale sunlight streamed into the gorge. Freedom beckoned.

But the small bird of hope that fluttered in his chest was soon crushed.

A bluff with a fifty foot drop to the river below fell open before him. He slid to a halt and turned to face his pursuers. The last member of his warband cleared the canyon and joined him on the shelf. It was Vasch, an adolescent with just a few seasons of experience behind him. Cudgels in hand, they waited. Thirty hooded trolls charged out of the gorge. Bergtatt and Vasch met the rush head on, smashing bones, crushing limbs and sending trolls plummeting to their deaths on the jagged river rocks far below them. The pup fought well, conceded Bergtatt, as Vasch hammered an uppercut to a troll's chin. But no matter how many they killed, more filed out from the gorge to take their place. Bergtatt knew it was only a matter of time before they were overwhelmed. No, they would have to risk the plummet and the rocks below.

Bergtatt grabbed Vasch by an arm and swung him out into void. The troll flailed his limbs in surprise until he hit the water. Bergtatt turned and seized the next troll who came at him by the crotch and throat, and threw him back at his comrades. Then he took a running leap and launched himself after Vasch.

The river rushed towards Bergtatt. He hit the water feet first. A sharp pain exploded up from his crotch, making him wince. The cold stole his breath from him. It filled his mouth and burned his nostrils.

Spears cut the water around him into bubbled ribbons. This river will not beat me, raged Bergtatt. His feet touched the bottom and he pushed off hard. His breath gave out a few seconds before he broke surface. Bergtatt spluttered and coughed. He rolled onto his back and looked about. The current had carried him to safety. There was no sign of Vasch.

The river took Bergtatt northwards for some miles before he managed to latch onto some overhanging branches and pull himself out on to the east bank. He trekked back downriver in the hope of finding a crossing point.

Trumpets blared nearby. The staccato of shod feet announced a mounted party nearing his position. Trolls didn't ride horseback, but there was a human settlement in the Pervilhelns and they often passed through troll territory. They always rode in large numbers and were better equipped than the trolls, though they tended to avoid them. Better be cautious, thought Bergtatt, as he flattened himself against the ground, hoping to pass notice.

Mounted alvor rode into view, armed with lance and bow. Bergtatt cursed his luck. Alvors were the sworn enemies of trolls. He had seen them a few times in the distance, riding patrols all the way up to the river, but never crossing into the mountains. They would kill a troll on sight and it was the same if it was the other way around. Bergtatt pressed himself closer to the ground until the loamy spell of earth filled his nostrils.

An alvor spotted him and shouted to his companions. The horses veered and galloped in his direction. Bergtatt jumped up and made a run for the river, but the alvor quickly flanked him and threw a weighted net over him. He tumbled to the ground, struggling to break free.

The alvor jabbed at him with their lances as one of them dismounted to manacle him. The alvor gasped a single word and pointed at Bergtatt's face.

THE CHANGELING KING

His captors argued angrily with each other for a few moments. Up close, he found himself admiring the slimness of their limbs, the lightness of their complexion and their beautiful bird-like eyes. Then one of them nudged Bergtatt with his foot and indicated for him to get up. An alvor clipped a chain to Bergtatt's manacles and secured it to a horse's saddle.

The alvor rode at Bergtatt's pace, keeping his chain slack. They offered him water when they stopped for a break and some fiery crusted bread.

They rode for nearly a day and a half before they came to a large city. Bergtatt looked on, curious.

The city reminded him of the craggy mountains along the western coast of Pervilheln, where the sea and harsh weather had eroded them into towers and misshapen stacks. Wherever Bergtatt looked, the wide streets were lined with dark glossy walls.

The alvor escorted him to a large square with cages suspended from a viaduct. There were seven cages in all, only one of them occupied. An alvor on top of the bridge lowered a cage until it was just a foot off the ground. Another alvor took off his manacles and forced him to climb inside at spear point. The alvor locked the cage and signalled to his fellows to raise it up. The cage swayed alarmingly. Bergtatt gripped the bars to steady himself and watched the guards walk away. He glanced over to the other occupied cage. Its tenant was an exceptionally ugly goblin, with puffy eyelids, sharp cheekbones and nostrils. He was dressed in a filthy blue robe, probably sourced from the humans, with the hood up to shield him from the sun.

'What are you being held for?' asked the goblin in fluent troll.

'Nothing. They caught me by the river and brought me here,' replied Bergtatt.

'My name is Vermin. I burnt two alvor alive. I am a shaman amongst my people,' said the goblin.

'Why don't you magic your way out of this?'

'Because, idiot, that would take components. A rock crystal, dried larvae and slug-juice. They took all my pouches away from me before they stuck me up here,' said Vermin.

Bergtatt grunted and then made himself comfortable as best as he could.

NOOR A JAHANGIR

Over the next few days Bergtatt watched the alvor go about their business beneath him and listened to Vermin's stories. Occasionally, scraps would be dumped on the cages from the bridge.

On the fourth day, the guards returned and lowered him down and took him out of the cage. They clipped a chain to his manacles and then led him through the city streets towards a large sprawling building that dominated the skyline over the gabled rooftops of lesser houses. The closer they drew to this large structure, the smaller Bergtatt felt. Scores of windows glowered orange in the lofty walls, like the eyes of some monstrous creature staring out of the gloom. The dread within him intensified as the gates opened with a groan. His chest constricted with fear. Some fell destiny awaited him inside, he could feel it. Something perhaps worse than death. The gates gaped open as the guards led him into the building's maw.

Bergtatt tried to dig his heels in as the guards dragged him on by the chains through a series of claustrophobic passages, up a broad flight of stairs and into a small chamber.

Three alvor sat talking around a table, in high backed chairs, sipping from crystal goblets. Their conversation fell silent as he entered. The first alvor looked old with his long white hair, the gold of his skin faded to a pale-yellow. His posture, however, exuded strength and authority. The other two alvor looked much younger, except one had a silvery complexion.

'This is no strange breed of troll, I fear. It is a changeling,' said the white haired alvor, 'was not one born to your wife, Lord Telemnar, not so many years ago?'

The silver skinned alvor nodded his head without looking up.

'It would have been a child of eleven winters now, Archmagus. This . . . abomination looks to be at least thirty . . .'

'Changelings grow at an accelerated rate. Their physical attributes outstrip their mental and spiritual faculties. Fear not, Telemnar, you did the right thing. It would have only brought you shame and grief. Changelings are possessed by evil humours that drive the host to murderous madness.'

'Could we not have fashioned some kind of care home for these poor unfortunates, perhaps ease their suffering?' queried the third alvor.

THE CHANGELING KING

'Do not be foolish, general,' chided the Archmagus.

The alvor called Telemnar rose and approached Bergtatt. He gazed intently into Bergtatt's eyes as if searching for something hidden there. Something about Telemnar spoke to Bergtatt at a subconscious level. It was a distracting and uncomfortable feeling.

'Take it away and throw it back in its cage. Let the wretched thing die of starvation,' said the Archmagus, a look of revulsion on his face.

A memory beckoned of a cold rock and a gathering. Chanting and the burning of incense sticks and cold faces. One face rose up from his memory, of an alvor with eyes like twin pools of quicksilver and a voice echoing through the ages, 'I would give it a name. I name it Bergtatt, the ill-fated.'

Bergtatt roared and yanked his arms free from the alvor restraining him, his fingers closing tightly around Telemnar's brittle throat.

The guards battered him with their spear but Bergtatt held on grimly.

The alvor gasped for breath, his soft narrow hands trying to pry loose Bergtatt's vice-like fingers. Telemnar's face had turned blue and his eyes bulged.

A chair smashed against Bergtatt's head and knocked him to the floor. Telemnar fell beside him, his eyes fixed wide and accusing. Bergtatt cried out in anguish, oblivious to the blows that continued to rain down on him.

When Bergtatt came to, he found himself back in his cage. Vermin watched him with a strange look on his face. He seemed agitated.

'You have a great destiny ahead of you. I know it,' said the goblin.

'What are you talking about?' asked Bergtatt.

He tried to sit up, but was confounded by the various hurts that had been inflicted upon him.

'I have been sent a vision by my masters. You will become a force to be reckoned with in these lands. You will reign over all the races of Kryllon. This city will be your inheritance. With the aid of my masters, none will be able to overthrow you.'

NOOR A JAHANGIR

There were a couple loose teeth in Bergtatt's mouth. He yanked them out and then spat a mouthful of blood through the cage floor.

'My destiny is to rot here, right next to you.'

'You are a powerful leader amongst the trolls and I am influential amongst the goblins. We could raise an army and destroy this city. We could wipe the alvor off the face of Kryllon. What do you say?'

'I say you're crazy. We are going to die here, unless you can magic us both out of the city,' mocked Bergtatt.

'Throw me those teeth and I will be able to open your cage with a spell. Then if you are able, you must climb up the chain to the bridge and lower my cage.'

'Lie to me or try and betray me, and I'll swing over there and bash your brains out,' said Bergtatt before pelting the goblin with his molars.

'It will take me some time to prepare the incantation; you may wish to sleep awhile. Once we leave, we won't have many opportunities for rest. The alvor are not normally given to torturing their prisoners. Why did they beat you so?'

'I killed one of them,' said Bergtatt.

Bergtatt dozed restlessly for a few hours. His body healed quickly, bones mending, swellings shrinking and wounds closing themselves. By the time he rose, he was completely healed.

Vermin clutched Bergtatt's teeth between both hands and mumbled an incantation into them. Then the goblin pointed at Bergtatt's cage and the door swung open.

Bergtatt pulled himself up and out of the enclosure and grabbed a hold of the chain. The cage swung wildly with his movements as he climbed hand-over-hand, his arms aching from the effort of holding on, his hands slipping from his own sweat. His eyes were fixed on the bridge above, watching for signs of movement.

Finally, he made it to the top, grateful for the feel of stone under his fingers as he pulled himself onto the bridge. He rolled onto his back and waited for his strength to return before attempting to haul up the goblin's cage.

THE CHANGELING KING

'What's the matter with you, are you trying to kill yourself? You were supposed to find the winch and lower me down,' complained Vermin as he clambered out of his cage and onto the bridge.

Bergtatt growled at him.

'Maybe your way was better. Alright, follow me and try not to make too much noise,' said the goblin.

The city slumbered as they moved from shadow to shadow, circling away from the odd patrol. Bergtatt could see the castle drawing closer in the gloom.

'Where are you taking me? The gates are in the other direction,' he growled.

'There will be guards watching the gates. You must trust me. I know of a hidden way, a secret way. It is much safer.'

Vermin stopped at a drain and raised the grate. He gestured for Bergtatt to jump in. Bergtatt growled again. Vermin shrugged and disappeared feet first into the darkness. Bergtatt followed, trying his best not to breathe deeply. The sewers were quite clean, but not entirely free of rats. The goblin snatched a passing rodent and tore its head off with his teeth. He looked at Bergtatt and offered it to him. Bergtatt declined with a sneer.

The sewer led them to a tunnel. From there they travelled up into the marsh beyond the city's walls.

The changeling and the goblin travelled together for three days, silent and watchful. On the fourth day, they left the marsh and crossed an old stone bridge that had been built by a human king, centuries past. Off to the north, Bergtatt spotted something sparkling on the horizon.

'What is that?' he asked, curiosity overcoming his revulsion for Vermin.

'That is the city of Maidenhall-on-the-Sea. They are said to be different from the alvor of Ranush, but no more tolerant of our kind,' said Vermin.

'More alvor. I shall destroy them too,' said Bergtatt. 'You go and prepare your people. In two years I will come to the underground realm of the goblins. If you do not keep your promise, I will destroy the goblin tribes first.'

Bergtatt set off at a run.

By nightfall, Bergtatt had reached the mountains and his hunting grounds. He snuck up on a sleeping sentry and snapped his neck. He used the troll's helmet and cloak to disguise himself. Last of all, he picked up the troll's axe and then boldly walked into the camp, lay down by a fire and promptly fell asleep.

The next morning he rose early, re-arranged his disguise and sat down to watch. The trolls awoke eventually to move sluggishly around the camp. He listened to the various conversations and learnt that his missing half-brother, Thark, had returned from the dead to lead the party. Noont had died in an ambush and Bergtatt was rumoured to have drowned. Stunned, he remained concealed for several more hours, mulling over these turn of events.

Around midday, Vasch entered the camp with a sharpened piece of slate in his hand. Bergtatt was pleased to see him alive. He was a good fighter.

'Come out, traitor!' he yelled.

Bergtatt tensed. Could it be that Vasch had been in on Thark's plan? Had he somehow found out that Bergtatt had returned? He grabbed his axe by the haft and made himself as small as possible. Vasch crashed about the camp, kicking aside dozing trolls. He continued to shout and rant until Thark stepped out of his cave.

'What is this noise?' asked Thark, nursing a clay keg. Bergtatt noticed for the first time how sibilant his foster-brother sounded. 'Are we under attack?'

'Traitor, you betrayed Bergtatt. You arranged the ambush. I saw the bodies. The fallen on both sides were from our own party. You murdered your own brothers,' said Vasch.

'He was mad. He needed killing,' said Thark dismissively.

Vasch screamed and ran at Thark with his weapon raised. Thark sidestepped and struck him with a club he had concealed behind his back. Vasch fell hard. Thark stalked forward and swung the club downward, smashing Vasch's arm, sending his slate skittering away from him. Thark raised the club overhead for the killing blow.

THE CHANGELING KING

'Stop,' shouted Bergtatt.

Thark turned around to see who had dared to interfere. Bergtatt stood up and threw the cloak aside. Then he took off the helmet and cast that away too. Some of the trolls fell back with cries of fear. Thark blanched and began to back away. Bergtatt flexed his thick arms and hefted his axe.

Why deny myself the pleasure, thought Bergtatt. He would kill him with his bare hands. He let the axe slip from his fingers. Thark smiled and threw his club aside.

Thark lowered his head and charged forward, spearing his shoulder into Bergtatt's stomach and slamming him down onto the ground. Winded, Bergtatt barely got his arms up as Thark pounded him with a flurry of punches.

Bergtatt twisted free and scrambled to his feet, then threw a kick to Thark's mid-section. Thark took the hit and wrapped his arms around Bergtatt in a bear-hug and squeezed.

Bergtatt smashed his forehead against Thark's nose. Blood spurted from his nostrils but he only squeezed harder. Bergtatt continued to head-butt Thark, marking the trolls face, breaking his nose and opening cuts over his eyes. Finally, Thark dropped him and took a few shaky steps back. Bergtatt closed in on him and threw a punch to Thark's sternum. He followed it with a jab to his abdomen and a haymaker to the troll's throat. Finally, Bergtatt jumped up and struck him with both feet, catapulting Thark into the throng of onlookers.

A troll pushed Bergtatt's axe into Thark's hand. Bergtatt scooped up Thark's discarded club.

Thark charged straight at him. Bergtatt stepped forward to meet him. The club swung out and struck Thark just above the elbow. A second blow landed behind Thark's knee, making the troll's leg buckle. The third broke Thark's jaw.

Bergtatt stood over the broken body of his brother and threw aside the club. He looked at the trolls around him as Thark lay dying at his feet. Some of the faces were new, but none moved to avenge Thark. Such was the troll way.

'All who oppose me will die. Bergtatt died in the river. I am the Trollking,' he roared.

NOOR A JAHANGIR

The trolls looked at each other in confusion. Vasch walked over to Bergtatt and raised his arm. 'Blood and glory for the Trollking,' he shouted.

The trolls took up the chant.

CHAPTER 28: A SHORT-LIVED RESPITE
KRYLLON

Nathan had not felt this refreshed since leaving Alvorn Reach. The hot bath had done wonders for his tired body. Justine had laid out clean clothes as promised. They were a good fit. But he wasn't able to enjoy the experience fully. Logan hadn't said a word to him yet. The last time Logan had been like this was when Nathan had taken Logan's bike without asking and bent the front wheel against a high curb.

Nathan sighed and wondered whether he should break the silence first. He and Logan were the only ones in the dining room aside from a young couple enjoying each other's company as much as the food. Nathan watched them wistfully as they whispered, giggled and held hands underneath the table, oblivious to the rest of the world. He wondered whether the four of them would ever get the chance to behave like teenagers again.

The sound of chatter from the common room paused momentarily. The innkeeper entered the dining room escorting two beautiful women. Nathan did a double take as he realised that the women were Salina and Katrina. They were dressed in a similar fashion to the young lady at the other table, velvet skirt and bodice over a white blouse. Salina's hair was piled up on top of her head and held in place by long pins. Katrina's cropped hair had grown since their arrival in Kryllon and had been brushed out on to her shoulders. Nathan and Logan stood as one to pull out chairs for their ladies.

'You both look absolutely stunning,' said Nathan. Logan bobbed his head in agreement; dumbstruck.

'You don't look too shabby yourselves,' said Salina. Katrina fluttered her eyelashes at Logan and laughed in delight as he turned bright red. Justine cleared her throat.

NOOR A JAHANGIR

'I'll have your food brought in.'

The meal was as lavish as any they had eaten on Earth. They started with savoury vegetable soup, followed by stuffed aubergines and sausages with a fruity mint sauce, served with Justine's house wine. Once the used dishes were cleared away, Justine brought in dessert, apple-pie spiced with cinnamon and smothered with cream.

'How is Haldrin? I haven't seen him since he went out on patrol some weeks ago,' said Justine. 'How did you meet him?'

'We kind of bumped into him in the mountains. He was kind enough to escort us into town,' said Nathan.

'Where exactly are you from?'

'Oh, just a small fishing village on the south coast, I doubt you'll have heard of it,' said Katrina.

'We don't see many humans from the south; its alvorn country isn't it? I'm surprised they let you pass through their lands. Those two-faced, donkey-eared devils can't be trusted,' said Justine, her face taking on a sour look.

Nathan wondered what the alvors had done that they were so disliked by Kryllonian humans.

'Oh, we stuck to the river most of the way. We didn't really see much of them,' said Katrina.

'Wait, you went through the Belt? You four must have remarkable luck to have passed through alvor country and the Belt without a scar to show for it.'

Not unscathed, thought Nathan, not unscathed.

'Well now, I've other customers to see to. I'll have some nettle tea sent out to you. Let me know if you need anything else.'

Justine cleared the table and headed back to the bar. Suddenly, Nathan found three sets of eyes staring at him. Nathan sighed inwardly and shifted uncomfortably in his chair. He had eaten too much and the dining room felt too warm.

'Well, I guess this is as good a time as any. Katrina, I was way out of line. I'm an ass and a pig. I lost my temper and I shouldn't have. Please forgive me. I'm a big stinking idiot,' said Nathan.

THE CHANGELING KING

'Nathan, we were both out of line. These past few months have been difficult for all of us,' replied Katrina.

'It's understandable, right? I mean, who else has a better reason to be freaking out? We're light-years from home and have had to grow up pretty fast,' said Salina.

'Yeah, so let's just put all this behind us. Besides, if we had followed you, we wouldn't have got caught by them goblins,' said Katrina.

'If you hadn't come to the rescue, we might have been killed,' said Salina.

'Of course, there remains the question of who will lead us,' said Katrina.

'I understand. I'll go with whoever you guys decide on,' said Nathan, though his heart sank to the pit of his stomach.

'I think we all are in agreement on this. After all, you've got us this far, Nathan,' said Katrina, smiling shyly.

'We haven't been killed, maimed or seriously injured yet,' said Salina.

'Besides, no one else wants the job,' said Logan with a warm smile.

'I promise I won't let you down again. I'll get us home,' said Nathan, his voice choked with emotion.

Embarrassed by the intensity of the discussion, they smiled sheepishly at each other.

'I'll stick a knife in the first person who suggests a group hug,' said Katrina.

The dining room hushed as the four burst out laughing. An elderly couple shook their heads in disgust, making the four laugh even harder. Justine had to tell them to quieten down, and even then Katrina and Nathan had the giggles for another ten minutes.

After their late lunch, they walked over to the trading post. The store had everything from dry rations to travel clothing and even tooled leather saddles. They managed to get a good price for the alvorn trinkets that they had collected over time. It seemed people in Erskine were happy to purchase alvorn goods, despite their hatred of them. The four had plenty gold left over to get their weapons serviced and purchase mounts. Justine's son gave them directions to the best smithy in town and to a horse-master.

The smithy, a bear of a man named Brand, was busy filling orders when they arrived. Money exchanged hands and the blacksmith took one of his apprentices off some other work to get their equipment ready right away. He assured them that the apprentice was capable. Logan insisted on staying to observe the work despite the blacksmith's objections. Nathan and the girls continued on to the horse-master.

They were met at the stable gates by a boy with an unruly mop of hair. He led them inside and then went off to fetch the horse-master. Nathan and the girls sat down on a bale of hay to wait.

The boy returned shortly with a handsome middle-aged man. He had bright, crinkly eyes and the same unruly hair as the stable-hand. The girls shot to their feet as if they had been stung and began to quickly brush straw from their clothes and straighten their hair. Nathan got to his feet too and strode over to shake the man's hand. His grip was strong and warm.

'Good day, young man. My name is Rodan and this is my boy, Raeborn. How may I be of assistance?'

'I'm Nathan Celic and these are my friends, Salina and Katrina.'

Nathan paused as Rodan inclined his head to the girls. He blinked. The girls seemed confused, their hands fluttering as if they didn't know what to do with them. Rodan flashed a smile and gestured for them to follow him. He led them past a small riding yard and into the stables.

'We're friends of Captain Haldrin,' said Nathan, hoping that the name would have the same effect on Rodan as it had on Justine.

'Ah, and did the good Captain send you to me?'

'No, actually it was Justine's son who gave us directions,' said Nathan.

'Ah. Well then, what are you in the market for? If you're after pack animals, I don't deal in them. My horses are the best in Kryllon, better even than the nags the alvors ride on.'

THE CHANGELING KING

Nathan felt his heart sink. Justine's son had sent them to the best horse dealer in Erskine. He was no expert in evaluating horses, but he knew a little about shopping. The best always charged the most.

'I'm not sure whether we can afford your prices,' said Nathan.

Rodan stopped and gave him a hard look.

'I haven't told you my prices yet.'

'I don't want to waste your time, sir. But we don't have much gold left,' said Nathan.

'Show me.'

Nathan pulled out his money pouch and passed it to the horse-master. The man sifted through the coins with a thick finger.

'I see. How many horses were you looking to purchase?'

'There are four of us and we have a long way to travel.'

'Four,' muttered Rodan to himself.

Rodan tightened the drawstring and threw the pouch to Raeborn, who had followed them in. The boy snatched the pouch out of the air and tucked it into his shirt. Rodan took them through a door into an adjoining stable then led them out into another yard. Four horses stood drinking from a water trough. There were two chestnuts, one grey and a black. Nathan had never been near a horse before Kryllon but could tell that these animals were happy and well-fed. They were slightly larger than the horses kept by the alvor. Nathan and the girls walked over to the animals to stroke their shiny flanks and glossy manes.

'Do you like them?' asked Rodan.

'We love them, but I don't think we can afford them,' said Salina, as she possessively stood between the grey and Katrina.

'They're yours. I'll even throw in the tack and saddles.'

'We couldn't possibly take these horses,' said Nathan.

'Aren't they good enough? I tell you, you won't find better horses than these anywhere. They are from the finest stock, bred right here in Kryllon by my family for centuries.'

'What the hell's the matter with you two? Let's grab the horses and go. You can be all noble about it afterwards,' Katrina whispered. 'We'll take them.' She added aloud.

NOOR A JAHANGIR

Raeborn took the steeds away, while Rodan lectured them on the proper care of horses and warned them against using bits on his animals. Eventually, Rodan ran out of things to say and then just glowered at them as if he was having second thoughts about selling the horses. Raeborn returned with the animals, covered in quilted blankets, blinded and bridled up. Rodan spent a few minutes whispering to the beautiful creatures whilst stroking their snuffling noses. Finally, he thumped their flanks and handed over the reins to the three.

Nathan and the girls left the stables, occasionally glancing over their shoulders, expecting to hear a shout, or see Rodan running after them saying there had been mistake. They reached the end of the street and there was still no sign of him.

'I'm having the black one,' said Nathan as they walked the horses down a busy avenue.

'What are you going to call it?' asked Salina.

'Darth Vader.'

'You can't call it that. Give it a nice name.'

'It's my horse, so I can call it what I want.'

The sound of metal striking metal could be heard over the hubbub of the streets. Before long, they could see the smoke that billowed from the blacksmith's chimney as sparks skittered out onto the street. Salina and Katrina watched the horses while Nathan entered the forge to find Logan. It didn't take him long.

Logan, stripped to the waist and wearing a leather vest, held a fiery blade flat on an iron anvil with a pair of tongs. The blacksmith and his apprentices shouted encouragements as Logan bashed the blade with a huge hammer. Nathan watched as Logan thrust the blade into a large basin of water, filling the forge with steam. By the time it had cleared, Brand was examining the sword with a critical eye. He put the weapon down and slapped Logan's back, almost knocking him over.

'You're a natural, boy. Are you sure you don't want to apprentice yourself to me?' asked Brand.

'I'm afraid I can't, master. There is something that I have to do,' said Logan.

'Well, that's a great shame. If things don't work out, come back this way and we'll make a blacksmith out of you yet.'

THE CHANGELING KING

'Thank you, master,' replied Logan.

'What was all that about?' asked Nathan as the blacksmith went about his business.

'Oh, nothing,' replied Logan as he wiped the sweat from his body with a rag.

An apprentice brought out their weapons and armour, individually wrapped in parcels of muslin and twine. Logan pulled on his shirt and tunic. Brand followed the apprentice out, carrying a smaller parcel in one huge hand. He undid the twine and revealed an exquisite dagger, finished with an ornate hilt.

'This is one of mine. I want you to have it,' said Brand.

'I can't accept this. It's much too fine a gift.'

'Who said anything about a gift? This is payment for the work you've done for me and an incentive to come back.'

Logan took the dagger and admired it with reverent hands. He bowed before the blacksmith in thanks. The blacksmith chuckled in pleasure and waved him away.

'Remember, my offer stands for as long as I live. Apprentices are a copper a dozen, but a gifted apprentice is a rare thing. Farewell, Logan.'

Logan and the smith clasped wrists one last time and then Brand headed back into his forge. Logan carefully slid the dagger into his belt as if it were a fragile flower rather than a weapon. Nathan shook his head in wonder.

When the four returned to The Silver Penny, Logan hit the bathhouse again. Nathan watched the girls pampering the horses with the help of an eager stable-boy. The animals responded to the attention by nudging the girls playfully with their heads and nuzzling their hands. The girls had come to a happy agreement that Salina would have the steel-dust gelding and Katrina would get the bay, leaving Logan the chestnut. Nathan felt a surge of contentment and optimism. The four of them were closer now than they had ever been. Then, through the open stable doors, he caught sight of the goblin again.

***

NOOR A JAHANGIR

The sun set early over Erskine, disappearing behind the snow-topped mountains and setting the gathered clouds on fire. A pretty maid came up to inform them that Captain Haldrin was waiting downstairs.

Haldrin stood by the bar speaking quietly with Justine. A mug of ale sat untouched before him. The ranger looked up as they came down and patted Justine's hand before walking over to them.

'There's been a change of plan. Gather your gear. I've already instructed the stable hand to prepare your horses,' said Haldrin.

'What's going on?' asked Nathan.

'A goblin named Jarnak was spotted watching the inn.'

'Yeah, we saw a goblin earlier today ourselves. Is this a problem?' asked Logan.

'Jarnak is Dross's second-in-command. They're the ones that have been asking around about you.'

'I get your point. What do we do?' said Nathan.

'Get your things together and I'll tell you the rest while we ride,' said Haldrin.

The four changed back into their travelling gear and belted on their armour. Haldrin waited for them in the courtyard with their horses. They stashed their belongings into saddlebags and then mounted up. Shame, thought Nathan with genuine regret, it would have been really nice to sleep in a soft bed again. The sound of shod feet echoed loudly on the cobbles as Haldrin led them out onto the street. There they were joined by five rangers. Nathan recognised them all from their encounter in the caves. They looked rested and ready for action. Haldrin rode beside Nathan and Salina.

'So, where are we headed, Captain?' asked Salina.

'We are to meet with the Lord Mayor at a secret location. He wishes to speak to you before you leave town,' said Haldrin.

'Do you suspect a trap?' said Nathan.

'The Mayor keeps his own counsel and his motives are known only to him. There is the possibility of a trap, but nothing is certain as yet.'

'Why not just ride out of town now?' asked Logan from behind.

THE CHANGELING KING

'The town-gates are bound to be under watch. The only way you're going to be able to leave is with the Mayor's blessings. I've already dispatched someone to scout out this secret location. If the meet is compromised, we will be forewarned.'

Nathan looked over his shoulder to exchange a glance with Logan and Katrina. At the first sign of treachery, Nathan would take Haldrin hostage. As much as they liked Haldrin, they weren't going to trust him blindly. Nathan rotated his sword-belt to a position from where he could draw his sword quickly. The streetlights produced a greasy fug overhead, making it difficult to see if they were being shadowed on the rooftops. A couple of good archers could take them out without the riders ever seeing them.

Nathan could feel himself starting to sweat, despite the chill mountain air. They rode under an archway and into a walled graveyard. A woman stepped out of from beneath a drowsy willow. Nathan's sword whispered from its scabbard. Haldrin held up his hand. It was the ranger, Kira.

'I'm sorry, she came out of nowhere,' said Nathan quietly. The woman nodded dismissively and began her report to Haldrin.

'The Mayor's brought five men: three out in the open with halberds, two crossbowmen hidden in a grove. Jaim and Flinn are keeping an eye out for Dross and his animals.'

'Well, Nathan, does that set your mind at ease? The Mayor isn't the most courageous of people. If he planned on ambushing you, he would have arrived with a whole regiment. Kira, you've done a good job. Once the meeting is over, get a hold of Jaim and Flinn, and head back to the barracks.'

Kira nodded and slipped back into the shadows. Haldrin flicked his reins and guided the party through the maze of gravestones to a private area dominated by a single crypt entrance. To Nathan's dismay, Haldrin rode straight into the crypt. Nathan's father hadn't been a church-goer, but it still felt like sacrilege to ride into the last resting place of some poor soul. He gritted his teeth as the riders behind him crowded his horse forward.

The crypt steps were broad and the horses descended easily enough. Several mummified bodies were ensconced in niches along the walls to either side. The crypt was well lit by torches. Wood shavings littered the stone floor muffling the sound of their passage.

NOOR A JAHANGIR

Nathan had expected the crypt to stink of death. Instead he felt a breeze cool his cheeks, infused with the attar of roses. The ground turned to dirt and suddenly they emerged into the open air again. Stars twinkled above them as they entered a grove.

The mayor stood wrapped in a heavy cloak with a fur-lined cap on his head. His guards stood attentively around him. Two quivering bushes gave away the hiding place of the crossbowmen.

'Finally, you make an appearance. I was about to send out a search party. Welcome to my gardens, my lords and ladies. Please accept my apology, as I must rescind my offer of dinner. It seems my Captain and honoured guests have knowingly misled me,' said the Mayor.

'I beg your pardon, Your Grace. It was a necessary subterfuge,' said Haldrin.

'Are you going to dismount, or do I have to keep craning my neck?' asked the mayor.

Haldrin and the four companions swung down from their steeds and approached the Mayor.

'You may want to call your crossbowmen out before they damage those beautiful mulberry bushes,' said Haldrin.

The mayor sighed in exasperation as the men stepped out shamefaced from their cover.

'Someone better explain to me who these four southerners are and what is going on.'

'We're not going to the coast,' said Nathan.

'That much I gathered.'

'We're headed to Ranush.'

'So it's true,' whispered the Mayor, 'you are going to slay the Trollking.'

Nathan glanced at Logan and the girls. In a heartbeat the four sprang into action. Salina rolled to the left, sweep-kicking a crossbowman off his feet. She rose from the ground, then snapped out another kick and knocked the man unconscious. Katrina loosed an arrow and pinned the second crossbowman's arm to a tree before turning to cover the halberdiers that Logan had disarmed. Nathan crossed the grove in three steps and lifted the mayor up by the throat.

THE CHANGELING KING

Haldrin and the rangers stood frozen where they stood, shocked by the speed and ferocity of the attack.

'Let . . . go . . . of . . . me,' rasped the mayor.

'If he wanted to betray you, he wouldn't have called us here. He would have sent assassins to kill you while you slept,' said Haldrin.

Nathan relaxed his fingers. The mayor took in a grateful breath of air and massaged his neck.

'Thank you, Haldrin, for your belief in my integrity,' said the Mayor in a dry voice, his eyes taking on a calculative look.

'You are not of this world, are you?' said the mayor, removing his hat as he spoke to run a hand over his shiny bald pate. 'No, you're not. I have old books in my personal library, journals of the early settlers, predating even the rise of the High Kings. I thought them to be mere flights of fantasy, fairy tales for children. The journals spoke of travel across the stars through gateways from other worlds. Our own folklore suggests that we once possessed strength and speed such as yours. This, of course, changes everything.

'I have no love for the Trollking and his minions. His taxes have increased year on year. I curse the day that our great-grandfathers made that terrible pact with him. His foul servants have walked our streets ever since, stealing from our honest folk. No, I bear no love for the Trollking's evil.'

'Even if we are these legendary warriors from the past, what chance do we have of defeating the Trollking?' asked Katrina, her voice dripping with ire. 'Do you think for a moment we can walk up to the gates of Ranush, through all the goblins, trolls and scumbag traitors? I'm sure the Trollking will lie down, a willing sacrifice for the good of Kryllon. You make me sick. Every one of you is happily ready to send four kids to their doom, you cowardly lords of mighty halls.'

Nathan drew his sword and rested it casually on the mayor's shoulder. The man flinched and looked to Haldrin for support. Haldrin shrugged.

'When the Trollking finds out that you let us slip through your grasp, he will crush Erskine and scatter its stones all over these mountains. Why would you risk everything now?'

NOOR A JAHANGIR

'Wait, I have news. Haldrin reported he saw a fleet of longboats several miles out to sea on a northerly heading. Word of a coming war has reached even here. It is said that the dvargar are marching too.'

Haldrin nodded in confirmation.

'All the more reason to kill you now,' said Nathan, sliding the flat of his blade along the Mayor's shoulder towards his neck.

'Killing me will not help your cause. I am willing to overlook your bad manners. You have good grounds for grievance against the people of Kryllon. Your coming has given us all a reason to hope. Humans amongst the alvor, the alvor allied with dvargar and the heroes of legend once more walk the land. The Trollking will have too much to deal with without concerning himself with a minor irritation like us. Whether the battle is won at Ranush or not, Erskine will have thrown off its yoke. We have enough warriors now amongst the rangers, the town guard and the militia to take back the town.'

'Well, I'm glad for you,' said Katrina, gritting her teeth in anger.

'I'm sorry, but there's nothing more we can do for you. Haldrin will lead you out of town and then you are on your own. Ride hard,' said the Mayor.

Nathan sheathed his sword and walked back to his horse. Katrina, Salina and Logan put up their weapons too, allowing the angry guards to stand up.

'If you betray them, I will kill you myself,' said Haldrin, as the rest of the party mounted up and turned their horses around.

The town was quiet, except for the raucous singing of the odd marauding band of drunken goblins. The four kept a vigilant eye out as the rangers guided them down twisting roads and through dark alleys. Haldrin finally called a halt at the back of a shabby warehouse, beneath the high walls.

'This exit is known only to my rangers. Go under the care of the ancestors and never forget that you have friends here in Erskine,' said Haldrin.

The four thanked Haldrin and his rangers, and then rode through the hidden exit. Moments later, the horses trotted out onto a mountain path with the town of Erskine behind them.

CHAPTER 29: DREAMS

ENGLAND

Vasch removed the horn from his lips and waited. The horses were getting restless. Sigberd and Haig tried their best to keep them calm. Soon Udulf and Grenld came loping out of the woods.

'Who blew the horn?' asked Udulf immediately.

'Me,' said Vasch. 'Where are the others?'

'We split up to cover more ground. Grenld and Agilerd were covering the east.'

'Grenld and Agilerd. You took eight trolls with you. What happened to the others?'

'The female warrior killed Durke, Thark, Eberherd and Ludherd. She has some kind of magic at her disposal,' said Udulf.

'Magic? Nicor-dung. The humans have mechanical weapons, just like our crossbows. There is nothing magical about them. One human warrior and a boy killed four of my warband? You disgust me, Udulf. You are not worthy of serving the Trollking.'

Udulf scowled, his lips parting to reveal his yellow tusks, deep ridges appearing above his nostrils. Vasch straightened up and thrust out his chest. Just then, Lang came running out of the forest at full tilt. He didn't slow until he saw Vasch and Udulf facing off. He clutched a bleeding stump, raggedly severed from the bicep. His face had picked up some cuts too.

'Agilerd?' asked Vasch.

'That demon-woman got him. Look what she's done to me. That was my good arm,' said Lang.

'What about the orb?'

NOOR A JAHANGIR

'I've got it. I picked it up before I engaged.'

Vasch sneered at the self-pity in the troll's voice. He never should have allowed Udulf to take command. Udulf must have read his expression for his hand moved to his axe. Vasch could feel all his aches and pains and wondered whether he still had enough strength to take down Udulf. The troll removed his axe and threw it into the hard-baked earth.

'You are no longer the commander here,' spat Udulf. 'They answer to me now.'

A bout to decide leadership wasn't the best thing right now for the mission, but Vasch doubted Udulf gave a damn about the timing. If it had been up to Vasch, he would have slit the upstart's throat quietly at night. But he couldn't afford to back down in front of the troops, wounded or not. He removed his own axe and threw it down beside Udulf's.

'You're not fit enough to lead a bunch of shebaks, let alone a crack warband, Udulf,' said Vasch.

Udulf roared and pounded his chest before stalking towards him. Vasch adjusted his stance to better protect his broken ribs and took up a low guard. The manoeuvre was made clumsy by the splint on his ankle. Udulf swung a haymaker at his head.

Vasch raised an arm to block, and then slid it over Udulf's before locking it up with a twist. He hammered his fist into Udulf's side.

Udulf managed to slip free and came back with a left-right combination that snapped Vasch's chin back.

Grenld and Lang began to shout encouragements to Udulf. The trolls formed a half-circle around the combatants. Sigberd and Haig called out advice to Vasch.

Vasch moved into Udulf's guard and clinched Udulf's head, drawing it down for a knee to the face. Udulf took the hit and then powered out of the hold, blood dripping from his snout.

Vasch could feel his energy waning. He had to end this fight quickly, before his body gave out. He needed to find some way of turning the tide, otherwise Udulf would happily pound him to death.

Vasch fought back as best as he could. Udulf's face bore testimony to Vasch's efforts. But a right hook, followed by an uppercut and a straight laid Vasch out flat. His vision swam and he fought to hold onto the distant pinpricks that were the stars above.

'Enough,' said Vasch, his voice barely a croak.

Udulf stalked forward to stomp on his face. Vasch didn't have the strength to raise an arm, not even in defence. Sigberd stepped in and shoved Udulf back.

'He said enough. You've won. You are our undisputed leader now,' said Sigberd.

'Why should I spare him?'

'The orb,' said Vasch and pointed to Lang.

'He's the only one who can read the orb,' said Sigberd.

Udulf held out his hand to Lang and received the orb from him. He knelt down beside Vasch and raised it to his face. Vasch saw his own battered visage reflected on its surface.

'Well, what does it show you? Where are the demon-woman and the boy?'

Vasch breathed on the orb and it came to life. Two images flickered under the glassy surface.

'You will find them at a point, six miles west of here. They will be in metal-cattle.'

'Now make it obey me,' said Udulf.

Vasch looked at the troll and curled his lips.

'Do it and I will spare you,' said Udulf.

Vasch pressed his lips to the orb and mouthed a word. The ball flared up and then turned dull again.

'Mount up. We move out now,' said Udulf, pushing the bauble under his breastplate before standing up.

'What about Vasch?' asked Sigberd.

'What about him? I've spared his life, but that doesn't mean he's coming with us. Leave the spare horses here. He can have one if he can catch it.'

Vasch lay quietly and listened to the sound of his comrades riding away. The stars seemed so cold and far away from this world. Vasch wondered whether one of them was Eridani.

NOOR A JAHANGIR

Adam's eyes snapped open, the vestigial afterimage of his nightmares fading slowly from his mind. The sun had risen and its rays shone through the green canopy of the woods. Karen's handbag propped his head up and her coat lay over him like a blanket. The coat smelt nice. Karen sat beside him, the shotgun resting across her legs. Her face was bruised down one side and her lips were swollen.

'How you doing, partner?' asked Karen.

'I think I've had better days. Thank you for looking out for me.'

Karen smiled warmly. She held her hand over his face, splaying her fingers, with her thumb and index finger forming a circle.

'How many fingers am I holding up?'

'Three?'

'You asking me or are you telling me?' said Karen.

'Three.'

'Good. Can you stand up?'

'I think so,' said Adam. 'Have you been crying?'

'I had something in my eye, but it's okay now.'

Karen helped Adam up before retrieving her handbag and coat. Adam noted a strange pile of grey dust on the ground nearby.

'What's that?' asked Adam.

'It's what's left of the troll I shot dead last night. It just kind of disintegrated around dawn.'

'Like vampires?'

'I guess so.'

'We're probably both going to need therapy after this is all over,' said Adam, grinning despite the banging pain in his head.

'Are you good to walk? I want to put as much distance between us and this place as possible. Those things might come back with reinforcements.'

After an hour of walking, in more or less a straight line, Karen and Adam found their way out of the wood. They crossed a field full of grazing sheep and climbed over a stone wall onto a road.

THE CHANGELING KING

Eventually, they came upon a small sleepy village identified by a roadside sign as Peel Brook. The village seemed virtually deserted. Just like in a horror movie, thought Adam. They found a cottage tearoom that was open for business. There were no customers inside but he could hear someone working in the kitchen. They made their way to the rest room at the back. It turned out to be small but clean, with a single toilet cubicle in the corner. Karen let Adam use it first, whilst she cleaned herself up in the wash basin. Adam flushed the toilet as Karen dried her face and arms using paper towels.

'Adam, use the soap and wash off as much dirt as you can. We don't want people asking us questions we can't answer.'

Karen helped Adam brush the leaves and dirt out of his hair, then applied some foundation to cover up the bruising on her face. They wiped down the sink with some wet paper towels and used a brush and dustpan to clean the mess on the floor. Once Karen was satisfied with their efforts, they vacated the rest room and sat down at a table.

A petite, elderly lady walked through from the kitchen and looked at them as if they had appeared by magic.

'Well, hello, you must excuse me – I didn't hear you come in. Most of my customers come in around lunch or teatime. There aren't that many hikers about at this time of the year. Do you know what you will be ordering?'

'Could I have a pot of Earl Grey, please? And I'll have a slice of carrot cake too, if you have any. How about you, Adam?'

'I'll have a blueberry muffin, a chocolate éclair, a cream donut and a tall vanilla milkshake, um, please.'

'Dear me. Anything else, young man?' asked the tearoom lady with a wide smile.

'No, I think that's it. No point in being greedy.'

The tearoom lady chuckled and went back into the kitchen. She returned a few minutes later with their order.

Karen found a crumpled banknote in her pocket to pay for the food and then asked if there was a payphone nearby. The tearoom lady pointed her to the cloakroom. Karen went and made a call whilst Adam eyed up the carrot cake and wondered what his mum was having for breakfast.

NOOR A JAHANGIR

'You want to go halves?' asked Karen as she strode back to their table.

'Yes, please,' replied Adam eagerly.

Karen cut through the moist cake and pushed her plate to the middle of the small table. Adam dug in and finished his half in three generous mouthfuls. He raised his glass and washed it down with several gulps of milkshake.

'Karen?'

'Yes?'

'Sometimes I see things in my dreams. Things that have happened, or things that might happen. It started after Salina drowned. Sometimes I see things happening in another place. I'm not even sure if it's Earth.'

'Where are you going with this?'

'I had another dream while I was unconscious.'

Karen glanced over to the kitchen. The tearoom lady had half shut the door. Karen nodded for Adam to continue.

'You just went to call a taxi now, right?'

'Yeah...'

'We were sitting in the back of a dark blue Toyota Avensis. It had fluffy dice hanging from the mirror, with a cow-skin print on them. The driver had white hair. We were driving on a country road, just like the one we walked along to get here. The trolls came charging over a hill on horses and started firing arrows at the car. One jumped in the middle of the road and the driver tried to dodge it. He lost control and slammed into a wall. The car exploded.'

Karen looked at him with such intensity that it made him want to squirm. She blinked and turned to look out of the window just as their car arrived. It was a blue Avensis. She looked at Adam in a way that made him feel like a freak.

'Adam, we have to go,' said Karen.

Adam allowed Karen to lead him out, his heart thumping wildly. What was happening to him? Did he have some kind of superpower, or was it a curse? The visions were never pleasant. Someone was always getting hurt in them.

THE CHANGELING KING

The driver was a middle-aged man with hair so blonde it looked white. Hanging from the rear-view mirror were a pair of cow-print, novelty dice. Karen whipped out the shotgun from under her coat and walked to the driver's side door. The driver looked at her as if she had gone mad.

'Get out of the car, sir. I have to commandeer your vehicle,' she shouted.

The man opened the door and stepped out with his hands raised high in the air.

'What the hell is going on?' he said, his voice quaking with fear.

'My name is Detective Karen Rainbow. I'm a police officer. I'm sorry. I have no choice but to take your car. It's an emergency.' said Karen. 'Move over to the side of the road.'

Adam watched dumbstruck as Karen got into the car. He looked apologetically at the driver and then climbed into the passenger seat. Karen turned the car around and then accelerated away from the village, throwing Adam around in his seat as he struggled to fasten his seat belt.

'That was cool,' said Adam.

'I'm glad you approve. What now? I mean we've already changed the vision, right? I'm driving the car now.'

'I don't know. This is a first for me too.'

A sharp bend loomed up ahead and Karen sent the car careening around it so fast that the back kicked out a little, but she quickly got it back under control. Adam was pushed back into his seat as the car surged forward. Maybe if Karen drove fast enough, they would be able to outrun the moment of the crash. Adam looked at her speedometer. The needle was steadily climbing from sixty to seventy miles an hour. Adam's eyes were drawn to the ascending line of the hill.

Karen swore loudly. Just as Adam had predicted, the trolls crested the rise and continued at an angle that would bring them down on top of the car. There were five trolls, mounted on what looked like Shire horses, armed with crossbows. The trolls began to fire as soon as theywere in range. The iron-tipped bolts punched into the vehicle's aluminium body with a screech. One of the trolls came alongside the Avensis. Karen jabbed at the electric window button until it slid open.

NOOR A JAHANGIR

With one hand steadying the wheel, she stuck out the shotgun and squeezed off a shell. The shot went wide but the noise spooked the horse. The others were forced to pull up as their companion toppled to the ground in front of them. Adam turned in his seat to watch the monsters recede behind them.

Buoyed by a sense of hope, he turned back to grin at Karen. A strange look passed over her face. She reached over her shoulder to feel her back. Her hand came away covered in blood.

CHAPTER 30: THE END OF AN AGE
KRYLLON (AGE OF THE ALVOR)

After a bloody year of in-fighting, the Trollking led a horde of thousands across the river and into the treacherous marshes of the North East.

The Trollking's purpose was so fully fixed on Ranush, that he paid little heed to the nettling guerrilla action from Maidenhall as they passed through alvorn lands. Frustrated by the lack of an enemy to stand and fight with, the Trollking pushed on. Such was the terror of his wrath upon his troops that none dared to desert, despite the scores that died from injury and disease on the long march. Finally, the city of Ranush appeared before them, wreathed in the coils of marsh vapours. The horde's cheers were dampened as they were met by a torrent of arrows.

To the Trollking's delight, the alvor had marched out and formed ranks before the walls. He was tired of chasing enemies that melted away before his fighters had time to react. But despite their seeming preparedness, there was still a diminishing stream of refugees piling in through the city's only gateway to the south-west. He instinctively knew that the alvor would expect him to rest his troops first before launching the siege. Bergtatt roared orders to attack immediately.

As predicted, the alvor were caught off guard. The Trollking waded into them with his huge T-bladed sword, swinging left and right, outpacing his own warriors. The alvorn commander yelled orders from the ramparts to rally his troops, but the Trollking's horde ploughed on through their ranks.

Refugees scattered as the Ranushan cavalry rode out of the gates and thundered along the open ground. Bronze armoured lancers and five thousand pounds of horse flesh crashed into the horde's right wing.

NOOR A JAHANGIR

The wing buckled, the shockwave flowing through the ranks. The Trollking, having hacked his way to the wall, pushed his way through to the lancers and began to cut them down.

The riders struggled to disengage as the Ranushan infantry retreated to the gates. A hail of arrows fell from the walls to cover their withdrawal. Missiles bounced off the Trollking's human-forged armour as he strode after the lancers. He marched right up to the gates as they slammed shut behind the last of them. He roared a challenge to the city, daring them to come out and fight him. Slowly, his horde gathered behind him. His challenge went unmet.

The months that followed were less dramatic than the opening gambit of the siege. Regular shipments by longboat from Maidenhall kept the city from starving, whilst his own followers fought over the meagre rations delivered over land, by their reluctant human allies. The local wildlife was hunted down to extinction until even the birds knew not to fly anywhere near the city.

The Trollking's forces dug trenches around the city, planted stakes to discourage cavalry charges and set patrols to keep a watch on the walls. Any scouts or refugees captured were tortured in plain sight of the walls. But the gates remained closed.

When violent squabbles broke out amongst the goblin-tribes and the trolls, Vermin suggested a distraction. Teams were organised and sent back into the marsh to attempt the capture of nicors. Vermin hoped to break them in and train them for use as cavalry. Other teams were despatched to the heavily forested hills to chop down trees to make a battering ram and ladders.

The battering ram failed to make an impression on the gates of Ranush, but it did elicit a response from the defenders. Boiling oil was poured over the ramparts of the gatehouse onto the ram-crew. The ladders proved much more successful and led to the first all-out attack on the city walls.

The assault lasted three hours, as defenders desperately threw down ladder after ladder. A great cry went up, from both sackers and defenders alike, as the goblins established a foothold on a small section of the wall.

The occupation lasted a full ten minutes before the bodies of the goblins were thrown back down.

THE CHANGELING KING

The battle ended when the alvor realised it was more effective to pull up the ladders instead of throwing them down. The goblins returned to camp shamefaced and were given a flogging for their failure. Morale flagged and that night marked the first desertion from the Trollking's force. It was not to be the last.

More ladders were crafted and Vermin ordered the units to attack different sections of the wall, to work out where best to focus the attack. Hills were quarried for stones to use as missiles.

The siege continued as summer turned to autumn, and autumn turned to winter. The price of failure grew steeper as the Trollking started to butcher his own troops. More of them slipped away into the hills.

The supply wagons failed to arrive as the first snows rimmed the hide tents and frosted the tops of the city walls. Vasch was dispatched with a warband to investigate. He returned a week later to report that Maidenhall had taken to raiding the supply route.

Starvation quickly set in and the winter began to take its toll. The weak amongst them died and became food. There were no more deserters, but the city gate's remained closed.

The Trollking took to riding a big bull nicor along the west wall each evening. The odd arrow would bounce harmlessly off his armour, but the Ranushans remained behind the gates, knowing that it was only a matter weeks before the Trollking's horde would break or begin cannibalising itself. It was then that Vermin entered the Trollking's hut.

'I have a plan, but it is highly dangerous. Especially for me.'

The Trollking snorted in derision. He had opened the last cask of ale and was sipping slowly from the rim.

'Within the keep, in the main tower, there is a room warded by seals. Within this room is a cauldron pool that is a source of magical energy and a gateway to the Void.

'Though you are my liege in this world, I have other masters. They are beings of great power that exist in a different dimension, far from our world. If we can reach the pool, I can summon them to aid you. But there will be a cost.'

NOOR A JAHANGIR

'How will you enter the city? Have you forgotten the walls and the alvor?' Bergtatt chuckled, the edge of madness glimmering in his eyes.

'Do you not recall how we escaped from Ranush all those years ago?'

The Trollking was silent for a few moments.

'Worm, why did you not remind me of this path before now? We could have sent down our troops and taken the city from inside.'

'Forbearance, my liege, I beg you. Do you not remember how narrow the passage was and how quietly we had to proceed? We would never have been able to get enough troops into the city without being found out.'

The Trollking put down the cask and stood up, towering above the goblin, a giant even amongst the trolls. He grabbed Vermin's robes in a gauntleted fist and hauled him up to his deformed face. The goblin began to speak rapidly.

'My lord, I plan on only five of us entering the city. I will need three shamans to assist me in breaking the seals and opening the gateway. We could slip in quietly and do the deed before anyone is any wiser. What other choice do we have?'

The stench and the darkness of the tunnel brought back memories that he had buried with his name; of cages, of torment and the murder he had committed. Down he followed Vermin and his shamans, into the sewers and then on to the dungeons. They climbed up into the keep, slitting the throats of slumbering guards and hiding the bodies in dark corners. The killing and the threat of capture intoxicated the Trollking, until his blood sang in his ears and his mind fluttered ever closer to madness.

Ever higher they climbed until Vermin signalled that they had reached their destination. The shamans set to marking the reinforced doors with symbols that crawled across his vision. The Trollking clutched the hilt of his sword, his senses in a swoon as the strangeness of this night drew closer to its climax.

Finally, Vermin let out a long drawn out a sigh.

'Is it done?' asked the Trollking.

THE CHANGELING KING

Vermin nodded. The Trollking drew his sword, threw the doors open and strode into the chamber beyond. The goblins lit torches, flooding the room with light. The cauldron pool stood in the centre, its surface dark and flat. He walked around the pool and over to a stone throne, built into the far wall. He drew his sword then settled down, resting his blade across his lap. Vermin began to chant and his assistants sketched more shapes and symbols on the pool's rim with charcoal.

The pool began to bubble.

A dark form rose up through the oily surface.

'My master,' said Vermin, dropping to his knees and bowing his head.

'Why has my servant summoned me?'

'Master, we are in need of your aid. I bring you Bergtatt, the Trollking, Overlord of Kryllon. He wishes to make a pact with you.'

'I require sacrifice,' said the wraith as it struggled to maintain definition.

Without warning, the Trollking leapt from the throne and cut down a shaman. The others tried to flee, but he was faster. Soon all three lay on the ground crying pitifully for mercy. They knew what was to come next. He carried the writhing goblins one-by-one to the pool and threw them in. The bodies disappeared without even a bubble on the pool's surface to mark their demise.

'More,' said the wraith.

The Trollking clenched Vermin's arms from behind.

'No, you need me,' pleaded Vermin.

'Yes. Your sacrifice will serve both of your masters,' said the Trollking.

Vermin struggled to free himself but the Trollking raised him up and cast him in. The goblin's thrashing limbs did little to help him. He sank as quickly as the others. The wraith's form shuddered.

'I serve only myself,' said the Trollking, waving a clenched fist to emphasis his words. 'You will do as I demand, and in return, you will get all you desire.'

NOOR A JAHANGIR

A dry rattling sound came from the demon. Laughter. The Trollking suddenly felt very cold and alone.

Vasch woke that night to the sound of the sky falling. Sulphur burnt holes in the ozone as smouldering meteorites pummelled Ranush. Terrible screams rose from the city. The gates were thrown open as alvor poured out in all directions. The Trollking's lieutenants quickly marshalled their troops and fell upon the terrified refugees.

Vasch found a barely touched cask of ale in the Trollking's hut. He took it outside and settled down to watch the slaughter.

CHAPTER 31: MAIDENHALL
KRYLLON

Nathan leaned low over the neck of his horse, fighting to keep his eyes open. The girls had talked him out of calling it Darth Vader. Instead he had settled on Onyx. Salina, the most experienced rider amongst them, had taken the lead on Moonlight. Katrina and Logan brought up the rear on Chocolate and Fire.

They had walked their horses for most of the night, afraid of laming them by misstep. Daybreak had brought the first rain of the autumn. The trail led them to a valley through the northern range of the Pervilheln Mountains. The valley was verdant and busy with small creatures desperately preparing for the winter's hibernation.

By afternoon, they cleared the mountains. Tired and wet, they set up a cold camp under the lea of a jutting rock face. They hadn't rested long before they heard the first horn blowing in the distance.

'Mount up, quick time,' shouted Nathan.

The four scrambled their gear together and clambered onto their horses.

'I see them,' said Salina.

They all turned to look. A posse was quickly moving along the valley floor. Nathan tugged on his reins to turn Onyx around and then heeled him into action. The others followed suit. Behind them, they heard the whoops and cries of their pursuers as they were spotted.

The uneven ground provided a number of opportunities for injury, made even more hazardous by the rain. Precious time was spent in navigating the toothy maze of rocky outcrops. Nathan desperately scanned the distance for open ground.

NOOR A JAHANGIR

Black-feathered arrows whistled over their heads.

Nathan turned in his saddle for a look. A warband of trolls and goblins, mounted on nicors, were clambering straight across the spiky terrain. Their leader didn't seem concerned by the loss of a few troops as they fell from their terrible steeds.

'They're gaining on us,' called Logan.

'Come on, ride harder. I can see open ground ahead,' urged Salina.

'I can't see it, are you sure?' said Nathan.

'Yes. It's not that far ahead.'

They urged their horses to gallop even faster until Nathan was sure one of them would fall. All around them he could hear projectiles clattering and smashing on the rocks. An arrow grazed his shoulder. Nathan gritted his teeth and leaned lower over his horse's neck. They crested a thrusting fault and leapt down to the promised open ground. Finally, given their head, the horses streamed away from the warband like ribbons caught in the wind. The nicors, though sure footed and powerful, were not built for speed. Soon the warband were left in the distance.

The four rode on at full steam until the horses tired, their flanks heaving and covered in frothy sweat. Nathan estimated that it would take the warband at least an hour and a half to narrow the gap. They continued at a more leisurely pace for another half hour. The rain stopped as the clouds rolled on to the East. Something sparkled on the horizon.

'What is that?' asked Katrina.

'It's like a part of a star broke off and fell to the earth,' said Salina.

Katrina snorted derisively. Salina glanced at her and smiled.

'It's Maidenhall, the city of the alvor. We'll be at its gates by nightfall,' said Nathan.

At midday, they came upon the river and walked the horses along its bank until they arrived at a fork. They persisted on until the current seemed slower and the water so clear that they could see the smooth, blue and grey stones that formed its bed. Bullet shaped fish, black, brown and dusty blue, darted about beneath the surface to avoid the snapping beaks of long-legged herons and diving kingfishers.

THE CHANGELING KING

The four stopped to drink from the river and fill their canteens. They used clumps of grass torn from the banks to the wipe down the horses and let them drink too. A little further on, they found a natural ford where they crossed over to the other side. The land was lush here, with leafy foliage spotted across the grassy landscape.

Maidenhall grew on the horizon until they could see its marble clad walls glowing gold in the waning sunlight.

'It's awesome,' said Katrina. 'It's like the whole wall has been crafted from a single sheet of marble.'

'The alvor summoned it up from the very ground and moulded it to form the city,' said Logan.

'You remembered that from our history lessons?' said Nathan incredulously, 'I thought I was the only one who ever paid attention during class.'

They rode along the wall until they came upon the towers that flanked the main city gates. The warband wouldn't venture this close to the alvorn city, reasoned Nathan. Arazan had told them that the alvor spellweavers had cast a spell on the city to keep out all sentient beings. This would be as safe a spot as any for them to camp. After seeing to the horses' needs, they huddled together under their blankets and quietly munched on oatcakes and apples. Autumn in Kryllon was just as cold and dreary as autumn in England.

The sound of goblin horns roused them from a fitful slumber. They scampered to their feet and grabbed their weapons. It was still night but the sky was clear and the moon rode low over the horizon. The horses were nowhere in sight. Nathan cursed himself for an idiot. He should have insisted on tying them up for the night. Either way, it was too late for escape.

The warband had formed a semi-circle and advanced on them out of the night. Dross, the troll from Erskine, stood at the centre of the twenty-strong band. He wore a simple iron breastplate and fauld over a leather codpiece. The troll was heavily scarred and clenched a large, serrated blade.

The four fanned out to face off with the enemy. They had not practiced their close-quarter combat skills since their training. Only Nathan had been involved in the skirmish with goblins near Erskine.

Surprise had played a big hand in that victory, thought Nathan. This would be much more difficult. If any one of them hesitated, it would mean death for them all. Nathan couldn't let that happen. He had to do something, but what?

Logan raised his sword and stepped forward.

'Hey, you, ugly butt-munch, why don't you come out from behind your scummy cronies and take me on, one-on-one?' said Logan.

'You challenge me, pup?' snarled Dross. 'I'll tear out your guts. I'll hang them from them gates for the crows to eat. I am Dross Alvorslayer, the vilest, most vicious demon-spawn to have climbed out of the abyss. My sword has drunk the blood of heroes. You are nothing but a maggot to me, unworthy of my lowliest minion.'

'Great. Of all of the trolls in Kryllon, I picked a fight with the one that likes to talk. Stop gassing on like a goblin shrew and fight me.'

The troll roared.

'What's he doing?' asked Katrina.

'Trying to be a hero,' said Nathan, wondering if his brother was a match for this brutish warrior.

'I fear no one. I will crush you, worm. I will crush you beneath my boots,' said Dross.

'Yes, but what guarantee have I got that your underlings won't stick a knife in my back?' said Logan, swinging his arms back and forth to warm up his muscles.

'None of my warriors will interfere,' said Dross, 'can you say the same for your comrades?'

'You'll do us a favour by ridding us of him,' said Katrina, playing along, more confident in Logan's abilities than Nathan was. 'We've had to listen to him brag all the way from Alvorn Reach about how many trolls he was going to kill.'

Dross snorted and stalked forward. The troll dwarfed him by at least three feet in height and two feet in girth. Dross swung his cleaver down at Logan's head, but Nathan's brother span away to the side and swept his sword at the troll's legs. Dross parried the blow.

Logan twisted and brought his sword around clockwise, to chop at the troll's neck.

THE CHANGELING KING

Dross back-pedalled and countered with a blow that would have felled a tree. Logan rolled and tried to kick the troll's legs out from under him. Instead, Dross caught Logan in the chest with a heavy foot, sending him sprawling to the ground.

Despite being winded, Logan managed to regain his feet as Dross bore down on him with several slashes. Logan ducked and parried, making space with his footwork.

He followed through with lightning quick strikes of his own, coming in high and then low, intermittently. Dross managed to block a few, but his armour bore the brunt of the rest.

Raging, the troll let down his guard further to get in a mortal strike. More blows crashed against his armour, leaving silvery scars behind. The goblins jeered and shouted obscenities at both combatants, revelling in the violence.

Logan picked up the tempo. He followed a series of blows to the chest with a rising vertical cut that split the troll's black lips. Dross, blood gushing over his chin, charged at him again.

Logan sidestepped and slid his sword under the troll's arm. Dross dropped Logan with the pommel of his cleaver to the back of the head. Then he reversed his grip on the sword and raised it to pin Logan to the ground.

Nathan's heart lurched hard against his ribs. Salina's hand flew to her mouth and Katrina covered her eyes with a sob. The goblins leaned forward, frothing at the mouth in anticipation.

Dross coughed, a puzzled expression crossing his face. The cleaver dropped from nerveless fingers and the troll toppled forward.

Logan rolled clear and scampered to his feet. Sword held low, Logan moved cautiously towards Dross and pushed him over with his foot. The troll didn't stir.

Gasping for air, Logan staggered back to his companions. Katrina threw her arms around him. Nathan grinned with relief. The goblins exchanged confused glances, caught in an unexpected situation.

'What are you pus-suckers waiting for, kill the worms,' roared Jarnak, Dross's lieutenant.

The goblins attacked.

NOOR A JAHANGIR

Logan lay into the enemy with quick slashes and stabs, giving Katrina the space she needed to use her bow. Nathan and Salina fought back to back, wheeling around to defend each other.

The goblins closed in around them, forcing the four together. Soon the press of bodies made it difficult to swing their swords. Twice, they tried to break out from the siege of swords, but both times they were pushed back. These goblins were much more skilled than the ones Nathan had fought under the Pervilheln Mountains. They were clearly used to fighting as a unit. Only two of them had fallen so far. Nathan wondered which of his friends would die first.

A loud groaning, like a giant's yawn, brought about a momentary lull in the fight. The goblins fell back as the gates of the cursed city cracked open behind the four humans. Nathan and the others staggered back with them, as a blinding ray of dawn-light shot through the gap. Was it possible that the city had a defending force inside? Why hadn't Arazan told them about it? His heart quickened with hope.

A single warrior, armed with two curved-swords, stood silhouetted in the nimbus of molten light.

CHAPTER 32: UNEXPECTED ENCOUNTERS
KRYLLON

The sole warrior charged out of the alvorn city. Nathan felt despair touch him as he realised that salvation didn't wait beyond the gates. The warrior flew past Nathan and into the incredulous warband.

He moved through the enemy as if they were a mist parting for his blades. A trail of blood and death followed in his wake. His movement were conservative and minimal and yet his speed was inhuman. Nathan had never seen anyone fight with such fluid grace and deadly artistry. Not in real life anyway.

'This guy's kicking arse,' said Logan, wiping blood from his face. 'Come on, we have to help him. We can't let any of them escape. We can't risk them telling the Trollking that we're coming.'

The four re-entered the fray. Scattered by the newcomer, the goblins seemed to have lost their cohesion and with it their mystique. Heartened, the four fell on them with renewed vigour, letting their training take-over their movements. The fight was short.

When the adrenalin charge subsided, the stench of bodily fluids and churned earth hit the four with the consequence of their victory. All around them lay dismembered limbs and bodies bearing terrible wounds. Salina dropped to her knees, her body shaking with nausea. Nathan too felt his stomach churning, his mind beset by the horrific vista created by their weapons. He doubled over as the contents of his stomach spewed from his mouth.

Once the spasms had passed, he looked at the others, careful to avoid the bodies scattered around him. Katrina and Salina sat huddled together with their arms around each other. They rocked slowly back and forth, their eyes closed to the horror. Logan walked over to the wall and leaned against it, gazing at the sky, lost in thought.

Meanwhile, the stranger moved from body to body, seeing the grisly task through to the end.

Nathan walked over to the girls. His muscles had started to cool and he could feel the stiffness setting in. Sunlight flowed over the city's wall. Nathan offered both of his hands to the girls to help them up.

'Let's get our things together and get away from here,' said Nathan.

Logan straightened and raised his blade in warning. The stranger approached. There was something regal about his gaunt face, despite the dark circles under his hazel eyes. A burr of hair shadowed his upper lip and chin. His armour wasn't really made of gold as Nathan had first thought. It was contrived of curved strips of burnished bronze. It seemed to be designed for an alvor, but fit the painfully thin warrior snugly. He held his swords in a relaxed grip by his side.

'Thank you for helping us,' said Nathan in the alvorn tongue.

The wild-haired warrior shrugged and jabbered something back in a language that Nathan had never heard before. Nathan tried again in Common. The warrior became agitated and began to speak even faster, his wide eyes flitting from face to face. Finally he yelled in exasperation and signalled for them to follow him into the city.

'What about the curse?' asked Salina.

'Well, it's probably safer in there than it will be out here,' said Nathan, reverting back to English. 'I say we play along with this guy and see what we can learn from him, though I don't know how. He must be from the continent. His skin is too tanned to be native to Kryllon.'

'Ha,' yelled the warrior, causing them all to jump. 'Ha, Ha,' he yelled again. He began to jump from foot to foot and jabbered to himself.

'This guy's stark raving bonkers,' said Katrina.

The warrior stopped and looked at Katrina as if waiting for her to say something else. When Katrina didn't speak he began to scratch his head furiously. Then suddenly he stopped and fixed them with an intense stare. He began to speak slowly, as if trying to remember the correct words. The four looked at each other and shook their heads.

THE CHANGELING KING

The warrior shook his head too and then motioned for them to follow him through the gates.

Nathan's eyes devoured his new surroundings as the strange warrior guided them onto an avenue lined with generously proportioned houses and shops made from unlined marble. Quartz obelisks stood on each street corner, engraved with alvorn symbols, naming the street and providing directions to public spaces. The gates closed shut behind them, to the sound of clinking chains. They followed the warrior up the main avenue, marvelling at the way trees, grass and flowers greeted them in the most unexpected places. They thrilled at the fountains raised at exact intervals.

The deeper they went into the city, the more spectacular the architecture became. But despite its beauty, its emptiness began to wear on their nerves. The market squares, parks and playgrounds were vacant. Even the birds had abandoned its sky.

Nathan came to a startled halt as the warrior spun around and began to speak rapidly again.

'He's speaking a European language,' exclaimed Salina from behind him, 'It sounds like Portuguese or Spanish or something.'

The others crowded forward as the stranger shook his head, more to himself than at them and spoke again. This time they all understood what he said, despite his archaic accent.

'You speak English?'

'Sultan bin Suleiman, Prince of Azamabad? That's your name then?' asked Nathan.

The warrior nodded his head vigorously.

'And you came here how, exactly?'

'I myself do not understand how. One second I am in a cave meditating, then suddenly I am not.'

'Does this mean that there is another portal that leads to Earth?' asked Katrina.

'If our friend is who he says he is, the portal doesn't lead to our time,' replied Nathan.

NOOR A JAHANGIR

The enigmatic Sultan led them deeper into the lost city. He seemed to be taking them to a large palace with spires that rose high above the quartz-tiled roofs of the smaller dwellings.

'How is that possible?' asked Salina.

'It's like Shadel'ron explained to us. The portals exist outside of the normal continuum of space and time,' said Nathan.

'What does that mean in English?' snapped Katrina.

'It means that if you're lucky enough to find a portal that leads to the world of your choice, it may not take you to the time of your choice. For example, the portal we came through is in twenty-first century England. Sultan, on the other hand, is from the Indian sub-continent, a few hundred years before our time.'

'Which means, we're stuck here unless we can somehow penetrate a city guarded by goblins and trolls, slip into the fortress of a freak that makes Hitler look like Mandela, and then locate a paddling pool that doubles as a magical gateway,' said Katrina.

'Well, you don't have to sound so cheerful about it,' sulked Salina.

Katrina grinned.

'So, um, friend, how did you come to learn English?' asked Nathan.

'An Englishman taught me.'

Sultan suddenly cocked his head to one side as if listening for something. He turned around slowly on the spot, his eyes shut tight. Salina jumped as his eyes snapped open again. He raised a finger to his lips.

A dozen shadows detached themselves from the cover of nearby buildings and surrounded them in a ring of spearheads. A dozen more appeared on the rooftops. More still charged up steps from the boulevard below until there was no direction for escape. Nathan raised his hands and called to the others to remain calm. These were not trolls or goblins, but armoured and helmeted alvor.

'Stand down, stay your weapons,' commanded a familiar voice.

An alvor stepped through the closed ranks of spears and removed his helm to reveal the bronze hair and diamond-hard eyes of the Captain of the Alvorn Guard. Arazan. Salina and Katrina squealed in delight and threw their arms around the flustered alvor.

THE CHANGELING KING

'So, my friends, how have you come to be roaming the streets of Maidenhall?'

The alvor had escorted the five humans to the harbour district, to a wharf which, for the first time in almost a century, had an Alvorn longboat in dock. The vessel featured a single mast mid-deck and a row of oars on either side. Alvorsong was the name carved into the hull. The Alvorn fleet flecked the coastal waters beyond.

Nathan and the others exclaimed in wonder.

'How goes the war effort, Captain?' asked Logan.

'General Tinuvil has thirty longboats, with a hundred alvor on each, numbering my own Alvorn Guard amongst them. The Archmagus has communicated that Lord Gillieron and Lady Merenwen have been successful in garnering the support of the dvargarn kings. Ten thousand dvargar now wait south of Ranush for our signal.

'But you still haven't answered my own question yet. This city was enclosed in the most powerful force-field our Spellweavers have ever created. It would have taken the concentrated effort of twenty of them to lift the spell.'

'We didn't do anything, Captain, honestly,' assured Salina, afraid that they had somehow offended the Alvorn people.

Nathan quickly told the alvor about their journey from the watchtower, leaving out any mention of Shadel'ron and the shadow-wolf. He ended with the skirmish outside the walls and the role that Sultan had played.

'His colouring is different from yours, how can you be sure he is of your home world?' asked Arazan.

'He speaks the languages of our world and doesn't understand a word of Common,' said Logan.

'He could be a spy.'

'The way he cut into those goblins, I wouldn't think so.'

'The Trollking has no qualms in slaughtering his own to accomplish his goals.'

NOOR A JAHANGIR

Nathan looked at Sultan, who gazed at a lonely cloud in the sky with the intensity of someone searching for answers. Then, rather abruptly, he looked his way and gave him a big goofy smile. Disarmed, Nathan found himself smiling back.

'Even if he isn't a spy, it still does not explain how he came to be here,' Arazan continued. 'The barrier-field erected by the spellweavers extends above and below the city. Neither a bird, nor a mole could enter.'

'We haven't really had much of a chance to speak to him yet,' said Nathan.

'Though he's really useful in a fight,' added Logan.

'We will take him prisoner until we can present him to Lord Gillieron or Captain Tinuvil,' said Arazan.

'No, he doesn't belong here,' said Logan, moving to stand beside Sultan. Katrina moved to join him, as did Salina. 'He is not of your world. He will stay with us.'

'As you wish. I was only thinking of your safety,' said Arazan, his ears drooping slightly.

'You are going to the horrible place?' queried Sultan tentatively. 'You are going to the city of monsters?'

'Yes, we are headed to Ranush, the city of the Trollking,' said Salina.

'You've been there?' asked Katrina.

'I escaped. That is a bad place. Do not go there.'

'What is he saying?' asked Arazan.

'He's been to Ranush,' said Nathan.

Arazan drew his sword. 'He will tell me everything he knows, or I will strike him down as the Trollking's spy.'

In between moments of panic and hysteria, Sultan related his nightmare journey out of Ranush. When Nathan finished translating Sultan's story into Alvorn, Arazan sat back and stroked his ears.

'Do you realise what this means?' said Arazan. 'This madman, if you can convince him, can lead you straight into the keep itself.'

'That's good, because, we were still a bit sketchy on that part of the plan,' said Nathan.

THE CHANGELING KING

'This changes everything,' said Arazan.

'It does?' said Katrina, not liking the emphasis on everything.

'Absolutely it does. I'm going to reassign a squad of twelve of my best to accompany you to the city. Once you penetrate the keep, you will continue your quest alone. Their mission will be to get the gates of the keep open. If we capture the keep, the battle will be over. However, increasing the size of your party also increases the risk of discovery. All of this depends on whether this human remembers the way back and is willing to guide you.'

'Sultan, will you take us to Ranush?' Salina asked in English.

'You want me to take you to the bad place?' Sultan asked incredulously.

'Yes, but only if you want to,' said Salina squeezing his hand between both of her own.

'I get to kill the monsters that hurt me?' asked Sultan.

'Very likely,' said Nathan.

'Then I will take you. I will kill the evil ones,' said Sultan, with such finality that it sent a shiver up Nathan's spine.

'Great,' said Arazan, bemused. 'The fate of our world hinges on the fancy of a lunatic. It's usually Lord Gillieron who banks on such odds, but here I am. Squad Leader Anaemus will lead the warriors I am sending with you, but ultimate command will fall to you Nathan, at least until you reach the keep.'

Squad Leader Anaemus, a particularly prosaic looking alvor, with gold-dust skin, nodded and went off to select his squad.

'Nathan, Logan, Katrina and Salina, I must beg leave of you now. Our scouts will be returning from the rendezvous with Lord Gillieron's dvargar. Farewell. May Kige watch over you.'

CHAPTER 33: HARWOOD TOWER
ENGLAND

'Karen, you're bleeding. Stop the car.'

Karen looked pale. The car slowed until it was barely doing twenty miles per hour.

'I can't reach it. Adam, can you see what it is?' she asked, her words starting to lisp together.

Adam nodded, even though he felt like he was going to throw up.

'There's an arrow sticking out of your back. You have to stop the car,' said Adam.

Karen looked ready to pass out. Adam caught sight of a sign out of the windscreen for a picnic area, two hundred yards ahead. Karen steered the car into a small car park and parked haphazardly. Adam unclipped his belt, got out and ran around to open Karen's door. Karen took his hand and allowed him to lead her over to a wooden picnic table, covered in scribbled doodles and mildew.

'Adam, I need you to be brave for me,' said Karen. 'I need you to pull out the arrow.'

Adam found himself struggling to hold back tears of panic. He didn't know what to do. Desperately, he prayed that Karen wouldn't die. She leaned over the table and braced herself. Adam wrapped his fingers gingerly around the bolt. Karen winced.

'Adam, I want you to yank it out – as straight as you can. The arrow might be barbed, so we don't want to risk damaging anything in there, okay? Now, I'm going to count to three and then I want you to pull. One, two . . .'

Karen screamed as Adam tugged at the quarrel until it slid loose. Blood welled up to fill the puncture hole and began to gush out.

THE CHANGELING KING

Karen went limp against the table. The blood continued to flow. Adam felt panic clawing up his throat. He felt like screaming for help and running away, but he knew he couldn't leave her. She would die if he didn't do something right away.

He ran back to the car and grabbed Karen's coat from his seat. He tried to tear a sleeve off but the stitching held firm. So he used the whole coat to press down on the wound.

How long was he supposed to do this for? He had no idea, so he kept checking every few minutes to see if it had slowed. It seemed to be working. Adam went back to car, hoping that the taxi driver had a First Aid kit. He searched in the glove compartment and found an old mobile phone. It had one bar left on the battery. He shoved it in his pocket and continued to look around the inside of the car. Finally, he opened the boot and was relieved to see a green box strapped to one side. He took the box over to the picnic table and tipped the contents out next to Karen. She was still out cold.

Adam pulled out the phone from his pocket and keyed in a number from memory. The call went straight to voicemail.

'Dad? It's Adam here. Your son. I don't know if you're still alive somewhere. I really hope you are. Maybe you've lost your memory and have a new family or something. But if you get this message, I want you to know that I miss you a lot.

'The thing is, we... mum, Salina and me... we're in a lot of trouble and could really do with you coming home. Dad... I love you and I'm... I still believe in you.'

By the time Karen awoke, he had cleaned and dressed the wound as best as he could. He helped Karen sit up slowly. She reached back under her shirt to feel for the wound and was surprised to find it bound up. Adam blushed.

'Did you do this?' she asked.

'Um, yeah. I made a bit of a mess of it. I ended up using all of the dressings. Um, I had to lift your shirt up.' said Adam, his face glowing bright red.

'How else would you have put it on?' said Karen. 'Adam, you may just have saved my life. Thank you.'

NOOR A JAHANGIR

She leaned forward and kissed Adam on the cheek. Adam's heart pounded so hard in his chest that he wondered how Karen did not hear it. He could not help grinning. Karen stood up slowly, breathing hard and obviously still in pain.

'I don't suppose you know how to drive?' she asked.

'I'll give it a go,' said Adam. 'Can't be too different from the games.'

'I was kidding,' said Karen.

The driver's seat in the Avensis was saturated with Karen's blood. Adam retrieved a tartan-patterned travel blanket from the boot and draped it over the seat. It took Karen a couple of minutes to manoeuvre herself into the car. She struggled to turn the key to start the car but couldn't raise her arm high enough.

'It looks like you're going to get to drive after all. My arm is too stiff and it'll only get worse as we go on. I'll just have to give you a quick tutorial.'

It took Karen five minutes to get out and get back in on the other side. Adam slid into the driving seat and clutched the steering wheel eagerly.

'Adjust your seat so you can comfortably reach the pedals,' said Karen, 'There should be a lever under the seat to slide the seat forward. There is another lever to the side that adjusts the seat height. Good. Now adjust the mirrors so you can see behind yourself. Now turn the key in the ignition to start the car.'

The car started with a rumble. Karen was about to continue her tutorial when Adam stuck the automatic gearshift into drive, released the handbrake and jammed both feet down on the accelerator. The car bounced over the kerb and tore across the grassy verge. It swerved onto the road, the tyres still spinning from the sudden acceleration.

'Yup, just like the games,' said Adam. 'The accelerator is a little more sensitive but the handling is a lot better.'

'Does your game follow the British Highway Code?'

Night drew its shroud over the world. Karen had dozed off again. Adam glanced at the speedometer for the hundredth time to make sure he wasn't breaking the speed limit. He was getting the hang of this. As long as he didn't have to turn left or right, Adam was fine.

'What time is it?' asked Karen, rubbing her eyes with her left hand.

'Just gone past six, Karen. It's getting too dark, I can't see anything.'

'Try switching on the headlights.'

'Oh, okay. Yeah, that's much better, thanks.'

Karen opened the glove compartment and rooted around to see what the driver kept in there. She found a pair of reading glasses, a bar of chocolate and a bunch of street maps. She switched on the overhead light and began to take a closer look at the maps.

'Adam, we should be coming to a side-road soon. On the right, I think. I want you take it.'

'Side-road, got it,' replied Adam. 'Is this it?'

Adam slowed the car right down before attempting the turn. Luckily, there weren't any other cars on the road; otherwise, he may have bottled it. The tyres squealed dramatically as he pulled on to a steep un-surfaced road. The road grew increasingly narrow and bumpy with potholes. Eventually it levelled out and the tower house loomed out in the headlights. Adam stomped on the footbrake, stopping the car as suddenly as he had started it. Karen swore as a fresh bout of pain shot through her shoulder.

'Sorry. Where did that come from?' said Adam.

'Harwood Tower's been here for over five hundred years. Put the gear into park and pull the handbrake up. This is where we're spending the night.'

Karen felt light-headed and weak. Her shoulder was on fire. Adam had done admirably to patch her up, but the wound needed to be checked by a doctor. Even a little bit of dirt or cloth from her shirt could turn the wound septic. But that would have to wait until tomorrow. The tower wasn't the most hospitable location, but they needed to get off the road and get some rest.

The darkness obscured all but the three storey height of the tower and its square base. Karen banged on the door, not expecting anyone to be in. The door creaked then fell inwards, sending up a cloud of dust that left them coughing.

'Well that was lucky,' said Adam.

Once inside, Karen spent a few minutes looking for a light switch. Grimy tube lights crackled to life. The tower smelt of damp and urine. Dust lay thick over everything, but scuffed prints on the ground suggested that someone had been here quite recently. It took both Karen and Adam to lift the heavy door up and to push it back into place. They barricaded the door with a couple of rickety chairs, a wonky table and a heavy display case, which they pushed across the protesting floor.

The first floor was almost as bland as the ground floor, with three narrow windows and a couple of empty display cases. There were more display cases on the second floor, as well as a number of sturdy wooden benches. The third floor proved more interesting, with five suits of armour standing vigil, complete with weapons, draped with lacy patina of cobwebs. Moth eaten tapestries hung on the walls, depicting battle-scenes in faded colours.

'These will make good blankets,' said Karen aloud.

'Karen, there's another set of stairs back here,' said Adam, who had been inspecting the armour.

'They must go up to the battlements. Adam, help me with these tapestries, they're heavy. There's a bit less of a draft on the second floor. We can sleep on the benches.'

Back on the second floor, they dragged the benches together to form a cot for each of them, over which they spread the tapestries. With the housekeeping done, they set about checking their ammunition and reloading the weapons. Finally, they turned out the lights and lay down on their improvised cots.

'These benches are too hard and the bits in the middle stick into my back,' moaned Adam.

'You could always sleep on the floor.'

'No, that's okay, it's not too bad if you slide down to one side,' conceded Adam.

Karen lay on her good side, with her arm folded beneath her head. The arrow slits had been widened at some point in the tower's history to accommodate windows. A little bit of celestial light managed to penetrate the grime. It wasn't enough to see by, but it served to fool her eyes into forming shapes in the darkness. The shapes became faces from her past.

She was still awake a few hours later, when the sound of screeching metal woke Adam. Something was wrecking their stolen car. A glance out of the window confirmed her worst fears. The trolls had found them again.

CHAPTER 34: MORBIUS MARSH
KRYLLON

Nathan and the others spent the night in a beautiful villa in the eastern quarter of Maidenhall, the hereditary home of squad-leader Anaemus. The villa was built of smoky white quartz, fitted together like an elaborate jigsaw puzzle, with verandas enclosing all of its elevations. The awnings were tiled with over-lapping hexagons of mother-of-pearl.

When dawn broke, despite the quartz spangled sunlight, none of them felt like getting up. In the end, the promise of a hot bath and the delicious aroma of a cooked alvorn breakfast drew them out of their silken cocoons.

After breakfast, Anaemus took them to the armoury and found them some new plate armour and helmets that bore curved cranial ridges. Each segment of armour was embossed with a sunburst over four wavy lines.

'What does this symbol mean?' asked Katrina, running her fingers over the blaze.

'It's the device of Maidenhall's City Guard,' Anaemus replied. 'Here, use this oil to blacken your armour. It wouldn't do for us to be spotted shining like slivers of amber in dragon dung.'

They left the city through the main gates and then walked along the wall and across a prairie. Anaemus set an economical pace. The grass underfoot was made slippery by a morning shower. Nathan felt clumsy in his new armour, uncomfortable with the way the plates moved and rubbed against his body. Besides, he had always hated cross-country running. The alvor moved soundlessly and silently, using hand signals to communicate with each other. To Nathan it seemed like they hardly even breathed. The five humans, in comparison, sounded like a stampeding herd of elephants.

An hour later, they arrived at a crumbling ruin of a bridge spanning the eastern branch of the Caprice. It would have been troublesome for an army to cross, but the party leapt the distance without mishap.

Sultan took the lead as the terrain deteriorated into a squalid and smelly marshland. Dirty grey-brown bogs dotted the landscape. The alvor began to lose their unassailable cool as the air became thick with grotesquely fat meat-flies. Heavy, oily vapours rose from the ground, so dense that even the brave sun had difficulty penetrating its recesses. Their boots squelched and sank into the greedy mud, releasing a sulphurous gas each time they wrenched them clear. Nathan tore some material from the frayed edge of his cloak and shoved a piece in both of his nostrils. Progress was slow, though the madman's route seemed the best they could hope for.

The armour that they had so admired in Maidenhall now seemed like an excessive burden. Their eyes streamed from the stench and their noses dripped mercilessly. From all around them came the chirping of insects, the bass grumping of bullfrogs and the sinister sound of snakes rasping their scale together in warning. Salina swore after a huge meat-fly nearly flew into her mouth. Nathan smiled despite his own discomfort. He took even greater satisfaction from the suffering of the alvor. Their sensitive noses must be going through hell.

'This is ridiculous,' said one of the alvor as his right leg sank all the way up to his knee in an exceptionally smelly puddle. 'We're not getting anywhere. We shouldn't be following this mad human.'

'Silence your belly-aching and use your nose, soldier,' said Anaemus. 'There is a definite hint of sea-air blowing from the northeast. Mad he may be, but the human has a keen sense of direction.'

Darkness came early in the marsh and with it the clamour of the nightlife. Large predators that spent the day asleep beneath the mud emerged to hunt. Nathan spotted a nicor slipping through the reeds, a three meters long snake dangling from its maw as it slid into a murky pool. A torch or two would have been comforting, but Nathan knew that Anaemus wouldn't allow it. Instead, he grabbed Salina's hand and gave it a gentle squeeze. She smiled in return and moved closer to him.

'How do you know where you are going?' Nathan asked Sultan.

'I'm following my tracks. My tiger tracks, then my snake tracks,' replied the madman, pointing to the ground. 'Then more tracks.'

'Why did I even ask,' said Nathan aloud.

One of the alvor stepped on a marsh viper and narrowly avoided being bitten. The viper hissed angrily as it slipped away. It was getting too dangerous to travel without light.

They found a fairly dry patch of heather and settled down for a cold meal and another night under the stars. Anaemus assigned watch to his squad, allowing the humans to sleep undisturbed. Nathan was glad the alvor had come along. He had been dreading this part of the journey. Now some of the uncertainty had been lifted off his shoulders. It would have been even better if they had come along the whole way with them.

The night air was just as soupy and infested with flying insects. The ground heaved with all manner of creepy-crawlies. Nathan shuddered as a small bog snake slid over his hand, trying to get into his bed roll. He picked it up between two fingers and threw it in the direction of the nearest puddle. A fire would have been really nice, he thought to himself.

Everybody was up early the next morning and out of sorts. They shook out their sleeping rolls and picked out bugs from their hair and clothes before making quick work of breakfast. By dawn, they were on their way again.

An hour before noon, they ran into an enemy patrol.

The alvor fell upon the goblins without preamble. It was over in under a minute. The alvor cleaned their blades and dumped the bodies in a bog. Nathan looked down and saw that his own sword was in his hand and dripping blood. The blade slipped from his fingers. Salina and Katrina looked pale and close to being sick again. It was becoming too easy to kill.

At midday, they spotted a greasy smudge shimmering in the distance. Sultan stopped in his tracks and began to shiver.

THE CHANGELING KING

'I think you should tie my hands now.'

'Don't be daft, we're not tying you up,' said Logan.

'No, it's best if you did. I do not have many moments of lucidness, I know. But now I need you to put your trust in me and tie my hands,' said Sultan in earnest.

'What is he saying?' asked Anaemus, his eyes narrow with suspicion.

'Please, I beseech you, do this for me. I fear my memories of that place will unman me. You must do as I ask.'

The four companions stared silently at Sultan. For a moment he seemed transformed, mysterious and majestic. Katrina stepped forward with a length of rope and did as he had asked. The alvor watched incredulously as Logan took one end of the rope and began to walk beside Sultan.

'He requested we tie him up, in case he goes berserk,' explained Katrina in Common.

The party encountered two more patrols on their way to the city. The first they despatched in a similar fashion to the last. The second time they hid in the tall reeds, to avoid being spotted from the city walls.

The day had waned by the time they came upon the tunnel entrance. The stench of carrion rose from the hole, carrying over the smells of the marsh. The madman began to shiver uncontrollably. Logan placed a hand on his shoulder to reassure him. Even the alvor stepped back, daunted by the sense of evil emanating from within. This had once been the seat of the High Kings and a city of alvor. Now it was a charnel house of misery and doom. Nathan suddenly found himself unwilling to step forward into the dark maw of the tunnel. He would have run, had not Salina squeezed his hand and stepped forward. The spell was broken. The others followed until the darkness swallowed them whole.

CHAPTER 35: THE LAST STAND
ENGLAND

The last shell in Karen's shotgun exploded into the top of a troll's helmet. The troll, who had been trying to scale the tower, fell back onto its comrades, followed shortly by the now redundant shotgun. Karen pulled her head back from the arrow slit just as a crossbow quarrel shattered against the stonework.

'They're going to come through the front door. Adam, we have to set up barricades, slow them down.'

Adam nodded and ran down the steps with Karen behind him. Together, they dragged the display cases to block the steps leading to the ground floor, before returning to the second floor and doing the same again. This was it, thought Karen. There was no other way out of this place. All that stood between them and the trolls was some ancient furniture. When they had dragged the last of the benches into place, they heard the front door being smashed open.

'We need weapons, Adam. I've only got one magazine left in my pistol.'

'How about the stuff on the third floor?' asked Adam.

Karen and Adam sprinted up to the next level where the dust coated suits of armour stood silent vigil. The swords were so rusty that they were stuck fast to the gauntlets that held them. Adam managed to pull a buckler free and slipped it onto his left arm. Karen salvaged a chain mace and a long triangular shield with a faded insignia painted on its face. Before they could start on the armour, the sound of wood splintering and glass smashing came from below. The trolls were already breaking through the first floor barricade. Karen took Adam's hand and led him to the battlements.

THE CHANGELING KING

The stairwell was narrow and steep, the steps covered in moss and fungus. At the top of the stairs they found a wooden trapdoor, warped and bearing the scars of water damage. Karen felt around for a lock mechanism until her fingers found a smallish padlock and a draw bolt. Karen grabbed the padlock and pulled, hoping that the rust had done its work here too. The draw-bolt creaked as if in agony. Karen pulled harder until the bolt and faceplate tore free, showering them both with chunks of rotten wood. Karen pushed the trapdoor upwards but it didn't want to shift.

'Adam come up here and help me push. Get your shoulder up against it.'

Adam slid alongside her and put his back against the trapdoor. Karen counted to three and then pushed with all her might, ignoring the twinges in her shoulder. The trapdoor groaned as they continued to exert themselves against it. It gave suddenly, falling away from them with a crash.

Karen and Adam ducked back down to pick up their newly acquired weapons. As they straightened, they were confronted by the snarling face of a troll.

The troll reached in through the stairwell and grabbed them both, in one hand each, yanked them up and then threw them across the ramparts. Karen landed hard and screamed in pain as her wound tore open again. The contents of her handbag, including the pistol, skittered away from her.

The troll stalked towards her.

Karen rolled onto her hands and knees and scuttled after the gun. The troll intercepted her with a kick to the ribs, lifting her off the ground. Karen cried out again.

'Karen, your weapons!' called Adam from behind her.

Adam placed the mace on the shield and slid it across the floor. The troll snarled at Adam. Karen lunged for the mace, her fingers curling around the chain and swung it at the troll. The monster skipped back and removed an axe from its belt.

Karen forced her right arm through the straps of the shield, despite the excruciating pain pulsating from her shoulder. White spots filled her vision as she forced herself to stand up. Karen gritted her teeth and swung the mace again but the chain clattered against her shield, the ball falling short of its target. The troll leapt forward.

Three blows struck the shield in rapid succession, denting the shield and sending devastating waves of pain through her back. She would have dropped it then if she could only manoeuvre her arm out.

The troll backed away, bearing its tusk. Was it finding this amusing? She examined its face in the dim light, making note of a long scar that cut across its right eye. A milky white film covered the pupil. Maybe she could use that to her advantage. She pulled her arm back and swung again.

The troll swayed out of the way and made a grab for the chain, then yanked the weapon out of her hand. It placed a foot against Karen's shield and pushed. Karen staggered back. This was hopeless. Without a gun, she didn't stand a chance.

The troll began to bash away at Karen's shield, forcing her to her knees. She closed her eyes and waited for the death blow.

It didn't come.

Karen took a hesitant peek and found the troll staring at a dagger sticking out of its side.

Gunshots echoed above the tower. The troll toppled forwards, revealing Adam standing behind it, a wisp of smoke rising from the Glock clutched in his hands.

'Not that I'm being ungrateful, but you really shouldn't be messing with guns. Someone could get hurt.'

Adam gulped and blinked his eyes as if he had just woken up.

'Yeah, look what happened to this guy,' said Adam.

Karen pulled the twisted piece of metal off her arm and then accepted her gun from Adam. All she wanted to do was lie down and cry herself to sleep. But she knew the rest of the monsters were making their way up inside the tower. She looked around for something to weigh the trapdoor down. The battlements were covered with old bird droppings, lichen and not much else.

'Adam, help me drag this troll over there,' said Karen.

Adam slammed the trapdoor shut. Then they grabbed a leg each and drag the unbelievably heavy body over the warped square of wood. Finally, they added their own weight to the fleshy barricade and sat down on top of the troll.

'Yuck, it smells.'

'I don't think regular baths are high on their priority list, Adam,' said Karen, massaging her bruised arm and shoulder.

'You're bleeding again,' said Adam.

'Nothing we can do about that now.'

The trapdoor jerked. Karen and Adam threw their hands out for balance. It jerked again. Growling voices argued beneath them in an alien language. The stairwell had been almost too narrow for Karen and Adam to stand side-by-side. It would be even more difficult for the trolls to work together.

'So, how long do we need to keep this up?' asked Adam.

'I don't know.'

'Do you reckon they'll disappear when the sun comes up?'

'No, I don't think so. They've attacked us during the daytime before, remember?'

'Do you think someone will have heard all the noise?'

'We're literally in the middle of nowhere. The nearest house must be at least five miles away, Adam.'

'Well, at least try sounding positive,' yelled Adam.

'Okay, okay.'

'Well then?'

'I've got about fourteen bullets left and I only counted six of them outside.'

'We're going to die.'

The troll they were sitting on twitched.

CHAPTER 36: RANUSH

KRYLLON

The descent into the darkness of the tunnel was as terrible as anything that Nathan had experienced so far. The stench of decay and excrement grew stronger the deeper they went. It lacked the alien quality of the Belt, but still felt oppressive to a degree that they walked in a close huddle.

The orange glow of torchlight up ahead coaxed them forward. The party crept on, careful that the jingle of bronze links or the slap of a scabbard didn't give them away. Nathan realised that his jaw was clenched in a rictus grin and that he was breathing loudly through his nose.

Sultan suddenly yowled with such terror and rage that Logan let go of the rope securing him. Nathan felt the hairs rise on the back of his neck. The madman charged forward. Two silhouettes parted from the walls to block his path. Sultan ducked under the sweep of a club and then continued on. Still silent, the alvor surged forward, their cold swords biting into the trolls before they could raise the alarm.

The rest of the party emerged out of the tunnel into a sewer. Sultan was nowhere to be seen. The alvor slid the bodies into the slow moving sludge below the ledge they stood on. The bodies sank sluggishly from sight.

'What about Sultan?' Logan asked.

'What about him?' Nathan countered.

'Are we going to go look for him or what?'

'If we see him, we'll try and get him back. This place is like one huge, stinking maze. God knows how many more of these monsters are lurking around. No, I'm not going to risk messing this up by getting any of us killed.'

THE CHANGELING KING

'That makes sense, Logan,' said Anaemus. 'You have to look out for yourselves now. We have to keep moving. The longer we linger, the higher the risk of being discovered. Your friend has been here before and he can take care of himself.

'We are not far from our destination. I will take the lead from here. Once we hit ground level, we must part ways.'

'I would prefer it if you alvor stayed with us,' said Nathan.

'As much as I would like to oblige you, Master Nathan, I have my orders and you have your priorities.'

'Fine, lead the way then, alvor.'

Anaemus stiffened, his ears turning up sharply. Without another word, he began to move along the slimy ledge.

They soon found a door set in the curved, goo-covered wall. The alvor raised their swords as Logan hauled open the door. Through the doorway, three goblins sat on wooden crates, playing with dice.

They died without a sound, their dead faces twisted in surprise'.

The room led to a corridor lined with empty cells. Impossibly, the stench here was worse than that of the sewers. The dungeon corridor led to a set of stone stairs that ascended to a second level of prison cells. The cells here too were empty, though some bore rust coloured stains on the floor.

The corridor began to thrum with the distant sound of thunder.

'The siege has begun,' said Anaemus, in a hushed whisper.

To the south of Ranush, the dvargarn siege train began its bombardment of the outer walls. The captains and commanders of the Trollking's force gathered their warriors and made their way through the slums onto the parapet wall.

As the full might of Ranush rushed to take up position against the dvargar, the first of the alvorn longboats stole into the unguarded mouth of the long abandoned harbour. Balanced lightly on the bow-spirit of the Alvorsong, Captain Arazan called back directions to the alvor manning the tiller. The boat slid smoothly into dock.

NOOR A JAHANGIR

Outside the walls, standing amongst the rows of trebuchets and ballistae arranged on the last rise of the Higard Moors, Lord Gillieron, dressed in his bronze plate armour, watched the dvargarn siege-crews adjust the tension and tilt of their engines. One month of living with the dvargar had still not disspelled his admiration for their efficiency and ingenuity. Rocks were loaded into catapult cradles, huge bolts were fitted to ballista arms. The first salvo from the engines had already done considerable damage to the integrity of the wall.

'Ballista crews, ready!' shouted General Dedric, five foot tall and the same across, with large brawny arms sticking out from a mail-hauberk, decorated with beaten plates of gold and bearing the crest of the Pervilheln dvargar kings. His thick iron-coloured hair and beard sat under a conical helm, the curved blades of a golden axe forming slits through which his ice-blue eyes glowered. 'Trebuchet crews, ready! Both crews will fire on my command.'

The dvargar general raised his war hammer above his head.

'Fire at will.'

Wood creaked, counterweights dropped, and the air screamed as the engines unleashed their charges.

The defenders milled about on the walls in disarray. The crews scrambled to prepare their war-machines for the next salvo. The earth rumbled underfoot from aftershock as the missiles pounded into the wall.

Behind the siege-crews, the first wave of the dvargarn heavy infantry formed up; ten deep and a hundred wide, carrying reinforced wooden shields and long-handled axes.

Once the siege-engines had finished bombarding the wall, the General would unleash the dvargar secret weapon: the new war machine that Gillieron had glimpsed in the underground workshopss of Amundborg. The Glyptodonts.

As the ballista crews once again began to crank their engines, the city's defenders sent their first salvo of arrows from the wall. The air buzzed as the sky darkened, before the arrows thudded into the ground, too far out of range. Grimly, Gillieron watched as the siege-engines fired their third salvo. Trolls and goblins fell from the walls.

THE CHANGELING KING

The steps from the dungeons opened into a round chamber. Without a map of the keep's floor plan, they had no real way of knowing where they were. Anaemus slid along a wall to peek out of an arrow slit.

'This must be the western tower,' said Anaemus. 'I'd say that the great hall is probably along the main corridor. The Trollking's chamber will be high up in the central tower. My guess is that you'll find the stairs near the entrance to the great hall. Here we part ways. Good luck and may Kige watch over you.'

The squad leader signalled for his elite troops to advance. Nathan watched the alvor slink into the corridor, his jaw clenched in anger. The alvor had used them yet again for their own goals, abandoning them as soon as it suited their needs.

'Well, which way now?' Katrina asked.

'I think we've got a better chance if we climb this tower to the first floor and then head over to the central tower from there,' said Nathan, opening a door to check what was behind it.

'What about what Anaemus said?' asked Salina.

'That's the way they're headed. That's the way trouble is going to be. But your guess is good as good as mine. The stairs are right here, so, what do you want to do?' replied Nathan as he pulled the door open wider so they could see.

The others shrugged their shoulders. With a sigh, Nathan drew his sword and began to climb the stairs. This leadership thing wasn't all it was cracked up to be. He'd always thought that being in charge meant people would do as they were told without question. All he seemed to be doing was apologise, get interrogated and do the things no one else wanted to do.

The tower was chequered with shafts of light intruding through arrow slits. Cold air blew in but did little to dissipate the smell of urine and decay. The steps were covered with dry bat-droppings and other detritus. There was very little to suggest that the tower was in use.

A door broke up the monotony, though the stairs continued on upwards. Logan pushed it open. Rusty hinges squealed and the warped door scraped along the floor. Logan winced as Nathan threw him a dirty look.

NOOR A JAHANGIR

A cry of alarm preceded the sound of running feet, echoing along a broad corridor.

The four stepped through and fanned out. Salina drew back on her bow as distorted shadows danced towards them. She released before she even saw her target. The cloth-yard shaft whistled through the air and shattered on a troll's breastplate. A second arrow punched into flesh.

The troll that Salina had shot bore down on Nathan, a huge axe clasped in its hands. Nathan turned the first blow with the flat of his blade. Salina drew her hunting dagger and slammed it home between the troll's ribs.

The second troll charged at them, dragging its halberd along the floor. Katrina and Logan moved around Nathan to engage the new enemy. The troll heaved the halberd around, aiming to cut Katrina in half, but the girl rolled under the swipe. Logan attacked with a double-handed cut, which the troll deflected with its forearm. Katrina hamstrung the troll with a slash from behind. The troll threw out its arms as it toppled forward. Logan whipped out his dagger and rammed it into the base of its skull.

Meanwhile, Nathan had disarmed his opponent. The troll was on its knees, bleeding from several cuts and bristling with arrows. The four gathered around the dying monster. The troll removed its helmet, which it placed on the floor. Its eyes blinked rapidly, its breathing ragged from internal bleeding.

'Finish me,' the troll grunted in Common.

Nathan blanched and stepped back. He couldn't do it. He wouldn't kill in cold blood. Katrina and Salina shook their heads.

'Do not leave me to suffer. Finish me! Give me a warrior's death.'

The girls suddenly screamed into their hands as Logan stepped forward and plunged his sword through the nape of the troll's muscular neck.

Nathan glanced around at his friends. They were all pale from shock. But in the aftermath of the violence, none of them looked like they were going to vomit. Perhaps we're getting used to it, he reflected. He wasn't really sure whether that was a good thing.

THE CHANGELING KING

Blades were cleaned, daggers and arrows retrieved and checked for damage. The four teenagers walked away from the carnage, feeling like something precious had been ripped away from them.

CHAPTER 37: THE SIEGE
KRYLLON

The last salvo from the trebuchet had brought down a huge section of the southern wall. The ballistae were quickly reset to exploit the breech, making living creatures the targets of the barbed shafts instead of masonry.

Gillieron was amazed at the lack of organisation in the Trollking's forces. A few seasoned captains had taken charge of various sections of the wall, but were mostly ineffective due to the lack of long-ranged weapons and poor communication.

'Unleash the glyptodonts,' called General Dedric.

The grind of machinery and the rumble of wooden wheels on packed earth struck up, as the armoured carapaces of the glyptodonts trundled to the fore. The dvargar cheered. The glyptodonts rolled forwards, heading for the city gates.

The glyptodonts oval hulls were sheeted with iron plates and bristling with spikes. Each carapace rested on a flat chassis with six wheels. The wheels were the height of a dvargar, around five feet, and the spokes were reinforced with strips of iron. Kill holes were interspersed along the sides and compact, crank-operated ballista were mounted on top. Each of the glyptodonts also supported an armour-plated battering ram up front.

Gillieron noticed increased activity on the wall as the defenders spotted the new threat. At first there was a lot of gesturing, perhaps to the defenders who waited on the ground behind the walls. Then they seemed to abandon the wall completely. Puzzled Gillieron ran forward, trying to make sense of the enemy's movement.

The glyptodonts were now within bowshot of the gates. A small number of arrows and fist-sized rocks bounced harmlessly off the

THE CHANGELING KING

armoured hulls. Surely the defenders have more archers than that, thought Gillieron. The glyptodonts were now within thirty feet of the walls, their mounted ballistae firing off a round each, which thundered into the gates, sending splinters of wood into the air. The glyptodonts picked up speed, their battering rams poised to smash through. Something was happening at the gates. Gillieron shielded his eyes against the glare of the sun. They were opening.

The glyptodonts thundered full speed ahead, their ballista-crews firing at will. Shaft after shaft slammed into the gatehouse, even as the gates opened wider. A dark mass of bodies poured forth, their howls and screams carrying to Gillieron.

'General?' shouted Gillieron, drawing his sword.

Dedric blew into an ivory horn and the dvargarn infantry moved forward in formation, to the beat of drums. The sound of a thousand marching dvargar sent tremors through the ground and drowned out all else.

Outside the gates, the glyptodonts were being overrun by the enemy as they swarmed over the hulls, like ants attacking a marauding beetle. The ballista crews were torn from the hatches and cast down. More defenders charged out of the city to meet the dvargarn infantry head-on.

The charge broke on dvargarn shields like a tidal wave, though the impact rippled through the dvargarn ranks. The horde struggled against the shields, pushing and wheedling for an opening. But the iron-discipline of the dvargar held. Shields overlapped to form a near impregnable wall. The dvargarn phalanx converged forward, increasing the breadth of the frontline, flanking and then hemming in the enemy in a horseshoe formation.

The horn sounded again. The defensive attitude of the dvargar switched to offence. The shields of the front ranks slid open to allow the second rank to engage their axe-blades.

The skirmish turned into slaughter as the horseshoe tightened into a noose. Some of the goblins broke away and fled back through the gates. The killing continued until not a single enemy remained standing. The gates slammed shut, leaving behind the wreckage of the secret weapon that was to have won the war.

Dedric signalled a retreat as arrows rained down from the wall. The dvargar fell back with their shields over their heads. Gillieron strode over to Dedric. The dvargar's face was as stiff as stone. The glyptodonts had failed. The bodies of their crews were carried back to the dvargarn lines on the shields of their comrades.

The Ranushan harbour district was taken by Arazan's Alvorn Guard with minimal resistance from gangs of adolescent goblins that had been in the process of looting warehouses.

Two hundred alvor had been ordered to remain at the harbour to guard the longboats. General Tinuvil would lead a battalion of eight hundred warriors to capture the keep. The remaining two thousand alvor were split into a further three battalions to take the inner wall. Captain Elanesse would lead a battalion to sweep the harbour district and take the market district gate. Captain Quinlan would take the westerly gate. Arazan, overall second-in-command, would lead his battalion to the main gates that separated the city proper from the slums.

Progress through the upper city was slow, as the alvor were forced to check each house, unwilling to leave a possible threat behind their lines. Mostly, they found children, but on a few occasions, women and elderly goblins. A unit of warriors had to be detailed to watch the captives. The house to house searches continued throughout the bombardment of the outer wall.

The first sign of serious resistance came within bowshot of the inner wall. The gates that led down into the lower city were open. Through them Arazan could see the Trollking's forces milling about, trying to avoid getting crushed by falling masonry. The Trollking had expended little or no resources in maintaining the city. Nor had he vested much interest in commerce or the training of a regular army. The Trollking's forces were made up of mercenary warbands who thrived on vicious politicking and backstabbing to gain ascendancy in the Trollking's favour.

Arazan could see the yawning gap in the outer wall, even from this distance. Hundreds of goblins were attempting to escape the battle by slipping into the upper city in the confusion. Nearly half of the deserters fell quietly to alvorn arrows. The survivors could not comprehend that they were being attacked from within the city. Their disbelief cost them their lives. The irony was that the city had fallen twice before in the same manner. Firstly, when the alvor had overthrown the human high-king, and then when the Trollking had summoned a demon in the heart of the city.

Whether by divine intervention or sheer dumb luck, the body of the Trollking's horde remained unaware of the imminent threat from within the city. With the deserters dead, the main-gates were taken and shut on the lower city. Runners soon arrived, reporting the capture of the market district gates. More looters had been found and put to the sword. Arazan dispatched reinforcements to the western gate to aid Captain Quinlan and his command. Within half an hour, the inner-wall was taken. Yet still, the enemy remained ignorant.

Standing on the battlements, Arazan drew three flare arrows from a quiver secured to his thigh. The arrows were tipped with slow burning brands, filled with the phosphates used in glow-lamps. He nocked all three arrows to his bow and dipped their heads into a nearby brazier. The brands caught fire quickly.

Arazan drew his bowstring back, until the bow-string pressed against his nose and he could feel the heat from the arrows on the knuckles of his bow-hand. With a whispered breath, the arrows shot high into the sky, above the milling crowds and over the lower city. Arazan closed his eyes to find peace, preparing himself for the carnage yet to come.

Nathan and the others stood at the foot of the broad stairwell that led up the central tower to the Trollking's chambers. Nathan felt a strange disquiet within himself.

Taking lives, even those of monsters such as these, should feel wrong, he told himself. *Perhaps we're turning into monsters ourselves*, he reflected quietly. But what if that was the price of success? He had sworn he would do whatever it took to get his brother and their girlfriends home. Was he prepared to kill in cold-blood like Logan had? Did the end justify the means? Would the ghosts of his victims someday come back to haunt him?

Enough, he told himself fiercely. He couldn't be thinking like this. It would only get them killed. Right, wrong... it was all subjective. All he could do now was act. So, with a snarl Nathan tackled the stairs at a run. His companions followed close behind him, weapons drawn.

NOOR A JAHANGIR

They were met halfway by a unit of trolls. The brothers took the brunt of the attack, huge poleaxes driving them to their knees with every blow. The girls stood back and peppered the trolls with arrows.

'Logan, we can't let them push us back to the landing,' said Nathan. 'There's no way we'll be able to take them all at once.'

'The stairs get narrower the higher we go. We need to push them back,' said Katrina.

'And how the heck do we do that?' asked Logan, as another blow crashed against his sword.

Nathan hunched under a horizontal slash and lunged towards the troll attacking Logan, spearing it through a gap in its armour. The troll turned to strike at Nathan, but its poleaxe clashed with its comrades' weapon.

Logan exploited the same gap and drove his sword up into its ribs. The troll shuddered as if it had caught a chill, and then blinked its eye stupidly before toppling on top of him. Together they tumbled down the stairs knocking the girls off their feet.

The other bodyguards quickly flanked Nathan, who wrenched out his dagger and fought desperately as he was surrounded. He heard Salina scream his name. The trolls gnashed their tusks in frustration as Nathan evaded their clumsy weapons by pushing, shoving and stabbing anything not covered in iron until a large foot struck him in the small of his back.

Nathan sprawled forward, urgently rolling to avoid being stomped, the steps bruising his ribs and thighs. A troll trapped Nathan with its legs and reversed its poleaxe to spear him. Nathan froze.

A blur of bronze screamed up the stairs like a human comet, crashing into the bodyguards. The troll standing over Nathan stumbled. Jolted into action, Nathan scrambled backwards on his hands. Arrows flew over him as Logan bent down to help him up. Nathan struggled to see through the mass of armoured bodies to find his rescuer.

The trolls were retreating slowly up the steps as they struggled to contain the fiery whirlwind that moved almost too quickly for Nathan's confused vision to follow. Two curved sabres flashed, and an unruly mass of black hair thrashed the air. Bits of iron, leather and troll flew up into the air. Sultan had returned.

THE CHANGELING KING

Nathan and Logan pressed forward, waiting for an opportunity to join in the attack. A horn blew. Nathan shared a glance with his brother. The horn would bring every troll and goblin within hearing.

CHAPTER 38: WOMAN AND BOY
ENGLAND

The troll's arm twitched again.

'Adam, where did you shoot the troll?' asked Karen.

'I don't know. I had my eyes closed.'

Karen scanned the troll's upper body and face. It didn't take long for her to discover that the bullet had struck the troll in the head. The wound wasn't deep. The bullet must have glanced off its thick skull. Karen reached slowly for the dagger that Adam had stuck into the troll's side. She carefully wrapped her fingers around the hilt and yanked it out.

The troll's eye flew open and it roared in pain and anger. Both Karen and Adam fell off the troll in fright. One-Eye cried out again as a spearhead burst through its stomach from below. The troll grabbed the shaft as a second spear tore through its chest. One-Eye's head fell back as its body continued to spasm past death.

Karen and Adam moved away from One-Eye's body as far as they could. Karen looked over the battlements. She couldn't see the ground in the dark, but it had to be at least forty feet. There was nowhere to go. No escape. Karen picked up the mace and the Glock and positioned herself at an angle behind the trapdoor. To Adam she passed the dagger. In his hands it seemed more machete than knife.

The trolls would have to come through one at a time. Karen had no qualms about shooting them the second they poked their heads out. If even one of those things got through, it would be disaster for her and Adam.

The trapdoor crashed open, dead troll and all. Burn-face was the first troll through, pulling itself up with its remaining arm. Karen pulled the trigger. Burnt-face slid back down the stairs. The next troll up was the one she had shot off the side of the tower. Its helmet still bore evidence of that encounter. It peered out over the aperture, no doubt trying to get a fix on her position. Karen waited until it turned its head in her direction before firing a bullet through the helmet's eye-slit. The troll bellowed in pain and ducked back out of view.

'That's right. Keep them coming,' said Karen.

The wind had picked up slightly and it moaned through the turrets. A third troll launched itself out of the opening and rolled away. As Karen took her shot, another troll charged out and leapt in the opposite direction. Karen moved her pistol and shot again, catching it in the thigh. In the meantime, another two trolls, Burnt-face and Helmet, had gained the battlement too.

Four trolls and ten bullets, Karen thought to herself. Come on, I can make this work. A few of the trolls didn't have as much armour as the other two. She would focus her fire on them. The first bullet caught the smallest of the trolls high in its shoulder, twisting its upper-body to the right. The second struck it in the back, pushing it towards the parapet wall. A third bullet sent it tumbling over. Its cry was cut off abruptly as it crashed into the remains of the car.

Helmet was closest to her. He drew a sword taller than Karen and ran at her. Karen kept shooting until the gun clicked empty and Helmet lay still on the floor.

The remaining two, Burnt-face and the biggest that Karen had seen yet watched her gun-hand with some trepidation, unaware that she was out of bullets.

'Adam,' said Karen quietly, 'I want you to stay low and make a run for that trapdoor as soon as you see an opening. Get out of the tower and head for the road. Don't stop running and don't look back, regardless of what you hear. Is that understood?'

'What about you?'

'I'll be right behind you.'

The Big One and Burnt-face began to inch their way towards her, growing more confident as seconds expired and the pistol remained silent. Karen let the pistol fall from her hand and gripped the mace in both hands. She let the length of the chain play through her fingers until the spiked ball hit the floor. She began to swing the mace overhead.

NOOR A JAHANGIR

Karen moved closer to the trapdoor, the mace hurtling about her like a deadly spinning top. Adam scuttled towards the trapdoor but the Big One lunged at him under the maces killing circle. Karen yanked on the chain, smashing the spiked ball into the troll's shoulder.

'GO, ADAM, GO!'

Adam dropped through the aperture, as Burnt-face closed in on her. Its fist connected with her jaw and Karen's world briefly became a whirling kaleidoscope before fading to black.

Adam tumbled down the stairwell, scraping his palms and back raw in the process. He began to run as soon as his feet touched the floor.

He didn't stop until he exploded out of the front door, only to realise that Karen wasn't behind him. His stomach lurched with fear. The trolls must have got her. He could only imagine the kinds of horror they would be inflicting on her. He had to go back. He had to save Karen. But what could he do? He was only a kid, and a small one at that. Karen was probably already dead and if he went back, he would be wasting Karen's sacrifice. But what if she was still alive?

The surviving trolls were standing around arguing. The larger of the two had some kind of crystal ball in his hands and he kept on gesturing to it. The smaller one, with the scarred face had his foot on top of Karen's head. She wasn't moving. Adam felt a ball of heat growing inside him, starting in the pit of his stomach. His head throbbed with all the anger he had so far kept under control. He was tired of being scared. He was tired of being hunted. He was tired of watching the people he cared about get hurt.

Too preoccupied with their argument, the trolls didn't notice him stepping on the battlements. He stood with his feet shoulder-width apart and arms akimbo. His hands were balled into fists. The trolls turned to stare at him. He couldn't tell what they were thinking. He didn't care. The trolls drew out their knives.

The fire within Adam felt as if it was burning every cell in his body, even his hair felt like it was shrivelling from the heat. *All you have to do now is let go of the rage*, a tiny voice whispered in his head. Let go and blow these monsters away. Adam howled, a deep blood curdling sound, as the fire poured out of him.

The trolls were thrown back as a wall of heat exploded out from Adam.

His fury spent, Adam fell to his knees as exhaustion claimed him. He crawled over to Karen and placed her head on his knees. The trolls stood up and glanced at each other. Adam closed his eyes to the monsters and began to pray for a miracle.

CHAPTER 39: THE FALL OF RANUSH
KRYLLON

The dvargarn army stood silently, ready to march. The siege engines had exhausted their ammunition, leaving ragged gaps in the southern wall of Ranush. A chill wind whistled its cold breath on Gillieron's exposed nape as the day rapidly cooled into a brooding dusk. There was nothing left to do now but to march on the city. The signal arrows fired by Captain Arazan had extinguished themselves in the damp, churned earth just a few moments before. Now the final assault would begin.

Dedric had split the army under himself and Gillieron, despite the grumbling amongst the older dvargar, who were shocked at finding an alvor commanding them. Gillieron would lead a brigade of five thousand to the city's gates. Three thousand heavy infantry, armed with axe and shield, with a further two thousand bearing composite bows and short-swords. The dvargar had crafted a rude battering ram from a dead tree. Leather harnesses had been fashioned to give the dvargar a means of carrying it between them. Though smaller than the giant conifers of Alvorn Reach, the tree was still an impressive specimen.

Dedric would lead the remaining dvargar to take the southern wall, armed with ladders, rope and grapple-hooks.

'Kige guide your axe, General,' said Gillieron as he leaned down to clasp the dvargar's arm.

'I never thought I'd see the day that I shared a battlefield with an alvor... without being on opposite sides, that is. I must declare that it has truly been an honour. Pay my regards to the lady alvor. She's a tad skinny, but she's a comely lass. Take care of my lads. It's been a while since they've swung an axe at anything but straw-filled dummies.'

THE CHANGELING KING

Gillieron bowed and then strode over to join Lady Merenwen at the head of his column. She wore a polished bronze helmet with a high crest and leaf-shaped cheek guards. Her upper body was protected by overlapping, cordiform-shaped plates, over a mail-shirt that came to her knees. Her bronze greaves and vambraces were decorated with scrollwork of earlwood fronds.

Gillieron pulled on his own helmet and took up position beside her. He drew his sabre, finding its silver-corded grip and balanced weight a source of comfort against the daunting task that lay ahead of him. He wondered briefly if the human children had made it as far as the keep, before his mind settled into a meditative calm.

A dvargar bearing the stripes of a sergeant on his helmet stepped forward with a bull horn in his hand. Gillieron nodded and the dvargar lifted the horn to his lips and blew. A deep, melancholic hum resonated across the hillside and over the city's walls. When the note finally drifted away, the column began to march on Ranush.

Arazan loosed arrow after arrow, standing fearlessly on the battlements, ignoring the counter-fire that clattered harmlessly about him. The enemy had ordered themselves into ranks facing the inner wall. The front rank bore oblong shields, painted with the wivere skull. Behind them, archers bent their bows. The sound of a horn from the hillside reached them, sending despair through the ragtag battalions. The odds were stacked heavily against the defenders. Soon the dvargar would be coming through the city's gate and over the wall.

The sporadic movement of a unit of trolls puzzled Arazan. They ran from cover to cover, though they were well out of the range of the alvorn archers. What were they up to? Arazan scanned the lower city until he spotted an enclosure made entirely from twisted strips of iron. Something moved within the corral, writhing and twisting in the shadows and mud. Nicors.

'Manalay, Halvrin, the trolls are heading for the nicor pen. We must stop them at all costs. Get a message to Captain Quinlan.'

The two alvor unstrung their bows and holstered them over their shoulders before pelting along the wall. By the time Quinlan understood the message, it would too late. I have to do something and I have to do it now, thought Arazan. Sending arrows into the enemy below, he ran along the parapets. The trolls were in range now. He focused his fire on them instead.

The trolls took cover. It would only be a matter of time before he was out of arrows. They would try to wait him out. They didn't know that he only had to keep them pinned until Quinlan got his message. As if on cue, arrows flew at the trolls from further along the inner wall. The trolls must have realised their predicament, for they suddenly dashed across the last few hundred yards to the enclosure, braving the deadly hail of arrows. Arazan continued past Quinlan and leapt up onto the western wall. The trolls were at the nicor pen now. He sprinted along until he was directly above them.

Arazan sent several shafts whistling through the openings at the top of the cage. The stench was overpowering. Halvrin, Manalay and several others joined him, but it was too late. The gate to the enclosure crashed open. The trolls rode out on their two-ton steeds and began to thread through the narrow streets of the shanty town. The barbed tails of the nicors whipped into hovels and stalls as they passed, smashing the rickety structures to bits. They were headed for the gates. Arazan couldn't allow them to make open ground. He remembered only too vividly what the nicor cavalry had done to the alvorn pike at the Battle of Heaven's Wrath. If the nicors got through the gate, it would be bad news for Gillieron and the dvargar.

Arazan led his small band of alvor in a mad dash to the bailey over the city gates. A platoon of twenty-five goblins burst out of the bailey and swarmed up onto the wall like rats trying to avoid a soaking.

The alvor didn't even slow down to take aim. Arrows ripped into the enemy with deadly precision, sending them tumbling to the ground. The Trollking's mercenaries looked up to see what was happening. A goblin captain waved another platoon up a set of ladders.

'Back to the inner wall,' said Arazan in frustration as the gates were thrown open and the heavy cavalry slipped through.

The gates of Ranush opened and out rode the one thing Gillieron had hoped not to face: the nicor riders. The bite of the dragon-like creature was said to be as toxic as that of a marsh viper. Its claws and barbed tail made for fearsome weapons in close quarters. Their riders were fully armoured and carried iron-tipped lances. Gillieron sensed panic rip through the dvargarn ranks behind him.

He had to think fast. The dvargarn shields wouldn't be much use against the nicors. The reptiles would just climb over a shield wall and attack from above. He had to figure out a way of splitting the riders up and then picking them off one by one. His eyes fell upon the wreckage of the glyptodonts. Perhaps the dvargarn technology would save the day yet. Gillieron raised his sword and began to run. The dvargar picked up the pace to match his speed. He called out orders as they neared the overturned carapaces of the glyptodonts.

The dvargar turned the least damaged glyptodonts back onto their wheels and pushed them nose to nose. The wrecks of the other carapaces were added to the ends to extend the barricade.

The troll cavalry were building momentum. The dvargar formed up ten feet clear of the makeshift cordon. They overlapped their shields into a vast wedge, behind which the skirmishers readied their throwing axes. Gillieron moved to the point of the wedge.

The cavalry was almost upon them.

'Here they come,' shouted Gillieron, his heart pounding hard against his ribs.

The first wave of riders smashed into the barricade, the shock of impact tearing through the varnished wood. Stunned nicor writhed in pain. The reptiles quickly turned on their thrown riders, their powerful jaws noisily snapping limbs. The second wave surged over the spiked carapaces, trampling their fallen underfoot.

'Now!' yelled Merenwen.

The skirmishers released their deadly missiles, piercing armour and flesh with little resistance.

The remaining riders charged around the cordon and attacked the dvargarn flanks. As predicted, the large reptiles clambered onto the shield wall, their long, muscular necks snaking to find gaps beneath their splayed claws. Merenwen's skirmishers cast again.

The wall parted briefly as axes felled riders, then snapped back together as more nicors snatched dvargar from the ranks.

Maddened by bloodlust, the reptiles began to gorge themselves on the fallen. At Gillieron's command, the dvargar surrounded the isolated nicors and began to hack at both beasts and riders without quarter.

A horde of goblins and humans poured out once again from the gate.

Gillieron collared his sergeant and tersely issued fresh orders. The dvargar nodded and blew several long notes through the brass-capped horn. The dvargar disengaged and formed a phalanx in front of the barricade, the skirmishers moving to the wings. Merenwen joined Gillieron at the front and centre. He smiled grimly at her before raising his sword again.

'For Kryllon!' he roared, and charged.

The dvargar took up his call and surged after him. Missiles flew back and forth between the two forces. Dvargar fell to Gillieron's right and left. The gap between the opposing sides diminished rapidly. He had time barely for one last prayer to Kige, before metal clashed against metal.

The lines held for moments before breaking into smaller skirmishes. Gillieron's arm lifted and fell of its own accord, as if the deaths dealt by his sword were the actions of another. The ground grew slick as he pushed forward, trying to keep Merenwen in sight. He could see her armour glimmer amongst the sepia tones of the enemies' equipment. She fought with the same economic grace that Arazan did. Her blade seemed an extension of her limbs as she whirled away from a rampaging nicor, swayed back under the swing of a club and danced aside from a thrusting lance.

Gillieron cut his way towards her, reaching out to pull her back. Unaware, Merenwen moved away from him, pushing off her back foot, her body fully extended to spear a goblin's chest. She withdrew her blade and span low to sever the limb of a nicor. Her sabre continued its trajectory over her head as she pivoted on a foot and then brought the blade down to ram it through the nicor's ridged and horned head.

Gillieron's own progress wasn't as graceful but much more productive. He cut his way to her side and then hauled her back by the arm. His sergeant and a whole battalion of dvargar pushed their way through to them and covered their retreat.

Gillieron shouted new orders to the sergeant over the clash of weapons and combatants. The harried dvargar buried his axe in a goblin and then drew his horn to his lips and blew three short notes. The skirmishers moved to box in the enemy on both flanks.

Exhausted, Gillieron cast a glance towards Dedric's command. The dvargar general had captured several breaches in the wall. The goblins manning the gatehouse and bailey had stopped peppering Gillieron's brigade with arrows and seemed to be abandoning their positions. Then dvargar appeared through the gate and there were alvor on the bailey wall. Gillieron whooped with joy.

The fight suddenly went out of the enemy. Combatants began to drop their weapons to surrender, whilst others tried to bolt for freedom.

'Give quarter to anyone that surrenders. Strip them of their armaments and then chain them up,' said Gillieron to the sergeant, a weariness coming over him unlike anything he had ever experienced.

Merenwen wiped her sabre clean with a handful of grass. There were tears in her eyes. After a hundred years of occupation, Ranush had fallen once again.

CHAPTER 40: THE TROLLKING
KRYLLON

The battle in the keep had spilled out onto the second floor. Alvor, goblins and trolls battled in the corridors and on the stairs. Nathan had sustained a vertical cut that had nearly taken his eye and another along the back of his arm. As he had feared, the troll's horn had brought a platoon of goblins to the fight. Even with Sultan's martial skills they were vastly outnumbered and fighting on two fronts. The way home was tantalisingly close. But their quest seemed doomed to failure.

The goblins cried out as more troops appeared behind them. Tired and close to tears, Nathan felt like screaming to God for help. But then he saw that the goblins were falling back. Only then did he realise that the fresh troops were friends. It was Anaemus.

The alvor cut a path to them and suddenly they were surrounded by bronze clad warriors.

'Master Nathan, we will hold the demon-spawn here. You must press on and complete your mission,' said Anaemus.

Nathan felt a wave of affection for the stoic alvor, and found himself regretting his earlier harsh judgement of the squad leader's priorities.

'Thank you, Anaemus.'

The alvor pushed the trolls up the stairs and onto a landing. Nathan and the others waited until the alvor had cleared a path, before slipping by onto the next flight of stairs.

The sounds of battle faded as they climbed higher up the tower. They paused to look out of a large window, covered with an iron grille, to see if they could make out how the battle was going.

THE CHANGELING KING

Cold sunlight touched on the city under siege. They could see as far as the inner-wall. Alvor had overrun the upper city, with sporadic fighting littering the streets. The city's harbour was clogged with longboats moored tightly besides each other. The Archmagus had been right about one thing, thought Nathan. Whether the four of them succeeded or failed now, the battle for Kryllon would soon be won. All that remained between them and the final truth was a set of arched double-doors.

'Everyone ready?' asked Nathan looking closely at his friends.

They nodded one-by-one.

The doors were etched with ancient alvorn runes, darker writings marked around them in a language they didn't recognise. Taking a deep, shaky breath, Nathan grabbed a black handle. To his relief, he wasn't struck down by a magical ward. He pulled it open wide enough for the five of them to slip through and then drew it softly closed behind them. They spread out, forming a half circle, with the girls on the outside, Logan in the middle, flanked by Nathan and Sultan.

The chamber was lit with smoky torches ensconced on the stone columns. Between each set of pillars, there stood the amputated statues of the kings of old. Bits of broken furniture lay here and there.

In the centre of the room lay the gateway, a sunken, pentagonal cauldron pool, ringed by a low wall. The pool contained a resinous substance that undulated as if its dark surface hid a great depth. On the far side of the chamber, a figure sat so still on its stone throne that Nathan mistook it for another statue. It was covered from head to foot in thick plate armour, studded with fragments of bone, shrouded by layers of cobwebs and dust. A great helm mounted with the skull of a wivere, cranial horns flaring down on either side, rested upon its head. A six foot blade of black iron lay across its thighs.

Salina screamed in surprise as a gauntleted hand rose to grip the spiked hilt of the sword. The figure rose, stiff joints cracking and armour screeching as rusted plates were forced into motion.

The Trollking towered above them like a brooding giant. Nathan took an involuntary step back. Only now did he truly understand the hopelessness of their predicament. They had been sent to slay a nightmare behemoth in its own lair. He felt nausea spread across his midriff as fear made his heart beat painfully against his ribs.

NOOR A JAHANGIR

The Trollking stalked forward shedding dust and flakes of rust from his armour. The ten foot monster raised his sword in a single-handed grip and scraped the paddle-like blade along the ceiling. Sparks sprayed onto his shoulders.

Sultan yelled and charged around the pool. Nathan shook his head to clear it. He glanced at his friends. He had a promise to keep.

'Spread out around him,' he ordered. 'No one try to take him head-on. No way is this tin-man going to stop us from getting home.'

Logan nodded and followed Sultan. Nathan and the girls flanked the Trollking from the other side. Sultan continued his mad rush straight at the Trollking. The huge sword came crashing down and would have cut his emaciated body in half, had not the mad prince leapt aside at the last possible moment. Slivers of masonry showered Logan. Sultan slashed at the Trollking with both sabres, resulting in lots of noise but little harm to the tyrant.

Logan moved in with a thrust. The Trollking stood impassively as the blade skittered off his breastplate. Sneaking up behind the Trollking, Nathan slashed and stabbed at his back, barely nicking the surface. The Trollking swung his sword around his waist, forcing the boys to duck. A chair smashed into the side of the Trollking's head, followed by a small chest as Salina and Katrina threw random pieces of furniture at the behemoth. Wood splintered against the great helm, but didn't even affect a glance from the Trollking. Instead, a football-sized gauntlet lifted Nathan by the scruff of his neck and threw him at the girls.

Nathan tried yelling a warning as he flew past a column and balled the girls over. Sultan leapt onto the Trollking's back. The pommel of the madman's sword crashed repeatedly against the great helm, smashing a horn off the wivere skull. The Trollking reached back and grabbed Sultan by the hair. He shrieked in pain as he was yanked over the changeling's shoulder and deposited in a heap on the ground. The prince rolled aside as a hobnailed boot came crashing down.

Logan launched himself into a double-footed kick against the Trollking's stomach. The behemoth's foot slid back slightly. His blade rose and cut across Logan's stomach. Logan crashed against a column and doubled over.

THE CHANGELING KING

Nathan scrambled towards his brother, fearing the worst. Sultan grabbed Logan's leg and pulled him clear as the Trollking's sword descended again.

Logan's armour had taken the brunt of the blow. He was still breathing, though his face was twisted in pain. Nathan grabbed a torch from a pillar and rushed in close to the Trollking. The Trollking roared in anger as Nathan thrust the brand into the narrow visor. The Trollking staggered back and slapped at the face of his helm, tainting the already stale air with stench of burning flesh.

The girls drew their weapons and entered the fray. The Trollking swung blindly. Katrina was caught by the flat of the enormous blade. Salina stabbed at the monster's leg, behind the kneecup. With a snarl, the Trollking grabbed Salina by her face. Her sword fell to the ground as she was lifted off her feet, her legs kicking in vain. Nathan screamed her name and thrust his sword through a gap in the changeling's armour, beneath the pauldrons and above the breastplate. Blood sprayed Nathan but still the Trollking held Salina aloft. She was weakening from the lack of air, her thrashing limbs slowly giving up their struggle.

Nathan twisted his blade, even as Logan and Sultan drove their swords into the Trollking's side, exploiting holes that had rusted through the breastplate. The monster raised his head and roared in pain. It was not enough. The Trollking pulled his arm back and flung Salina down the chamber.

Nathan felt like he was moving through water as he leapt after her with outstretched hands, his head turning to follow her trajectory. For a fraction of a second, he thought his fingers brushed the soft leather of a boot. The oily surface of the cauldron pool seemed to reach out to take Salina from him. There was no splash or sound as she hit the surface. Her eyes met his briefly before the dark liquid closed over her face.

Salina, he tried to scream, but all he could hear was the blood pounding in his ears. The cauldron pool seemed so far away. His feet slapped the ground as he pushed through solid air. He bunched his legs to launch himself after her, but the hands of his friends held him back. Sound returned.

'Nathan, you can't,' said Katrina, sobbing aloud. 'She's gone. She's gone.'

NOOR A JAHANGIR

'Bro, we need you. Don't do it. Stay with us,' said Logan, tears flowing unchecked from his eyes.

'Use the anger,' said Sultan. 'Use it against him. Don't let her death be in vain.'

His words lit a fire within Nathan. Rage burned through him. Nathan raised his head and roared his fury. Weapons in hand, the four humans walked towards the titanic figure of the Trollking.

CHAPTER 41: THE RETURN
ENGLAND

Adam hunched low over Karen, his lips moving silently in prayer. Fingers twisted through his hair and wrenched his head back sharply. It was painful, but Adam couldn't find a voice to cry out with. Above him was the face of a troll, its black lips drawn back over gnashing tusks. In its other hand, it clutched a large hammer. He closed his eyes as tight as he could.

Crack. Adam's whole body jerked involuntarily.

The grip on his hair slackened and Adam fell forward on to Karen. He looked up to see what new devilry had beset them. Both trolls stood with their faces upturned. He followed their gazes and gasped. Lightning flashed and clouds swirled in an angry ring above them. A darkness blacker than the night, tore open the sky. A comet appeared through the rift and shot towards the tower. Adam and the trolls cowered as the battlements were engulfed by cold fire. When Adam realised he wasn't dead, he moved his arms from in front of his face and saw an angel standing in their midst.

The trolls gaped at the newcomer, their weapons forgotten at their sides. Despite everything that had happened to him these past few days, Adam was dumbfounded by the appearance of this heavenly creature.

The angel was clad in golden armour that followed the curves of its limbs and torso. Its head was covered with a close fitting helm that revealed startling blue-eyes and distinctively feminine features.

The trolls snapped out of their reverie. Burnt-face ran at the angel, who met the charge with a straight left to the troll's jaw. Both combatants stopped to stare at each other with surprise. The troll snarled. The angel punched the troll again, this time on the snout, causing it to blink rapidly. Gnashing its tusks, the troll grabbed the angel around the throat. A gloved hand covered the thick fingers of the troll and twisted the hand away, then turned to the right and pushed on the troll's elbow with her left hand. Annoyed, the troll tried to pull free, but the angel continued to turn and push. The troll grimaced and found itself forced to the ground, its arm twisted behind its back, held in place by two dainty hands.

The other troll stepped behind the angel and swung a war-hammer at her head. Even as Adam cried out a warning, the angel rolled clear. The hammer smashed into Burnt-face, fracturing the collar-bone and dislocating the troll's shoulder. Burnt-face howled in agony. Its comrade grunted apologetically before turning to face the angel. She had picked up the chain-mace Karen had been using. The troll lifted its hammer to crush the angel's head. The mace whipped out, the chain playing through the angel's hand. The ball lashed around the troll's forearms. The angel twisted her whole-body, holding the chain tight against her. The troll staggered forward, dropping its weapon.

Burnt-face howled again as it pushed its shoulder back into place. It fixed its eye on Adam and drew a dagger from its belt.

'Hey, I need help,' Adam called to the angel.

The angel heard him and came running, but was intercepted by the big one. Burnt-face's mouth twisted in a horrid parody of a grin. Adam needed a weapon. He felt around on the floor but couldn't find anything. Someone grabbed him from behind and pulled him to his feet.

'Get behind me.'

Adam stopped struggling at the sound of Karen's voice. A surge of emotions ran through him as he turned to see Karen struggling to her knees. He wanted desperately to say something to Karen but his tongue felt thick and awkward. Instead, he moved to her side and helped her to her feet. Karen's face was badly battered, one eye closed shut and blood poured from a deep gash on her brow. She cradled her right arm against her chest, clenching the troll-dagger in her left. Adam found a sword on the floor and hauled the heavy blade on to his shoulder.

As Burnt-face lunged at them, Adam swung the sword with all his might and struck a glancing blow on its leg. A small cut appeared on the troll's thigh. Karen shoved Adam aside and then rammed her

THE CHANGELING KING

dagger into the troll's throat. Burnt-face looked at them incredulously and then collapsed where it stood.

'Are you okay, Adam?' asked Karen.

Adam tore his gaze from the dead troll and looked at Karen. Her face had turned extremely pale, making the cuts and bruises stand out even more. Then he noticed the knife buried to the hilt in her chest. A bloodstain flowered across her already soiled blouse. She stumbled. Adam moved to her side, letting her put her weight on him.

'Help me sit down,' said Karen. He could hear the gurgle of blood in her voice.

Adam's vision began to blur again. His throat felt like he had accidentally swallowed a big wad of bubble-gum. Gently, he propped Karen against the bulwark. Her breathing was shallow, lips pressed tight against the pain.

'It's my fault. You told me to stay behind you. I should've listened to you,' said Adam.

'No Adam, it's not your fault. It would have killed us both . . . I'm proud of you,' said Karen.

'Karen?'

'Adam, be brave now,' said Karen, 'I'm dying.'

'No, no, no, you can't die. I need you. Just hold on, I'll call an ambulance, just hold on, please!'

'Adam, it's too late. You know, you are the bravest person I've ever met. I'm glad I got a chance to know you.'

Adam threw his arms around Karen, hugging her face tight to his chest, his tears mixing with the blood clotting in her hair. Someone crouched down beside him.

'Adam,' said the angel.

There was something familiar about that voice. Adam looked up into the angel's face. She had removed her helmet. He felt like he should know her. The face was worn and exhausted, but those eyes and that nose... 'Salina?' Adam croaked in disbelief.

'Yes, Adam. I'm back.'

'Oh, Salina, please, you have to help her, she's dying.'

'I'm sorry, Adam. She's already gone.'

NOOR A JAHANGIR

Adam looked down at Karen, her head resting in his lap. The lines had disappeared from her face, making her seem so much younger, so much more fragile. Gently, he lowered her head to the ground, combing her hair straight with his fingers. Salina closed Karen's eyes and then pulled Adam into her arms. Once more, tears ravaged his face with their burning tracks. His sister rocked him back and forth in her embrace. Exhausted by his ordeal, his grief spent for now, Adam slept.

CHAPTER 42: EMPTY VICTORIES

Dvargar poured into the lower city. Skirmishes raged from street to street, as the defenders put up pockets of resistance, barricaded alleys and sought to hide in shacks and mud huts.

General Dedric had set up command in a large tavern called The Crooked Leg. Gillieron and Merenwen made their way inside, ducking beneath the low threshold.

'It's good to see you alive and in one piece,' said Dedric.

'It's good to see you too, General,' replied Merenwen.

'The goblins have scattered and slipped out of the city through the sewers and bolt-holes. A warband of trolls have holed up in a market square five minutes from here. They're all that's left to fight on this side of the inner-wall.'

'They won't last much longer,' said Gillieron.

'No, they won't. I have already reinforced the units here. Hopefully, your brethren have cleared all resistance from the upper city too. It is time for you to head on to the Keep and end this war.'

'General, I ask that you remind your dvargar to give quarter to any of the enemy who surrender their weapons. There is no need to tarnish this victory with a blood bath.'

'Of course, Lord Gillieron. We are not monsters,' said the dvargar, his eyes hard.

'War crimes are not committed by monsters, General. They are committed by people who have given into their base desires and the darkness that resides in all living things.'

The dvargar inclined his head in a mock-bow and then returned to tallying losses. Gillieron wiped his hands unconsciously on his cuirass as he left the inn with Merenwen. He relayed his orders to the dvargar under his command. The dvargar possessed endurance that exceeded any of the people in Kryllon, but the long hours of fighting had taken a toll on even their prodigious stamina.

'Look lively, comrades. You are about to meet my alvorn brethren. They are steady of hand and firm of foot.'

Gillieron's words had an instant effect. The dvargar drew their shoulders back and raised their bearded chins high. Merenwen gave him a sidelong smile. The inner-wall loomed large as they cleared the market district. Captain Arazan stood within the vaulted gateway to the upper-city. The alvor bowed to each other and, uncharacteristically, Gillieron clasped Arazan's wrist in the manner of the dvargar. Arazan looked slightly taken aback by the gesture.

'It's good to see you, my brother,' said Gillieron warmly.

'You honour me, milord,' replied Arazan.

Arazan bowed formally to Merenwen too. Gillieron noted the play of emotions in the lady's eyes. Culture and war had kept these two apart, thought Gillieron to himself. Perhaps with the Trollking defeated, Merenwen and Arazan would find some way to be together.

Gillieron's dvargarn column marched through the short tunnel into the upper-city. There they were joined by the eight hundred alvor under Arazan's command. They proceeded through the streets without challenge. All around him, Gillieron saw signs of neglect. Ancient buildings had been allowed to become derelict. Public gardens had been left to run wild. Pools and fountains had stagnated and fouled. This was not the city he remembered visiting in his youth. Beside him, Merenwen's ears drooped as she cried silent tears.

The keep grew in the distance. Here too were signs of disrepair. The battlements had crumbled and the towers looked ready to fall. Ivy choked most of the castle's walls. Gillieron recalled his last visit, nearly eleven decades ago. He had accompanied the Archmagus to discuss the 'dvargar problem' with members of the Council of Elders. His memories of that occasion had been tainted, having witnessed an old friend murdered before his eyes. Perhaps if the Archmagus had had his way then, the heartache of a hundred years could have been avoided. Instead, the changeling had escaped, only to return a few years later at the head of an army.

Gillieron grabbed a nearby alvor for a status report just as the first explosion rocked the Keep walls from within.

THE CHANGELING KING

Nathan drew in a long ragged breath. He pressed his hand hard against his thigh, where the Trollking's sword had punctured armour and flesh. The wound wasn't bleeding heavily but it still burned like a smouldering ember lodged under his skin. The others stood hunched nearby, nursing their own cuts and bruises. The Trollking had retreated back to his throne, his armour glinting with fresh scars. Coppery bloodstains blended with orange rust, testimony to the fact that, despite his impossible size and strength, the Trollking was just as mortal as them. The changeling was weakening, Nathan was sure, but so were they.

Vengeance still smouldered in Nathan's heart. Right now though, he was running on empty. The armour was weighing him down and even his sword felt like an unnecessary burden. But the end was close now. Once more, Nathan hefted his blade and signalled for the others to advance on the Trollking.

Logan feigned a lunge, which the Trollking ignored and instead moved to attack Katrina. Katrina threw herself back as the huge sword savaged the air displaced by her passing. In the meantime, Nathan had flanked the titan and thrust his blade between its cuisse and greaves. The Trollking fell to one knee but still managed to reverse his sword, catching Nathan with the flat of the blade on the side of his head. His ears tolled from the impact as he crashed first into the wall and then fell, stunned, at the feet of the Trollking. For a moment he found himself staring into the changeling's colourless eyes. The Trollking raised his sword again to finish him.

Nathan found himself wondering whether Salina would fall forever through the void or whether Shadel'ron had kept his promise. Perhaps if there was an afterlife, they could be together again, one day. Nathan followed the descent of the t-bladed sword, feeling nothing at the immediacy of his own death. Hands dug into his arms and dragged him back. Logan stepped into his field of vision to press the Trollking with a flurry of slashes. The Trollking parried and followed through with a blow that could have felled a tree. Blades met with a terrible clash and Logan's sword shattered, spraying razor sharp fragments in every direction. Logan fell back with a cry, his face a webbed mask of blood.

Katrina screamed in horror and ran to Logan's side. Nathan felt his own heart stutter with despair. He had failed Logan, just as he had failed Salina. The Trollking towered over Katrina as she hunched over Logan's prostrate body.

Logan stirred.

Relief washed through Nathan. His brother was still alive. He would not fail him again. He would see this through to the end. Nathan slowly staggered to his feet. Everything seemed to be swinging crazily around Nathan. Lights exploded behind his eyes as he shook his head to clear it. A few tottering steps later, he noticed Sultan perched upon the throne, sword in hand. The Trollking, his back towards the prince, seemed unaware of him. The madman leapt, the point of his sword finding a sliver of flesh beneath the behemoth's helm. The blade punched out through the other side, severing the chain-links holding the gorget in place.

The Trollking crashed about the throne room, a geyser of blood spraying from his throat. Sultan held on to the hilt like a man possessed. Finally, the great sword fell from nerveless fingers and the changeling king crashed to the floor.

Nathan limped over to where the titan lay and prodded the body with his sword. The Trollking did not stir.

'Help me. This thing weighs as much as an elephant,' gasped Sultan, still trapped beneath the behemoth's bulk. Nathan pushed the corpse off the prince and pulled him clear.

'Much appreciated,' said Sultan as he rubbed his legs.

Nathan went over to check on his brother. Katrina was engrossed in pulling out bronze shards from Logan's face. Nathan knelt down beside her to help. The cuts would no doubt scar him for life. Pity for his brother moved him to tears, causing his own wound to sting. The victory for Kryllon had come at too hefty a price for them.

Logan reached up to wipe Nathan's tears.

'Time to go home,' he whispered.

Nathan and Katrina wrapped an arm each around Logan and helped him to his feet. Together they walked over to the cauldron pool to peer into its depths.

'I can't go with you,' said Logan.

Nathan looked at his brother as if he had suddenly sprouted wings.

THE CHANGELING KING

'What? What do you mean? What the hell are you talking about?' asked Nathan.

'I'm not going back,' said Logan again, more firmly.

Nathan could feel his face flush as his anger found a new focus.

'Don't be stupid. We don't belong here. We have to go back.'

'Back to what exactly, Nathan? Back to our crappy flat on the council estate? Back to wondering whether dad's going to come home? Whether he's going to be drunk or sober? No, Nathan, you can go back if you want, but I'm staying.'

'That's not fair. You can't do that. What am I supposed to do? What am I supposed to tell everyone? When the hell did you even decide this?'

'Since Erskine, maybe even before then. I don't know why, but this place just feels right to me. This is where I belong, Nathan. I feel more alive here. I came all this way to make sure that you got home.'

Katrina had been standing quietly through the exchange. Now she cleared her throat to add her voice to the argument.

'I'm not going either, Nathan. All I want is to be with Logan. We're going to get married.'

Nathan looked from Logan's face to Katrina's and then back. He waited for one of them to say that they were pulling his leg, that they just wanted to see the look on his face. He wanted scream and yell at them, but all he could think about was how tired he felt and how much he missed Salina.

'You've given this a lot of thought, haven't you?'

They nodded quietly with sombre faces.

'You're sure about this? There's nothing I can say or do that will change your minds?'

'We will be happy here,' said Logan as Katrina squeezed his arm and smiled.

Lost for words, he grabbed Logan in a fierce embrace. His entire life Logan had been the one constant thing that he could depend on. When their mother had run away, Logan had taken care of him. When his father would come home drunk in the mood to dish out a beating, Logan would stand between Nathan and him. Now he had to let go and look out for himself. Katrina gave him a quick hug and kissed his cheek.

'What about you, Sultan?'

'I want to see if my family are alright. I will go with you. Perhaps this Shadel'ron can guide me to my time. I have a kingdom to claim.'

Still unbelieving, Nathan placed one foot on the rim of the cauldron pool and readied himself to jump in. He gazed back once more at Logan and Katrina.

'Look after each other,' said Nathan. 'Maybe one day we'll meet again.'

The black pool exploded outwards, a shrouded figure rising from its depths.

Bolts of lightning erupted from clawed hands. Nathan threw himself behind a pillar. Katrina and his brother followed suit. Sultan, caught in the open, was pinned to the ceiling as wave after wave of energy poured through his flailing body.

'It's going to kill him. We have to distract it,' Logan shouted.

'Let's rush it together,' said Nathan.

The three ran out from behind their cover. A mere gesture from the phantasm sent them hurtling back. Winded, they struggled to their feet and tried bombarding the demon with broken furniture. Everything they threw at it was instantly incinerated. Nathan looked up at Sultan. The madman's eyes were clenched shut and his mouth gaped open, so wide that Nathan feared he would tear the flesh of his cheeks. The wraith swung its head towards Nathan and shucked off its hood, revealing an almost skeletal face, with a ridge of horns protruding from the crown of its head. The demons eyes were milky white, set in deep sockets over a jutting upper-jaw, lined with pointed teeth. This was the evil that Shadel'ron had warned them about. This was the phantasm that had held sway over Kryllon for a century. Nathan could feel the hate pouring out of it in pulsating waves.

Sultan screamed a pitiful rasp, barely audible over the crackle of the energy consuming him. Nathan hefted his sword like a javelin and threw it with all of his might. The blade flashed as it passed through the wraith without hurting it. Sultan dropped to the floor, flesh charred, his hair completely burnt away.

THE CHANGELING KING

The demon raised its arms towards the ceiling. An invisible force began to tear out a large section of masonry. Dust filtered through the cracks as the keep rumbled ominously.

'Leave them be. Your business is with me.'

A second figure emerged from the cauldron pool. Grey tunic and black hair flapped around a pale face set with storm-grey eyes. Nathan whispered a prayer of thanks. Shadel'ron had finally come.

The wraith turned to face the Guardian of the Void, emitting a keening sound so high that it drew blood from their ears. Several crackling spiders of energy discharged from its hands and scuttled towards Shadel'ron.

The Guardian gathered the electrostatic energy to him, shaping it with his palms into a chromatic ball. Then the pulsating sphere was thrown back at the demon. The wraith spread its arms seconds before it was engulfed and sent crashing into the throne.

The demon rose up once more and hurled a barrage of fireballs, which Shadel'ron deflected with a construct of light. The blazing projectiles exploded against a pillar, collapsing a huge chunk of the ceiling on top of the Guardian.

The wraith chuckled, a dry and ugly sound.

The rubble shifted as a hand scrabbled for purchase. Dust plumed and fell from Shadel'ron's shoulders as he hauled himself out.

Wind blew through the chamber even though there were no windows in the room. Nathan shivered and drew his cloak around himself. The breeze grew stronger until a cyclone whirled into being.

'We need to get Sultan out of here,' said Katrina. 'It isn't safe anymore.'

'When has it ever been safe in here?' asked Nathan as he edged forward against the wind. Logan took off his cloak and the three of them gently rolled Sultan's burnt body onto it.

'God, he's still breathing,' said Katrina.

Nathan knelt over Sultan with an ear close to the madman's crisped lips. Breath still rattled tenaciously in his throat. Nathan exchanged an amazed look with his brother. By all rights, the time-travelling prince should have been dead. His body had channelled enough energy to light up a football stadium. Securely wrapped in the cloak, the boys lifted Sultan and carried him towards the exit. Behind them Shadel'ron unleashed a furious whirlwind.

The backlash caught them all up, including Shadel'ron and threw them into the doors. The throne end of the chamber disappeared in a wild explosion of rubble and dust. Nathan and Logan picked up their bundle once more.

'Is he alive?' asked Shadel'ron.

'Barely, but I don't think he'll last long,' replied Nathan.

'Get him into the antechamber. I will tend to him once I have finished with this devil spawn.'

Nathan looked over his shoulder. The daylight glimmered through cracks in the ceiling and wall as the dust settled once more. How could anything have survived that?

'Do not be deceived,' warned Shadel'ron. 'Its kind has survived eons in dead space. A little bad weather isn't going to kill it. Now go, get out of here before it's too late.'

'What about the portal? Did Salina make it? Is she alright? I have to go home.'

'The girl is fine. Now go,' roared Shadel'ron, pushing them out into the corridor before slamming the warded doors shut behind them.

'Nathan, Sultan is going into shock. What do we do?' asked Katrina.

'I don't know. I . . . I don't know,' said Nathan, desperately staring at the doors.

With every passing second, his chances of returning home to Salina grew slimmer.

The battle within the chamber continued for an hour, marked by explosions of various proportions. Vagrant energies crackled and sizzled, until the doors themselves disintegrated and the wall around them began to melt into slag. Nathan, Logan and Katrina cowered on top of the stairs, shielding Sultan with their own bodies. Half of the chamber had been completely obliterated. The cauldron pool now stood at the edge of a ragged precipice. There was no sign of the demon. The Guardian of the Void turned to face them, silhouetted by the open sky.

'You must leave the keep at once.'

'The only place I am going is through that gateway,' said Nathan hotly.

'That way is closed now. We cannot linger here. The portal has become destabilised and will soon implode. When that happens, this keep will be blown into space.'

'But we've come such a long way. I have to go home. I don't belong here,' said Nathan, his voice breaking.

'I'm sorry. The way is closed.'

'But Salina . . .'

'She is with her brother now.'

'But . . .'

'I am sorry, Nathan. I truly am. I must attend to your friend. He is fading,' said Shadel'ron, brushing past him.

For a few insane moments, Nathan considered dragging the Guardian back to the cauldron pool. But even in his state of desperation, he could see the foolishness in that. His brother wrapped his arms around him and pulled him close.

'I'll find another way home, you'll see. God's my witness, I'll find a way.'

'I know you will, but now we've got to go,' said Logan.

Nathan nodded and allowed his brother to pull him away from the cauldron pool.

Shadel'ron lifted Sultan easily in his arms, still wrapped in Logan's cloak.

'Evacuate the keep of everyone. I don't know how long it will hold.'

'What about you?' asked Katrina, 'aren't you going to help us?'

'I must take your friend somewhere that I can help him,' Shadel'ron held Nathan's eyes for a moment. 'If there is another gateway to your world, I will help you find it, you have my word on that.'

NOOR A JAHANGIR

Shadel'ron suddenly disappeared without fanfare or drama. One second he was there and the next he was gone.

They had succeeded in defeating the Trollking and had won back freedom for Kryllon.

Wounded, exhausted and heartbroken, the three descended the remains of the tower.

THE CHANGELING KING

CHAPTER 43: NEW BEGININGS

The victors watched from the safety of the inner-wall as the Keep lit up the night sky with a column of purple fire. The aftershock rumbled throughout the city. Ash fluttered down from the sky and covered the city in a snowy blanket.

When there was nothing left to see, the alvor and dvargarn forces set about burying their dead in a mass grave and burning the bodies of their enemies. By the time their sombre work was done, the dawn sun was once more in the sky. Despite their exhaustion, the alvor and the dvargar were jubilant. Nathan, Logan and Katrina found that they were unable to share in the good cheer.

Lord Gillieron held a post-war council after a cold breakfast. The Saviours of Kryllon, as the humans were now called, were also invited. The dvargar general announced that his people would continue on to the Pervilheln Mountains, to complete their pilgrimage to the dvargarn ancestral halls.

Lord Gillieron and General Tinuvil agreed that the majority of the alvorn force would sail back to Maidenhall to prepare the city for the homecoming. Arazan and Lady Merenwen volunteered to go with them to Maidenhall, before continuing on to Alvorn Reach with anyone who wanted to return.

The council agreed that the prisoners-of-war would be held in the ruins of Ranush, to await the judgement of the Guardian of Kryllon.

The Saviours of Kryllon were free to choose their destination. They would be welcome anywhere they went.

It took the allied forces the rest of the day to finish breaking camp. The sun rode low in the sky before Nathan, Logan and Katrina boarded a longboat with Lady Merenwen and Arazan. They had a long voyage ahead of them, back to Alvorn Reach.

NOOR A JAHANGIR

Nathan stood between his brother and Katrina on the poop deck of the Alvorsong. They watched the gutted city of Ranush disappear behind a wall of coastal waves. Nathan's tears mixed with the salt spray as he vowed once more to find a way home to Salina.

The sky rumbled with what sounded like thunder. Adam's eyes felt swollen and he felt a cold emptiness inside him that went beyond grief. He looked to where Karen lay. Salina had draped an old tapestry over her.

His sister stood frowning up at the clear sky. She seemed so much older now, though barely a week had passed since her disappearance. There was something about the way she stood, a confidence and strength that he had not seen in her before.

'How long did I sleep?' Adam asked eventually.

Salina looked down at Adam and smiled. Her cheeks weren't as round as they had been and her hair was much longer than she had ever worn it. But, more than anything else, her eyes told her story.

'An hour. An hour and a half, at the most. How are you feeling?' She had picked up a strange accent from somewhere too.

'Horrible,' said Adam his eyes drifting back towards Karen's shrouded body. 'But, I'm happy to see you again,' he added hastily.

'Don't worry about it, Adam, I understand. I really do. I've missed you a lot. I didn't think I'd ever see you again.'

Despite the warm smile, Adam heard a note of sadness in her voice and her eyes were drawn to the sky again.

'How's mum?' she asked after a short while.

'Last time I spoke to her, she was recovering quite well. They had to move her to another hospital though. The trolls trashed the other one.'

'It seems we both have a lot to tell each other,' said Salina, her eyes wide with alarm.

Adam nodded solemnly. He too felt irrevocably changed.

'Where are the others? Are we going to wait for them?'

Salina looked back up at the sky and Adam felt a wave of loneliness emanate from her.

THE CHANGELING KING

'I don't think they are coming. The rift has been closed and I feel that it will not open again. We should leave this place.'

Once more, Adam experienced a sense of empathy with his sister, of being set adrift. No one else on Earth had seen or experienced what they had. No one would believe them.

Adam and Salina said their goodbyes to Karen, Nathan, Logan and Katrina on top of the lonely tower. Then, hand in hand, they set off down the steps and out onto the road that would eventually lead them back to streetlights, people and a life that had once been carefree.

Footsore and exhausted, Vasch was glad to see the tower finally rising out on top of the hill. It had been a very long and arduous walk. No doubt Udulf would be disappointed at the fact that he was still alive. There would be plenty of time to kill him once they were back in Kryllon.

It wasn't until he saw Haig's body spread-eagled on a dead metallic cattle near the tower that he realised something was amiss.

The troll entered the building and slowly climbed up the stairs. He passed through disturbed barricades and on to the ramparts. The first thing he saw was Sigberd's body, riddled with scorched holes. That was sad. The pup had had a lot of potential. He would have made a fine captain. The bodies of Udulf and Grenld were a much more welcome sight. Grenld seemed to have got it the worst from the looks of him. No great loss.

Vasch settled down to wait. The wraith that had originally opened the gateway above the tower for them would return before dawn to send him home. He watched the alien sun climb into the sky. Then he watched as the bodies of his former comrades turned to dust and blew away with the first brisk wind. Something twinkled in the dirt that had once been Udulf. Vasch sifted through the dust and grinned as he recognised the orb. He gave it a rub on his arm and whispered his name over it. Nothing happened. Then something else caught his eyes. It was the dagger he had lost back in the temple of death.

'How did you get here?' Vasch muttered as he slid it into its vacant sheath.

The day wore on. Vasch sat in the open with only his cloak to protect him from the sun.

NOOR A JAHANGIR

By midnight, he knew that the wraith was not coming. He was stranded here on this alien planet.

Alone.

***

THE CHANGELING KING

Acknowledgements

I'd like to say a big thank you to my beta-readers Dr Bano Murtaja, Nerine Dorman, Christine Snyder, Lucy Schmeidler, Hikmat Khan and Annette Bowman. Thank you to Janny Wurts and David Farland for their advice and guidance. A special thanks to Omer and Zakarya Anwar for their constant questioning and proofreading at various stages of the book. Also, thank you to Mrs Christine Bracewell for reading *The Lion, the Witch and the Wardrobe* to my class all those years ago.

Connect With Noor A Jahangir Online:

Twitter:

@noorjahangir

Goodreads:

http://www.goodreads.com/author/show/4951592.Noor_A_Jahangir

Facebook:

www.facebook.com/NOORAJAHANGIR

Blog:

Web: www.trollking.co.uk

Printed in the USA
CPSIA information can be obtained
at www.ICGtesting.com